MEMORIES OF
METH

MEMORIES OF
METH

SEQUEL TO
"THE METH CONSPIRACY"

J.E. HORN

Order this book online at www.trafford.com
or email orders@trafford.com

Most Trafford titles are also available at major online book retailers.

Printed in the United States of America.

ISBN: 978-1-4907-2566-6 (sc)
ISBN: 978-1-4907-2565-9 (e)

Trafford rev. 01/30/2014

 www.trafford.com
North America & international
toll-free: 1 888 232 4444 (USA & Canada)
fax: 812 355 4082

For my favorite little people:
Stacy, Justin, and Morgan.

In Special Memory
Of Carissa Hinz

In the summer of 2012 I had just finished the final draft of the Meth Conspiracy and took on the project of creating a cover for the book. I mean, how hard could it be? Answer: Damn hard. I was completely lost in attempting to develop any sort of cover scheme that I was happy with. I fired myself a number of times.

Then in a discussion with my mother-in-law I learned that she worked with a woman whose daughter was currently enrolled as a student in Chicago's American Academy of Art, with an emphasis on graphic design. The daughter's name was Carissa Hinz. A few weeks later I was given her contact info and gave her a call.

My first conversation with Carissa was not very productive. Not by any fault on her part, but because I was completely at a loss for what I wanted in a book cover. She was very patient in her questions concerning the story line of the book, the plot structure and characters in an attempt to get a feel from me of what I wanted in a cover design. The phone call ended with me admitting that I really had no idea what I wanted but I would know it when I saw it.

What followed from that conversation was a three month collaboration which resulted in a cover that I absolutely love. I liked it so much that I kept it for this book as well and just changed the color scheme. Carissa was truly a lovely young woman whose patience with me was unending and her insight amazing. Shortly after the completion of our project Carissa graduated from the American Academy of Art and had her whole creative life ahead of her.

On June 14, 2013 Carissa was doing volunteer work at a local Chicago art center in the Bridgeport neighborhood. As she was crossing an intersection to empty some trash into a dumpster she was hit by a car running a red light. Carissa died because the driver was driving and texting at the same time. She was twenty-one.

As I am getting older in years, I find myself trying harder to find meaning and purpose in this world we live in. Yet, when I look to the absolute answers of religion and the open ended questions of philosophy, I can find no adequate explanation for something like this. I am stuck with the realization that there are things that happen in our world that I truly do not understand. Carissa's death is one of these.

SPECIAL THANKS

Special thanks to Jason Roberts, Richard Zell, and Michael Richards who spent their free time reading rough drafts, grammar checking, spell checking, and making sure I did not sound like a total jackass with this book. Thanks fellas.

CONTENTS

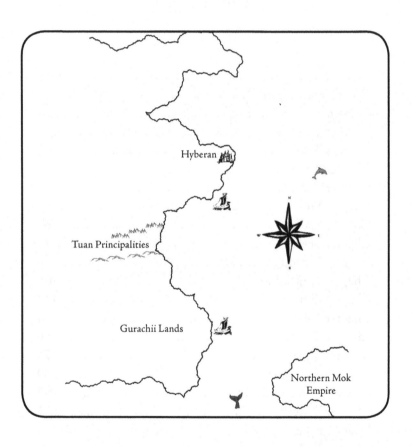

Hyberan

Tuan Principalities

Gurachii Lands

Northern Mok
Empire

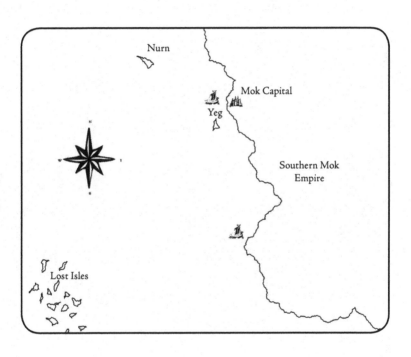

Nurn

Mok Capital

Yeg

Southern Mok
Empire

Lost Isles

What Came Before . . .

Methamphetamine (Meth) has become an epidemic in the United States. Such a social nightmare, that upon her election, the new President forms the Methamphetamine Control Agency (MCA). The MCA searched for the best prosecutors around the country to join this fight against Meth. Joining the MCA, Jonathan Champion was a federal prosecutor who had made his name prosecuting some of the most dangerous Meth dealers in the country. Dubbed the 'Golden Boy' by the press, Champion was the face of the MCA in the agency's early beginnings.

After losing his wife and young son in a car bombing, and with himself being horribly scarred, Champion withdraws from the world. He does his best to limit contact with those of his former life. He tries to simply exist in a world that now holds little joy or meaning for him. However, no matter how much he wants to simply live a purposeless life, events soon occur which shock him back to life. A strange tornado like creature offers him a bargain which leads him to another world.

Champion is met by a strange woman named Terra who explains that he is a mage and the only hope for his people.

He soon learns that humans, or mundanes, are considered a magic-less and inferior people to the other races of this world. Champion does not know whether he is dreaming, hallucinating, or had indeed been transported to another world.

In this strange world Champion meets two companions: the blue skinned Tyrell and the mushroom like Grach. While traveling, the trio shared a camp fire with the Mok merchant Calphan and his two mundane servants, Breg and Gret. The group of six then is attacked by a horde of rabid rodents under the control of three dark shrouded sorcerous beings. During the attack Champion discovers that he is able to call on the element of fire and burns the mesk horde to cinders, allowing the group to escape into an underground tunnel.

While traversing the underground tunnels Champion learns from Calphan about rawstones; the precious stones that are used as the main power source for this world. Champion is concerned by the smoky meth like smell that comes from the stones. Before he can discover further information about the rawstones Champion is separated from his companions and wanders lost in the darkness. Again he meets the strange woman Terra who gives him some intensive training in the command of air and fire. She tells him he must go to Hyberan, the Mages City, and find the librarian Mosha.

Meanwhile, Tyrell and Grach lead the remaining travelers to the surface. Grach returns to the tunnels to search for Champion and Tyrell is taken into custody by the Mages. Calphan the Mok merchant and his servants escape capture by the Mages by use of a Way Gate, a powerful rawstone powered magical traveling device. It becomes apparent that Calphan is not just a simple merchant.

Grach tracks Champion's movements in the underground tunnels and finds his friend in the company of a winged reptilian nightmare known as a Dracoth. The Dracoth, named Scorch was a prisoner who had turned on his masters. When Champion and Grach agree to free him, Scorch gives Champion powerful gifts with special properties; a helm, an ax, and a pair of gauntlets.

Champion and Grach make their way from Scorch's prison and travel to Hyberan, the City of the Mages. Upon arrival at the city, Champion obtains the aid of the Sublime Sisters to aid a sick child and meets the sultry Sister Kitla. Concerned about their inability to find Tyrell, Grach informs Champion of his decision to leave the city in search of their lost friend. Grach arranges for Champion to join the Green Guard before he departs.

Calphan also has his own plans in Hyberan. It soon comes to light that he is in league with those three mysterious beings who had attacked the group of travelers in the northern forests. Under the orders of the Mok Empress, Calphan is to provide assistance to these three dark allies in coordinating an attack on the Mages City. An armada of Mok warships awaits Calphan's signal to begin an attack on the city walls.

Champion's attempts to find the librarian Mosha have not been successful. Albeit, his efforts may have been a bit half-hearted due to the newfound contentment he has found with Sister Kitla. He also begins to form bonds of friendship with his fellow Green Guardsmen. For the first time since the death of his wife and son, Champion finds life worth living.

While escorting Eldest Sister to a meeting, Champion stumbles upon the abrasive librarian Mosha. After the exchanging of a few insults, Champion agrees to accompany the fat man to the library in the Mage Citadel. While at the library, Champion is shocked to find a man with the tattoo similar to one he recognizes from the day his wife and son were killed. He follows the man to the bowels of the Mage Citadel to discover thousands of mundanes, humans, being force fed Meth in order to power the rawstones.

In an attempt to obtain more information, Champion abducts a young tattooed boy, to the great distress of Mosha. Mosha and Champion then learn from the boy that the mysterious 'Orda' actually make the rawstones and that the 'white tar' or Meth, is somehow used in the rawstone process. The two men then release their prisoner and go to Mosha's quarters where Champion tells the librarian his story from the time he arrived in this strange world till now.

Meanwhile, Grach travels far but eventually finds Tyrell in the Ferrekei home lands under the care of his own clan. Though weakened from his imprisonment by the mages, Tyrell is adamant about returning to Hyberan to ensure that Champion is safe. The pair returns to the city to find that Calphan's servant Gret, has been horribly injured and left in front of the Great Temple of the Sublime Sisters.

Champion's reunion with his friends was bittersweet due to Gret's injury. Through his pain, Gret is able to tell the three friends that Calphan's other servant Breg, is in dire trouble. Grach and Champion go to aid Breg and find that their friend has been ritually mutilated and hung on a stone wheel. Through some dark magic, Breg is kept alive even through his gruesome injuries. Champion grants Breg's silent request to be freed from his pain by a merciful death.

Gazell and two other mages arrive to view Breg's horrible fate. Believing that the mages may have something to with Breg's torture and the mundanes being forced to use meth in the Citadel, a confrontation with Gazell seems inevitable until a grey clad Orda appears with a warning of danger. The Orda's warning is justified when the Mok Empresses' three evil allies appear and attack Champion, Gazell and her mages. With the Orda's help, Champion and Gazell defeat the three dark creatures.

In the meantime, the Mok Armada attacks the mage city. The mages defeat the Mok forces at great cost. During the chaos of the battle, Calphan makes a bold move and kidnaps Champion in an attempt to salvage something from the defeat.

Locked in the hold of a Mok ship, Champion is drugged into a comatose state to keep him from using his powers. In his dreams, he is visited by the woman Terra, who confirms his fears of the forced addiction of mundanes, humans, for the purpose of making the rawstones. With Terra's help, Champion is able to escape Calphan's clutches and a ship board cat and mouse ensues. Terra's instructions Champion attempts to drain the rawstone's from the ship's stone room to slow the Mok vessel down in hopes that his friends are pursuing the Armada. In a confrontation with Calphan, Champion loses control of his power and releases his powerful fire into the rawstones and burns the entire Armada to ashes.

Floating helplessly in unfamiliar ocean waters, wounded and almost mad from lack of sustenance, Champion is saved by a ship of Corsair pirates who have no idea what type of danger they may be courting.

Here ends "The Meth Conspiracy."

PROLOGUE

D reams are strange. Memories, urges, and wishful thinking all mixed together into a messy web of thought. Like being given a book with the first and last chapters missing and then asked to explain the plot. Yes, dreams were strange.

The landscape was a familiar one. A large open blue sky with small patches of wispy white clouds dominated the view. Somehow he recalled that the surroundings for miles around were known as "big sky country."

He sat in a wooden chair that creaked slightly as it rocked. Behind him he knew was a small brick farm house. He and the noisy chair were on the porch of the house. He never looked over his shoulder to view the house. He simply knew it was there, knew what it looked like, and his dream-self had no interest in confirming what he already knew. No, what had his attention was the building in front of him.

It was an unremarkable structure. Completely covered in a dull glass like substance it sparkled in spots under the dream sun. Through the glass vegetation of different kinds could be seen, mostly brown and withered. To the left of the glass building was a large stretch of old churned up earth, evidence of a large garden that had not seen attention for some time. His eyes roamed the outside of the building looking for any damages. It was vitally important that the structure was complete and whole. He did not recall why. A gentle breeze touched his face. He smiled.

"Hello Aeris."

A high pitched chuckle came from the air to his left. A moment later the elemental appeared. A tall willowy figure, the being was striking in appearance. Skin too pale to be called white almost glowed. No clothing covered the form. Aeris was entirely bare and hairless. Where proof of gender would normally appear a small bump of nothing existed. As the creature moved to stand next to the mage it stretched out long arms almost in benediction.

"Behold! The great mage! Master of Fire and Air! Scourge of the Bright City and the Big Frogs! Defender of lusty women and their whining brats! Behold his dream!"

Quiet descended on the pair. It stretched into a long moment bringing another smile. Aeris lowered its arms and turned, "Really, Master Mage. Such an omnipotent personage should have more interesting dreams. Sitting and watching dirt age is incredibly boring."

He shrugged at the observation, "This place was, is, important to me. I need simply to remember why. I will remember Aeris. I must."

He looked up at the elemental. No matter how often he prepared himself it was always a minor shock to look upon the form Aeris had chosen. Not because of the striking willowy body and pale glowing skin. It was the face. His face. His face, unscarred, unblemished. He looked away.

With a gusty sigh, Aeris sat down next to it's master. The man was a complete mystery. Not that it cared for human emotions attached to memories. What were they but bits and pieces of things in the past? Why remember them? Especially if they brought such sorrow and despair?

Aeris sighed again. It knew it had begun to take on some of the aspects of the mage. Aeris found itself sometimes thinking in living terms. It had sometimes referred to itself as "me", had begun to have strange thoughts and ideas. An elemental was not supposed to feel anger or remorse, not supposed to feel happiness or care if its master was in a dark mood. But it did. He did. Aeris sighed again.

Suddenly a ball of fire soared out of the blue sky striking the building. The pair watched in unsurprised silence as the glass melted off the building's wooden frame and fell onto the un-worked garden. After a few burning moments, the mage waived a scarred hand, the flames disappeared and the building again appeared whole and untouched.

A flaming apparition then landed in front of the porch. A dark red figure robed in fire and blackened smoke stalked slowly toward the silent duo. Smoldering red coal like eyes regarded the man and elemental with undisguised disgust. A raspy smoke filled voice demanded, "What is the meaning of this?!"

As if responding to a courteous greeting, the mage nodded his head, "Well, hello Cinder. What on earth has kept you?"

Growling and cursing Cinder took two steps forward and placed itself in between the building and the source of its annoyance. Sighing, the man was forced to look up and acknowledge the elementals presence. Cinder's form was as impressive as his airy companion was striking. Cinder was dressed in what looked to be a long coat and a strange hat with a large bill. Fire and smoke covered the coat and the head covering smoldered with a red and white fury. The man knew that the coat was a "trench coat" and the hat was one called a "cowboy hat." Like all knowledge of such things he could not place the memories associated with it.

Unlike Aeris, the angry face that regarded the mage was not unmarked. It was however, his face. His face crisscrossed with savage fire ripped scars. So much red and white scarring covered the entire visage that the flesh resembled so much thick spider webbing layered over and over. Blackened teeth poked through dry chapped lips in a ghastly sneer.

"You waste your time with this farce. This whining and mewling over things unchangeable; things that have little consequence. We have more important tasks to accomplish."

The mage turned his eyes back to the building for several moments. Just as Cinder was about to begin another vicious taunt the man spoke, "You two have knowledge that I need."

Blackened teeth clicked shut. Cinder met Aeris's glance with questioning eyes over the head of the mage. The pale elemental shook his head.

"No need to blame Aeris, my burning friend. I am just amazed that it took me so long to figure it out myself."

Slowly the man stood up from the chair never removing his eyes from the building, "Both of you know who I am."

Cinder paused a moment then snorted, "Of course we do. You are the most annoying, pig headed, won't live up to his potential . . ."

"Yes"

Cinder stopped in mid-sentence, mouth hanging open in shock. It looked to the source of its amazement. Aeris would not meet the glare. Instead, the elemental of air looked at the mage with haunted eyes. Again it said, "Yes.

We know who you are, or who you were. We are a part of you. How could we not know?"

The mage clinched his fists at his side. His back stiffened slightly. Taking a deep breath he asked, "Why?"

Motioning Cinder to be quiet, Aeris answered, "We see no need for it, Master. You have enough pain. Why do you need more? We kept your past from you because a part of you does not wish to know, but wishes to forget. We respect that wish and agree with it." He reached out with a pale hand and placed a feathery touch on the mages' shoulder. For several moments, the three waited in almost companionable silence.

Then shaking his head, the mage ordered, "Leave me."

Aeris nodded and faded away. Cinder stayed a moment longer. The fire of the trench coat burned a bit lower as if the elemental felt uncertainty.

"Master, I . . ."

"Leave me. Now!" With a yelp the elemental faded quickly away. The man stood alone on the porch lost in thought; dreaming.

CHAPTER ONE

The herbalist Thurga was a small man. Round-shouldered and stooped, he rarely looked into the eyes of his customers. He would nod continuously as he listened to their requests and, when they had finished, mutter, "Very well, good, yes, yes" as if complimenting them. His movements were quick and sure, his judgment of weight uncanny. He would tip powder or shredded leaf into small bags of muslin and rarely weigh them. Occasionally a new customer would ask to see the item weighed on his small brass scales. He would nod and smile, and say, "Very well, good, yes, yes." The scales would then show the exact weight in ounces the customer had asked for.

But then, the grey haired Thurga had been an herbalist for over twenty-seven years. Judgment to the quarter ounce, he considered, was a small enough skill to acquire in almost three decades and certainly not one to cause undue pride. Thurga was not wealthy, nor was he poor. However, a mund who had escaped the bonds of servitude in the Mok Empire could scarcely ask for more than he had. Thurga lived in a small house with a slate roof and a half acre of ground on which he grew many herbs. Other plants and fungi were gathered for him by women who lived in the brush filled areas of the higher hills. The herbalist Thurga had no close friends and no wife, for he was not a man comfortable with intimacy of any kind. Neither did he have enemies. He was not even disliked, which was unusual for a mundane who practiced his trade with such skill. In many communities in the isles, he would have been driven out of business long ago based on his race. Besides his skill, it was how he treated people that brought them coming back for his services. Thurga was punctiliously polite to all and never offered an opinion except on matters herbal and never entered into debate with anyone. It was, he had long ago decided, safer that way.

Thurga cast a quick, nervous glance at the grey eyed youth standing at his counter. He felt a bit uneasy around Kay, though in truth he could not think why. It had nothing to do with the young Gurachii himself, but with whom the man owed loyalty too. "Fever, you say? What is the nature of the fever Master Kay?" He listened intently as the young man explained of finding the Red Lady's son that morning in a state of ill health. The lad could keep down no food and had a strange pallor to his skin.

"The lady asked for you to select herbs that could be put in a broth or drink."

"Very well, good, yes, yes," said Thurga. "Please take a seat, Master Kay, while I prepare the necessary ingredients." Thurga was anxious to please the Red Lady, as she was commonly known. She had become a powerful personality in Haven and, truth be told, throughout the Lost Isles. More than fifty women were employed by her making dresses, shirts, blouses, and other articles of clothing. She had established a school in Haven open to all children whether they be mundane or not, orphaned or from a large well to do family. Rumor was she planned to open schools in other communities. The lady was remarkable. But, regardless of her accomplishments, and the high regard of the herbalist, it was due to the fact that she was the Mage's woman that made Thurga wish to please her.

Thurga stood for a moment surveying the scores of earthenware jars on his shelves. Each jar was marked with a symbol or a series of letters. The first he chose bore the picture of a leaf blackened in with coal mark. Uncorking the jar, he scooped out a portion of the contents, and then, with his left hand, opened a small bag of muslin into which he tipped the powder.

"What is that?" asked Kay. Thurga jerked. He had not heard the young man leave his seat and move once more to the counter. It unnerved him a little. Had it been anyone else, he would have asked him to politely return to his seat. But this young man was servant, or companion, to the most unpredictable Mage and his lady and therefore needed to be treated with a little more respect.

"It is the leaf of a black honeysuckle," said Thurga. "I shall give you four half-ounce bags. The powders must be boiled with sugar to make a type of cider. It will help dispel the fever.

"For the skin coloration I shall make up a potion with hamroot and suffix. The lady will know what to do with it. You may expect the lad to have some immoderate movements of the bowels in the early stages. To alleviate this I recommend tycle root extract. It is, however expensive. It is six golds a bottle, and you will need two bottles."

"Twelve golds?" Kay said, astonished.

"Aye, Master Kay. The Tycle tree does not grow in the Isles. Indeed, I have tried for years to grow just one shrub of the stuff on this side of the sea. The extract needs to be shipped from Hyberan and with the war 'shipped' means 'smuggled' and that raises the cost. However, the mixture is as effective as it is costly."

"I will take the one bottle," said Kay. "But I will have to send to the Manse for more gold."

"Not a problem, Master Kay. I trust you and your employer implicitly. Simply have the total sum waiting for me when I call on the honored Mage tomorrow afternoon." Thurga carefully gathered all the herbs and powders, then took up a willow quill and dipped it into a small pot of ink. In immaculate copperplate script he wrote out the details of the purchase and the sums required, sanded the finished receipt, and, when he was sure the ink had dried, folded the paper and handed it to Kay. The young man pocketed it and then heaved a large canvas shoulder bag to the worktop. It was already half full. Thurga opened the flap at the top and packed his powders and potions among the contents. The bottle of extract he placed within a wooden box with straw.

"Be careful with this, Master Kay."

"I will, Sir."

A commotion began outside, and Thurga could hear voices being raised. The outside door was thrust open, and a young mund pushed inside. He was red faced, his eyes wide with excitement. "There was a battle and old Spuros came into port with his crew beat up pretty bad. One of the Corsairs ships was taken crew and all by ambush. The Mage burned his way through and saved those that weren't spiked. They need hands down at the docks to haul the wounded off and help with repairs. Spuros wants the *Spite* refitted and with a few more hands so he can ship out with the tide."

"When do they plan to head out?" inquired Thurga.

"Not sure Sir, but the whole thing looks ugly."

"Thank you, my boy. Most kind of you to let me know."

The young man nodded excitedly, moved back to the street, and entered the bakery next door. His voice could just be heard through the thick walls, but only the occasional word sounded clearly. "Spuros . . . ambush . . . mage . . ."

"We live in perilous times, Master Kay," Thurga said with a sigh.

"I had best get back to the Manse. Be well, Master Thurga." Kay lifted the canvas bag to his shoulder, offered a short bow to the herbalist, and walked out to the cobbled street beyond.

Thurga could see people gathering in the street and wandered back into his storeroom, sitting himself down in an old wicker chair. Leaning back against the embroidered cushions, he closed his eyes. So much violence in the world, he thought sadly.

On the table beside his chair was a package of herbs and ointments he had prepared for the Mage only that morning, soothing balms for the old burns on the man's face and arm. Another package was for the Mage's head wound which was a near constant agony. He had almost died from that wound two years earlier. It had been the Mage's good fortune that Thurga had been summoned. There had been much internal bleeding but the herbalist had managed to stem the flow and halt the onset of infection. Even so, it was a full three months before the wounded man had recovered sufficient strength to walk unaided. Years later the wound was nothing more than a pale line of scarring hidden beneath the mages hair but still occasionally caused headaches and nausea that sometimes required bed rest.

Thurga sighed. Acts of violence were beyond his imagination. Never in his life had he desired to hurt anyone.

This latest conflict between the Corsairs and the Empire would change things. Until recently, the pirates simply identified rich targets and, sometimes with the mage's aid, looted and retreated into the Isles. The Empire had seen this as a mere annoyance before. Setting up this kind of ambush was different. Obviously the Corsair's activities were detrimental to the war effort. There would be more bloodshed and violence in the days ahead. Thurga felt the weight of sadness heavy upon him.

CHAPTER TWO

Fenn was cold. Shivering as a gust of water filled spray washed over the side of the ship; he tried to huddle further into his cloak. Just two more days he thought as he glared at the grey sky as if his anger could break through to warmer air.

Two more days and this stupid mission would be done. Two more days and he would be heading back to the Bright City, and back to the inns and the warm blankets of his room in the citadel. Tramping around the Lost Isles was a fool's errand and a total waste of time. There was nothing down here but pirates and runaway munds; Nothing that required the attentions of a mage.

Fenn's blue Ferrekei skin was getting wrinkled and raw from his time at sea. His people had little love of the sea and she returned the favor. Sea salt was famous for giving the blue skinned race horrible rashes. Though Fenn had avoided that particular indignity, he still did not want to press his luck.

The war was at a momentary stand still. The Mok Empress had taken large chunks of the Gurashii lands in the first few months on her march towards Hyberon but had met stronger resistance once the mages had organized. While the Mok's outnumbered the mages forces nearly five to one, the power that the council brought to the battle field evened up the odds. Thousands of Mok's died on the front lines from fire, storms, and earthquakes and yet still the Empress persisted. In two years of fighting nothing had been decided.

Once again his thoughts came back to his current predicament. A Mok missive had been intercepted that indicated magical activity in the Lost Isles. Located far to the south east of Hyberan, the city had very few dealings with the scattered communities in this lonely and isolated part of the world. According to the intercepted information several Mok ships had disappeared in the past year. Word had reached Hyberan that the Corsairs had appeared again in the past several months. This did not concern the council at the moment since the pirates would be more of a housekeeping problem for the Empress since the Isles were in her backyard; so to speak. However, any mage activity not authorized by the council must be investigated.

The *Swift* was a ship built for this type of mission. Sleek, and light of gear, bereft of cannon and with a near empty hold, she could fly across the waves even without the use of her stone room and the rawstones. The Gurachii crew was as efficient and capable as they looked disreputable. The kind of men you would not trust with your money purse or a woman, but who could sail the ocean's heart and live to tell about it. Fenn wiped his dripping nose on his sleeve and hoped the memory of hot cider could warm up his cold feet. Just as he thought he could feel his toes responding to the memory, a gust of wind knocked him from his feet. Scrambling back upright, Fenn forgot his discomfort and scanned the deck alertly. The crew went about their business seemingly unaware and not bothered by the weather.

That was a mage wind. Tentatively, he called up air and quested outward. He could sense . . . something. Up on the rigging a shape moved. Fenn channeled his will, bringing a funnel of air after the intruder. Shocked sailors leapt back from the whirlwind that appeared in the rigging and then seemed to bounce haphazardly around the deck.

"Clear the deck!" Fenn yelled over the sound of the creaking ship. As if poked by a hot brand simultaneously, the crew scattered to the galley and the hold. Only the captain and the steersman stayed.

Quietly watching the spectacle on his deck the captain called out, "Honored mage, what the hell is going on?" While Captain Drach held the same reverence for mages that most citizens in Hyberan did, he was still the ship captain and was owed an answer. The Gurachii captain stood calmly behind the steersman, his legs rocking effortlessly with the sway of the ship.

"When I find out I will let you know!" Fenn answered back. He gritted his teeth. Keeping the funnel moving was tiring considering all of the natural wind moving all over the deck. He could feel a presence on the deck that was definitely associated with Air. But not with the familiar attributes of a mage. What the hell was it? Fenn had no more time to answer his question as he was again buffeted off of his feet and the last memory he had was of hurtling toward the wooden planking of the deck, then nothing.

"He is coming around. Easy Honored Mage, you had quite the tumble." With a groan Fenn opened his eyes. He was lying on the deck with the face of the crew's healer greeting his groan with a relieved smile. With the healer's help, and a terrible headache the groggy mage leaned up to a sitting position. Off to the side were the captain and most of the crew, many of them held an assortment of weapons from cudgels to blades. Facing them, as if unconcerned, or unaware of their animosity, sat . . . . something.

Fenn's eyes grew wider as he studied the creature. Long of limb and pale, it appeared to be made out of air. The thing was humming to itself as it sat on the side rail of the ship with one foot resting on the deck and the other lazily swaying in the wind. A face complete with eyes, nose, and mouth seemed to be lost in thought as it stared out over the waves. As if it heard him slowly getting to his feet, the air creature looked over at Fenn and smiled, "Excellent timing, mageling. Your reawakening has coincided perfectly with the arrival of a personage of great import."

Feeling his legs steadying, Fenn ignored his aching body and approached the creature. Gently, he sent a probing of air towards the thing.

"Ah, Ah, Ah, now mageling. Only if you ask nicely." The being flicked a long finger and Fenn's probing dissolved suddenly. Pushing the healer gently away, Fenn now stood directly in front of the creature. What he was seeing was possible, but rare beyond imagining, "A manifestation."

"Excuse me?" The air man asked, cocking his, its, head to the side.

Licking dry lips, Fenn repeated, "You are a manifestation. I have read about it. But never have I heard of one that could . . . communicate."

With a soft chuckle, the creature replied, "Well, I do not know if I should be flattered or offended, mageling. I choose to be flattered." Another chuckle.

Being on his feet had steadied the pounding in Fenn's head somewhat. He could feel the anger of the crew behind him. This situation needed to come to a close before a confrontation occurred. The men would have no chance against the creature, but that would not stop them from acting. Recalling something Fenn asked, "You mentioned something about an arrival?"

"Indeed. You all are to be honored above many, mageling." Suddenly the creature stood up and spread its arms. The crew stepped back almost as one. In a hollow bellowing voice it intoned, "All here will bask in his magnificence; his wisdom; his beauty . . ." Lowering its arms the creature paused, then added, "Well maybe not his beauty. But mind your manners."

"That is enough Aeris." A voice said to Fenn's right. Turning, Fenn's eyes widened again as a mundane's face appeared out of thin air. As the mage watched, more of the mund appeared as if he were shedding a cloak.

"A concealment cloak." Fenn whispered. Long forgotten was Fenn's disappointment with the mission. If he did not survive the day, which was a strong possibility, he would still consider it worthwhile to have viewed a manifestation and a concealment cloak all on the same day. Now fully revealed, Fenn studied the mund.

Tall and thin, the mund seemed to be lost in thought as he took in Fenn and the crew. A well-made grey cloak contrasted with a pair of muddied brown boots. Thick brown gloves were covered with guantlets of a grey metal. A face horribly scarred seemed to belie the calm assurance the mund somehow exuded. One white eye and one hazel seemed at odds in the same face. Next to him the air manifestation stood but kept a step back as if in deference to the mund. With a start, Fenn realized that the mund and the creature each shared the same face, albeit the one without the scarring.

Captain Drach stepped forward. The mund turned his gaze on the Gurachii as the man moved to stand between himself and his crew. Fenn noted wryly that the Captain had not tried to step in between himself and the strange visitor.

"I am Captain of this vessel. All who are on it are my responsibility. Who you are to impede my ship?"

The captain's words were strange. Impede? Fenn looked around and suddenly understood that the ship was no longer moving. Stepping to the rail he looked down and gasped as the vessel was floating above the water, hovering still in the air. Stumbling back from the rail, the mage would have fallen had the healer not been at his side again. Taking some deep, calming breaths Fenn ignored the healer's reassuring words and instead concentrated on the captain and the mund.

As if digesting Drach's words, the mund spoke in a clear voice, "Do you carry rawstones, captain?" the quiet voice was filled with the promise of hidden violence.

Taking a half step back, the Captain nodded, "Of course. Our stone room holds rawstones in the event that we need them. In weather like this we use the wind and currents to speed our way. We are true sailors and use the stones only when necessary." Members of the crew nodded in agreement. Unlike the Mok Empire, the Mage Council only outfitted ships that could operate under full sail without the need for the rawstones.

Nodding slightly as if the answer satisfied him, the mund replied, "So, you will be able to return to your berth without the stones, correct?"

"Why? Are you demanding our rawstones?" The Captain could not keep the slight scorn from his voice.

"I did not say that I wanted the stones, but wanted to be sure you and your crew could return without them. For some reason I have a soft spot for the Gurachii. Though I am not sure why . . . ." The mund's voice trailed off as if he had lost his train of thought. As if dispersing a foggy memory, the mund shook his head,

"The Empire needs to be taught a lesson. I go to administer it. However, I cannot let you operate a vessel with rawstones. Therefore, I offer you a choice; you bring all the stones up to me now, or I destroy your ship and the stones. You have a few moments to consider." As if noticing Fenn for the first time, the mund approached. Feeling extremely vulnerable, Fenn still met the taller man's glare.

The mund let the silent moment last a bit longer before asking, "You are a mage?" There was a threatening undertone behind the question, as if he were asking Fenn to admit to something morally unclean. Fenn cocked his head to the side slightly considering his words carefully.

"I am. And so, it appears, are you. Although I do not know how this can be."

The mund's brow creased in response to Fenn's words and demanded, "State your meaning plain."

"You are obviously a mage and one of considerable power to have created a manifestation and be able to hold this vessel hostage. Still, a mund mage is something that I have . . ." Fenn was suddenly hanging in the air. Instinctually he called air and tried to undercut the strands holding him in place. The air bonds used to hold him might as well have been made from stone for all the good his power did. Slowly Fenn felt himself rotated upside down and he lost his bearing for the moment. Suddenly, the scarred face of the mund was inches from his own.

He could feel the hot breathe of the man's anger as he hissed, "I hate that word. Among all the things that I remember, that I know I hate, that is near the top of the list. I wish to use you as a messenger, but if you say that word again I will scorch your ass and then piss on the ashes. Understood?" Nodding his head in immediate understanding, Fenn felt himself being slowly righted. He breathed a sigh of relief as his soggy boots felt the hard wood of the deck.

Without removing his eyes from Fenn, the mund yelled across the deck to the captain, "Time is up Captain. Choose." Drach looked to Fenn, and at the mage's nod he shouted out orders. Three crew members dashed down to the hold. Minutes later they returned, each holding a leather case. Gently they placed the two cases in front of the mund and quickly backed away.

At a gesture from the mund, the manifestation stepped forward and opened each case. In the bland light of the grey mist filled sky, the rawstones flickered. Each case held eight stones capable of generating enough energy to power the vessel several hundred leagues. Slowly, the stones rose into the air, and floated toward the mund. As they approached, the mund closed his hazel eye and set his jaw in seeming intense concentration. The white oval of his right eye seemed to shine slightly. Fenn could almost sense something going on between the stones.

Suddenly, sounding little more like eggs being gently cracked, fissures appeared in the stones. Slowly, gentle wisps of colored smoke began drifting from their jeweled surfaces and filling the sea air with the unmistakable scent of rawstones. After several moments, the stones had gone grey and dark. Dead and empty, they fell to the wooden deck. Suddenly, the ship lowered into the chopping waves.

Fenn cursed as the vessel swayed into the water, making him stumble. After he got his bearings he and the mund mage shared a curious stare.

"Ware, Ships!"

The call shattered the almost solemn moment. Drach ran to the rail and swore at what he saw. Five Mok vessels were appearing on the grey covered horizon. Their speed indicated that they would take over the vessel in a matter of hours. With no rawstones, and an unpredictable wind, there was little chance of escape.

Captain Drach spat out some orders and the idle crew suddenly sprang into action. Rigging tightened, and hatches were secured. The steersman pulled hard on the wheel and the vessel lurched wayward, trying to grab and hold every ounce of the wind with canvas and sail. Stalking towards the mund, Drach pointed his finger in the scarred man's face.

"A damn fix we are in now, you ugly faced bugger! Sitting ducks without our stones! No chance! Was this your plan all along? Fuck us and then leave us to the green bastards?!" Pushing past the fuming captain, the mund approached the railing. Fenn joined him and the two mages watched the steady approach of the ships.

Fenn shook his head, "I might be able to shift air currents around one ship to lead it off course . . . but five . . ."

"We can handle this." As the mund spoke the manifestation stepped up next to him. Motioning with his hand he addressed Fenn, "Step back, Mage."

Through all he had seen, and witnessed, Fenn still bridled a bit at the mund's dismissive tone, "I am an Air Mage, Man! I can help you!"

Smiling almost cruelly, the mund answered, "We need fire to aid us. Now step back!"

Totally confused, Fenn did as ordered. The force of the command brooked no argument. Around them the crew's actions took on a more desperate feel as if the men threw themselves into their work to avoid thinking about the impending doom. Over the sound of the crashing waves and cursing sailors Fenn heard the mund's voice call out, "Cinder, attend me."

The apparition that appeared was something out of a nightmare or a fire mage's dream. Long coat, strange billed hat, and a scarred visage all covered in red flame.

"Aeris, start on the left, Cinder to the right. I will take the center ship. Disable their cannon first, then the ships. Go."

All three figures then leapt from the deck, soaring towards the approaching fleet. From this distance, it was difficult to see with any clarity. However, it was apparent that the three figures had approached the ships with amazing speed. The sound of startled cries of the Mok crews could be heard. Soon, the cannons began bellowing, bursts of colored rawstone smoke could be seen against the grey cloudy canopy.

With the ships sails at full blow, their own vessel began to move away from the conflict. Captain Drach joined Fenn at the railing. Silently, they watched as one, two, then three of the distant ships caught fire.

"That's not right." Drach mused out loud. At Fenn's questioning look, the Captain explained, "Those ships are burning from the holds. As if a fire was started inside the damn thing. Much as I hate the Mok's, they make a safe vessel. I do . . ."

An explosion blew his words away. Even from this distance the pair could feel a slight heat on their faces. Another explosion and then another. Soon, four great burning hulks drifted listlessly across the waters. The fifth, burning, but still moving on its own, slowly trudged sluggishly away from the scene.

Moments later, one small figure approached the ship. Slowly gaining in size as it neared, the mund mage soon landed softly on the deck of the ship. Drenched with wet, the man's hair plastered against his face, almost hiding the scarring. Holding his arms out under the cloak, he tried to shake off as much of the dampness out of the garment as he could, cursing as he did it. It was strange to watch the man do something as routine and ordinary as flush out his cloak given what they had just witnessed. With a shrug, he gave up and allowed his cloak to hang limp and wet from his shoulders, calmly regarding the duo in front of him.

With a low whistle, Captain Drach spoke first, "Quite a display. Now, what is the fastest way to get you off my ship?"

The mund smiled at that. To Fenn he said, "I told you I have a message. Are you capable of delivering it?"

Fenn nodded, "As long as you tell me what just happened out there."

Turning to look over his shoulder, the mund nodded towards the burning wreakage, "I think those ships ate something that did not agree."

At Fenn's irritated look, the mund threw back his head and laughed. Not a creepy maniacal laugh that Fenn would have expected, but a full, joyful sound, that even had the ship's Captain chuckling.

"Ah, blue man. You should see your face. It is a sight. Sorry for laughing. I have been told it is good to laugh at least once a day, helps keep the spirits up. I thank you for that." Smiling, if a bit ruefully, Fenn nodded. Motioning towards the rawstones that still littered the deck, the mund explained, "Recall what I did with the stones here on deck.

Now, imagine if I were to tell you, that the process you witnessed was one used to ensure that no damage was done to the good captain's fine ship and crew." At Fenn's hesitant nod, the man continued,

"The same process can be done at a much more accelerated rate. All that needs to change is the amount and discharge of the fire down the lines. Once a line is 'ignited' then the fire spreads to the other stones. Eventually resulting in . . ." The mund looked back over his shoulder. The four burning vessels had now been completely submerged while the fifth was nearly out of sight, making its way back to the safety of the Empire.

"Why did you spare one?" Captain Drach's question interrupted Fenn's thoughts as he tried to mentally grapple with what the mund had explained. Shrugging, the mund sighed,

"I was advised to let one get back to the Frogs. The idea is to make them hesitate before sending any more fleets against us. Probably won't work."

"Wait. Wait." Fenn held up a hand, "What do you mean by lines? What lines?"

Now a look of confusion crossed the mund's face. He exclaimed incredulously, "The lines connecting the rawstones; the lines! You mean, you can't see them?" At Fenn's head shake the mund took a moment collecting his thoughts, then spoke as if to himself, "I have forgotten so much, I don't know where things end and begin anymore. The stones are evil, I know that. They suck the life from my people like a never ending disease. I remember the grey wrapped man, I see hundreds of my people, trapped on beds that they can never get up from . . . ." Grabbing his head, the man swayed, his knees buckled and he crashed to the deck. Before Fenn or the Captain could come to his aid, the manifestation called Aeris appeared,

"Tsk, Master. This is most unseemly. What will the neighbors think?" Gently the creature eased the mund to his feet. Still groaning, he held his head obviously in great pain, now gripping the shoulder of the creature to steady himself. Turning towards the railing, the two moved as if to take flight again.

Sensing air being called, Fenn cried, "Wait! You said you had a message!"

At his voice the mund turned back. "Just tell the mages what you saw here today. That should be message enough." With that, the two took to the air. In moments they were small specks; in minutes they were gone.

Fenn slumped to the deck of the ship, his mind awhirl. Without the ship's rawstones the trip back to Hyberan would take weeks, instead of days. He would speed things up by giving his air strength to the sails. Still, the delay would be considerable and he would be exhausted before it was over. He had to remember and take note of everything now while it was fresh in his mind.

Pushing away the helping hands of Captain Drach, he ordered, "Captain! I need paper and ink, now! And a damn dry place to use them. Quickly! Quickly!"

CHAPTER THREE

Tyrell sat down with a grunt. As the fighting frenzy and the adrenaline faded, he could feel the new bruises and aches his body had recently purchased. All around him soldiers followed suit and tiredly took a breather in the lull of the fighting. Boys too young for fighting carried water skins and hard flat cake rations to those whose stomachs could hold it down. Though the idea of lukewarm water and the gritty bread did not sound appealing, he knew he would need the energy. After giving the lad a tired smile and thanks he took stock of his company.

The Duwvar busied themselves with attending to their plated armor. The yellow skinned warriors were used to fighting in close quarters underground which had adapted nicely to this trench warfare. The Mok's had learned early on the cost of charging a Duwvar shield wall.

Ferrekei, Gurachii, many black skinned Tuak, and others sat in small groups tending to wounds and resting; soldiers all. After he had swallowed the last of his ration, Tyrell stood and stretched. Catching the eye of Captain Hyad who was speaking to a Seren dressed in the uniform of a messenger, Tyrell motioned down the trench line. With a nod and a slight waive of his hand, the Duwvar officer turned his head back to the messenger. Tyrell knew he had only a short time before he had to report back to his company. Jogging now, he thought back on the past two years as he searched for Grach.

The Mok's failed attempt at taking Hyberan had lulled the golden city into believing the setback would cause the Empress to reconsider actions that might lead to all-out war. This was a terrible error. Within a few weeks of the attack on the city, the Empire invaded the Gurachii homelands. Tyrell shuddered at the memory of the stories of the atrocities that the Mok's had unleashed on the unprepared seafaring folk. Entire towns and cities were burned to the ground, Gurachii men were mutilated while their wives and children were made to watch, Mok games included releasing starved Garachii into pits with wild dogs to fight over rotten meat. In less than a year, the Garachii were overrun. Thousands of refugees fled north toward the Tauk principalities. The Tauk found themselves protecting their own lands from the Mok armies and roving bands of starving refugees.

In response, the Mages Council sent hundreds of mages south. The strength of magic alone slowed the advance of the Mok war machine; slowed but not stopped. By the time a significant defending force had been marshaled scores of mages had been killed in the fighting. Thousands of Mok soldiers had perished from the elemental magic unleashed but it did not seem to deter the Empress, as she seemed determined to have nothing less than total victory.

Those Gurachii who had been close to the water had fled in anything that could float. Hundreds of vessels struggled into Hyberan packed to the gills with the red skinned survivors. The mages had quickly turned the new arrivals into the beginnings of a formable navy and within a few months the Gurachii fleets had sailed south to ensure the Empress was halted at sea. The Garachii, all natural born sailors, fell upon the Imperial ships like wolves in a sheep pen. With mages and rawstone armaments to augment the new fleet, the Empress had little choice but to abandon any invasion by sea.

Geography, not strength of arms had come to the aid of the allied land forces. The southern Tuak lands were wide open grassy expanses well suited to herding and farming and also to the liking of the Mok generals who could use the open fields and their numerical superiority to surround and encompass any force arrayed against them. The situation was much different up in the northern principalities. Grasslands and rolling hills gave way to rugged mountains with few passes large enough to allow an army through, a perfect natural defense. Now with the Duwvar, Ferrekei, Tuak, and other allies the mages were able to make a stand and hold firm. For a year the Mok juggernaut had been unable to dislodge the much smaller force.

Lost in his recollections, Tyrell nearly missed his friend's hail. Jumping down into the muddied trench, he clasped hands with his Molden friend. A brown toothed smile split the gray skinned face like well churned earth.

After the Mok attack on the mage city two years ago, Grach had been called home. Tyrell had been mustered with most of the Ferreiki and other allied forces in the first few months of the war. It had been almost a year that the two friends had seen each other until the Tuak Campaign. Grach had arrived with a large force of Molden warriors that were welcomed by the allied command with open arms.

The Molden had proved invaluable in the defense. With their natural ability to tunnel and fight in tight quarters the Mok commanders had learned to avoid any defense works heavily manned by the strange grey skinned men. As a result, the defenders had divided the Molden force into several smaller units charged with the task of coming to the aid of any potential Mok break through. The strategy had been amazingly effective and had contributed to the standstill the Empress now faced.

Tyrell was preparing to return to his unit when the Seren messenger who had been talking with Captain Hyad approached them. Dog like in appearance, the Seren were not ideal soldiers in the type of trench warfare that had developed between the two armies. However, the ability to move quickly over the trenches and swerve through the massing troops made them ideal for carrying messages back and forth from the High Command to the frontline captains. The Seren were also known to be the preferred agents of the Mage counsel for tracking and dealing with problem citizens that the mages wished to be found or, some whispered, disposed of. With a lolling tongue the Seren flashed a fang white grin at the duo.

With a nod in greeting Tyrell gave the messenger his attention, "The Mages wish to speak with the two of you. Your commanders have been advised that your presence is required." After being around the Seren often in the past year it was easier to understand their growling speech.

Ignoring Grach's questioning look, Tyrell asked, "When?"

"Now, if you would be so kind?" A furry clawed hand beckoned them to follow.

The walk to the High Command was time consuming. While only a distance of a mile, rows of defensive works slowed the progress. At each defensive section, a password was required and the messenger had to show his mage's seal. Tyrell mused to himself that prior to the war he would have been frustratingly impatient to learn what the mages wanted of them. Now, he enjoyed the chance to stretch his legs outside of the cramped trenches and spending time with Grach.

Finally, the Seren escorted the pair through what had once been orchards of apple trees that had been prized for making spicy cider. The towering mountains on either side had given invaluable shade for the sometimes fickle fruit and had been the source of Tuak pride. Now the area had been mostly cleared of the fruit groves to make way for large supply warehouses and stocks for animals. Companies of soldiers and supply wagons swarmed back and forth transporting much needed supplies to the defenders in the trenches.

At the very foot of the pass a Tuak fortress had been built two hundred years before. The construction spanned the pass and would be the final line of defense if the Mok's managed to break through. Tyrell thought that the imposing walls would be little use against the type of rawstone artillery that the Empire could deploy. If the Mok's ever reached this far into the pass the only thing that the defenders could rely on would be the mages themselves. The narrowness of the pass would allow the mages to employ their talents to devastating effect against any massed enemy incursion. While he held no love for the Mok's, still the idea of that kind of destruction made Tyrell let loose an involuntary shudder.

The two friends found themselves quickly ushered into the fortress to wait on the convenience of the mages. Grach had said little until the messenger had left them to sit in an antechamber. Closing the door, they had been told, politely, to simply wait.

"Why do they need us now?" Grach's words were measured and gruff as usual. Many thought the Molden to be simpletons because of their practice of speaking slowly and with few words. From their friendship, Tyrell had learned that the Molden were far from simple but communicated with each other in ways other than speech. Using words was a secondary form of communication for a Molden and their slow way of speaking showed that.

Shrugging, Tyrell had no answer. Two years before he and Grach had been interrogated at length about their association with Johnathan Champion. The strange mund had appeared from a cave one evening in the middle of the two companion's campsite. With a horrible scarred face that hid a strangely tender and courageous heart, the man was nothing like any of the other Mundane's that Tyrell had ever associated with.

Humans, Tyrell silently chided himself. John always claimed he and other munds should be called *Humans*. Whether he was human or mund, whatever else could be said about him, John did not fit the typical profile of an inferior mundane. Indeed, quite the opposite. With mage like powers the man had been fearsome to behold. Tyrell owed his life to the man and had named him a feast brother. Since he had been taken by the Moks no one had seen or heard of Jonathan Champion. It had been a source of sadness for him and Grach that always seemed to be in their thoughts. Their lost friend.

The door opened, disrupting the momentary peace and quiet of the room. A small train of Tuak servants bustled in and quickly set up a pair of chairs and a table. Lastly they left a delicate tea set with four cups. Looking at the flowery design that seemed to overwhelm the plain white porcelain Tyrell had a sinking feeling in his bones as to who might be joining them.

He did not have to wait long. Two Ferrekei mages joined the pair. The old woman was dressed in the red robe of a fire mage and the man wore the white of air. He did not need to look to Grach to know that the Molden had crossed his arms; it was a sign that the normally polite Molden gave when they were unhappy with a guest.

The old woman looked the same as when he had last been in her power. She still wore the long flowing hair of a young unmarried Ferrekei woman with bits of shiny bronze work weaved throughout the white locks. Her gaze seemed to be that of a kind grandmother looking upon a child who had failed to live up to expectations.

The Air Mage had shut the door and now took a seat next to the woman. He seemed a bit frail and bruised as if he had traveled hard recently. He busied himself with pouring tea for everyone and then sat back in his seat and looked at the woman.

Gazell still held her gaze on Tyrell. When he had first met her she had totally dominated the contest of wills. Now, he simply looked back at her with a cold stare; unblinking. Letting the hard stare go on for a moment longer, Gazell picked up her cup. As if a signal, the other mage did as well. Tyrell and Grach made no move toward their drinks.

"MMMmmmm. Such a good vintage of Tuak tea. Pity more than half of the principalities are now under the Empress's control. I doubt she can appreciate the good stuff. Mok's have strange taste buds, you see. So, Tyrell, I see you are not wearing your oracle braid. Why is that?"

During his previous detainment by the mages, Tyrell had been handed over to a strange grey creature who called itself an 'Orda.' The thing had picked through his mind as if it were a book of some kind; his memories just so many pages to be carelessly turned. From that experience it was discovered that Tyrell had a slight skill in divination, or exploring possible futures through dreams. If it was a gift it was a fickle thing and his dreams had been of little use. However, all Ferrekei who had some of the talent were expected to wear a gold colored oracle braid. It was tradition.

He shrugged under the question, "Any type of colorful beacon like that might single me out as some sort of special officer that would bring me undue attention from the enemy. I am not the only one to remove such ornamentation."

"Humph . . . yes well, I am sure some things can be excused in light of the current situation." This brought an annoying grunt from Grach. The noise turned the mages attention to the Molden.

"And how have you been, Root Brother? I hear your brethren are acquitting themselves quite admirably in battle. You should be proud."

Grach rumbled, "There is no pride in killing, Mage Gazell. The Great Root will reclaim all her children in time. Such a war as this is an abomination."

Nodding in silent agreement, Gazell let the room fall into a moment of quiet as she took a slow sip. Placing her cup carefully on the table, she turned her attention to the mage sitting next to her, "Fenn here has an interesting story concerning a feast brother of yours, dear one. Would you like to hear it?"

The two companions gave an emphatic yes. Fenn spent the next hour giving a thorough accounting of his experience in the Lost Isles. The tale was amazing if not a bit confusing for a non-mage to understand. For Tyrell the important thing is that Jonathan Champion was alive. He is alive! But how did he escape the Mok's? How by the forest did he get to the Lost Isles? That was hundreds of leagues south, past even the remote parts of the Mok Empire. Tyrell thought with a faint smile, *John my friend, you never do anything by halves do you?*

"What were these . . . creatures that were with him?" Grach's voice almost growled.

Fenn leaned forward, his feet almost tapping with excitement, "Manifestations. They are truly amazing things! I nearly fainted dead away when I realized what I was seeing. And not one but two of them! You see . . ."

"What they are . . . ." interrupted Gazell as she gave Fenn a warning look. The man reddened slightly and lowered his gaze. ". . . is of little importance to you two. Let's just say we would like to very much speak with your strange friend again. On better terms and with a better understanding than the last time."

Tyrell's smile was almost a leer, "You mean when he is not putting the scare in you and then saving your creepy old bones from some snake skinned nightmare?"

Fenn sucked in a shocked breathe. No one spoke to Gazell like that. Her temper was outdone only by her long memory of those who have wronged her.

Gazell met Tyrell's impertinent glare. The leer only got slightly wider as the moment went on. With a shrug, Gazell blinked first, "Fair enough. However, the fact that he appears to have lost his memory, or at least portions of it, concerns us. That and the fact the Empress sees him as dangerous enough to send a small fleet. The destruction of her ships and crew will only make her more determined to deal with him."

Tyrell sat back in his chair and mimicked Grach's crossed arms. "Why are you telling us this? The Isles are a long trip, but a determined group of mages could make it there and back to open up any communications with him. You don't need us to do that."

"True." Gazell nodded, "If that was our only concern. However, your friend seems to have held onto one part of his memories, which is his dislike for mages. A large delegation from the Council could be seen as a threat of some kind. In addition, we are stretched thin as it is. Sending any significant force of mages to the Isles could weaken our defenses here. And . . . ."

"We are expendable." Grach voiced what Tyrell had silently concluded.

Gazell shrugged at the Molden's words, "Let's just say that you two have a unique chance of reasoning with your friend as opposed to a group of mages." The fact she did not refute Grach's statement was not lost on anyone. Gazell waited until both had given nods of agreement to rise and clap her hands once. The same servants entered the room and began clearing away the chairs and table. At an imperious gesture from Gazell they followed the two mages out into the hallway. Three doors down Gazell indicated for Fenn to open the door. What was revealed was amazing.

They were standing on a balcony overlooking a great open room. The height of the place was at least two stories. Below on the marble floor lay a map. But to simply call it a map was an insufficient description. This construction showed all of the lands currently involved in the war. Mountains, rivers, and oceans all could be viewed in stark clarity and seemed to jump out at the observer. What could also be seen in obvious relief was the distribution of the two armies. Green for the Moks and blue for the Mages. Below mages could be seen making changes to the illumination as orders were barked down from above.

One of the voices doing the barking stopped abruptly as he noticed them on the balcony. High Commander Rish was a Tuak Princeps, a ruler of one of the three free Tauk Principalities; he was also a mage. Mages were relatively rare amongst the Tuak and were given an elevated status in their hierarchy.

The Tuak were an awkward looking race at first glance. Tall and gangly, with black skin, ears that were so large they flapped in a strong wind, and equally large facial features. Awkward that is, until they moved. Rish did not so much walk over to the group as glide.

Standing at least a foot taller than Tyrell, the Tuak bowed low to Gazell and nodded to the others in turn. Taking his arm almost affectionately, Gazell purred, "Dear Rish, these three brave ones have agreed to partake on that matter we had discussed earlier."

Three? Thought Tyrell. Looking over at Fenn, the air mage's shocked expression indicated that this information was news to him. Sparing the air mage an almost sympathetic grin, Tyrell's attention was turned back to Rish who frowned slightly before speaking, "Ah, yes. The important matter that you hinted at but could not explain in any detail to me. The matter that takes valuable soldiers and a mage away from our current endeavor to go tramping to where again? Ah, yes. The Lost Isles." Rish was obviously not pleased by this course of events. Giving him a gentle pat on the arm Gazell said,

"I knew you remembered our discussion. Now, can you please show these three the best route on this wonderful creation of yours?" Indicating the map with a wave of her hand.

As he turned his attention back to the map, Tyrell thought, *It is just amazing what you could accomplish with magic.*

CHAPTER FOUR

*I*t is just amazing what you could accomplish without *magic,* Denna thought to herself. She sat on a chair near a window of the Manse. Below her lay the town of Haven. The place had definitely shed its fishing village status and grown and flourished.

The view allowed her to see the swirling activity of the market place. She could barely make out workers building up the harbor walls. Off to her left she could see the fields just below the rising hills that had produced their first edible crops. All this was accomplished through hard work and not a lick of magic.

Of course magic was one reason that this had been accomplished. The power of the mage and the secrecy of Haven's location allowed such prosperity. The Corsairs now attracted more island leaders and the fleet had grown. Yes, prosperity existed now where there was only a hope for simple survival before.

The thought made her look down at the small hand she held in her own. She turned her gaze to the small boy who lay in the bed next to her chair. His coloring was healthy now. Amazing to think that only last night the child had almost died.

She had to stop thinking of Sann as the child. He was her child. Her secret was out. The mage had recently found out somehow, or maybe he had always known. Unconsciously she put a hand to her face, and closed her eyes. He hit me. That was a first.

She had been one of the most sought after whores in all the Lost Isles, even though she was a mund. Pirates, merchants, and royal born would tread the waters seeking her pleasure. Shaff kept his girls moving from city to city to keep the customers wanting for more. Staying in one place too long was bad for business the brute often laughed.

It had just been coincidence that she had been with her master at the same time the Corsairs had arrived. A group of prisoners had been brought to the central square, all bloodied and chained. A slight drizzle of rain had begun to fall making the well packed earth of the square damp with traces of mud, the poor wretches had shivered with the cold wet as well as fear. Shaff had made a public spectacle of perusing the soon to be slaves and making crude comments. As always, she was made to accompany her master on this outing. She winced at the memory of the Mok striking her to her knees for failing to laugh at one of his cruel jests. The muddied ground had caused brown caked blemishes on her skin as she had struggled to her feet.

Out of the group of prisoners a tall mund made his way to the front, dragging those who shared his shackles. A head wound had been hastily bandaged and blood ran red down a scar covered cheek. The mund looked like some long dead sailor returning from the underworld like the stories told at one of the dockside taverns. He moved as far as the bonds allowed then spoke, "Touch her again, Frog, and you will burn."

Shaff seemed more surprised that the prisoner would speak to him at all as opposed to being affected by the words. Never taking his eyes off the obviously deranged mund, Shaff raised a booted foot and gave her a rough nudge back into the mud.

Fire. Shaff was on fire. One minute he was standing there, looking cruel and menacing, and the next he is on fire like some strange green torch with a high pitched scream of pain ripping from his lips. Scrambling away from the screaming Mok, the Corsairs looked ready to rush the scarred man until a barked command stopped them in their tracks. Pushing his way through the throng of pirates Captain Spuros came to stand in front of his men.

Spuros was not a large man, but he radiated that kind of dangerous authority that made you immediately dance to his tune or the consequences would be unpleasant. Like many of his crew, Spuros was a Gurashii; the rain had begun to fall heavier and it sent rivulets of water down his red seamed face. A black eye patch with a red jewel covered one eye and glinted through the rain. He stood there and watched as the fire consumed Shaff. The big Mok had fallen against the stone wall of a building and now lay motionless as his body turned to ash. The fire began to sputter as the rain made contact with the flames. Soon all that remained was a pile of blackened sludge that the rain slowly washed away leaving a darkened scorch mark on the stone wall.

Spuros turned his one eyed gaze to the tall mund. He slowly walked towards the man in a rolling stride that all sailors have who spend most of their time on the deck of a ship. Spuros stood before the mund and motioned toward the remains of the offensive Mok. The two began a quiet conversation that was drowned out by the rain to the others in the square.

With a nod, Spuros stepped forward and produced a square pegged key. With two swift turns the mund had his shackles off and was rubbing sore wrists. Spuros turned as if he expected the *man to follow. A quiet word stopped him. Turning back Spuros said something in a surprised voice. With a slow motion of his hand, the scarred man indicated his fellow prisoners.*

Spuros wetted his lips with a grey tongue as he considered the man in front of him. After a long wet moment, he shouted out an order. The sounds of shackle locks and quiet murmurs of thanks filled the wet night as the other prisoners were released from their bonds.

The tall mund then approached her. She had since risen to her feet and tried to remain calm as the scarred nightmare walked towards her. The rain had plastered the fire red hair to her head, and her drenched mud covered cloak was soggy with discomfort, but she stood her ground. For several seconds the scarred man looked down at her as if drinking in the sight. With a hesitant hand, he slowly placed a finger on her bruised face, speaking quietly, then she . . . .

"Lady."

She looked up as a servant quietly interrupted her recollection. Gently placing Sann's hand down, she nodded and left the room. When the mage summons, you obey.

THINGS HAD changed for the better. Definitely for the better, Thurga thought to himself. The sun had not yet risen, but its soft glow had begun to outline the brick and stone buildings as Thurga left his shop. He nodded to the crew of workers who were diligently refilling the oil lamps that lined the main boulevard. The lack of rawstones had led to a boom in the lamp oil business. Many of his fellow craftsmen had begun investing with merchants who were trying to find new sources of the fuel. One had even tried to convince Thurga that he had developed new, longer burning oils that would make them both rich. Since he liked the man, Thurga had given him half of the requested sum.

The community of Haven had seen strange times in the past two years. Ever since the Corsairs had arrived with ships bursting with plundered cargo the place had been a hub of activity and growth. The war had brought unexpected prosperity to a community of outcasts, runaways, and mundanes.

The start of the day was always a busy time. The fisherwives returning from sending their men and sons off for the daily sea harvest chatted excitedly with dock workers, farmers arriving with their goods and heading for the market stopped to listen to the local gossip, children picking up trash and sweeping the streets clean under the watchful eyes of the Mage's Men.

Thurga shook his head slowly in amazement. Many of these children a year ago would be begging in the streets or working for one of the local thugs stealing apples and cutting purses. Most were orphans or from broken homes and had nowhere to turn except the streets. Until the Mage arrived.

Thurga paused a moment to let his burden rest on the street. The sack was well made and he had little fear that it would break even with its heavy cargo. But his breathe had begun to come in heavier heaves reminding him that he was not a young man anymore. Slowly catching his breath he remembered.

The Mage had arrived with the Corsairs. It had been a thrilling and uncertain time for the community. Being tucked away in the midst of the Lost Isles, Haven was a difficult place to find. The old pirate Spuros was one of the few who knew how to navigate the isles and had a habit of unloading his cargo and hostages at the port town. Hostages meaning prisoners who were healthy and could either be sold as slaves or could be ransomed back to their families.

But the Mage had changed things. Well, the war had changed things as well, Thurga thought, but the Mage had done things . . . differently. Mundanes worked side by side with the other peoples of the community. The slavery and ownership of Munds was completely forbidden. As was the abuse and beating of women and children. This thought brought unbidden the image of the black burn mark in the center of the square. Thurga shuddered.

Shaff had been a demented evil fiend, for sure. Even for a Mok. Still, Thurga was not sure anyone deserved that kind of death.

Thurga shook his head to dislodge the gruesome memory. He hoisted his burden back onto a stiff shoulder. He turned his thoughts ahead to the current task to block any more unwelcome memories.

He was to see the Red Lady. At least, that is what she was commonly called. Thurga had never had the chance to make her acquaintance before she became the Mage's woman.

"Wha . . . the . . . ahhhhhh . . ."

Thurga was now flying. One minute he was lost in thought, ambling towards his destination, and the next he was literally swept off of his feet. He felt the sack ripped from his hands as he fell . . . upward. Hands over feet, head over heels, Thurga found his voice and screamed for help.

A light chuckle near his ear sounded out of place in the chaos, "Calm yourself. I am simply hastening you on to your appointment." The voice came from behind his ear. Thurga's eyes widened as he stopped swinging his arms and kicking his legs. He was flying. His heart still hammering painfully in his chest only felt like a slow thump as the wind gently caressed his face. The craftsman spread his arms out from his sides as if they were wings. Below, the street he had been walking looked to be a wide ribbon leading upwards. Past the millers alley and the tanners block the road suddenly rose to end at an elegant structure; the Manse.

Decades earlier a wealthy merchant had dreams of making Haven his base of operations and the Manse was to be the jewel in his mercantile crown. The building had been finished but the merchant had run upon hard times and had been forced to abandon the project. Rumors spread that the wealthy man now was a clerk for one of his former competitors.

The whispery voice chuckled again, "Hold on now." Instead of fear, Thurga felt the excitement and thrill of flying flow through his body. Instead of a shriek of fright, he shouted in joy as he hurtled towards the Manse. *If I am to die, this is how I would do it.*

Just as the cobbled courtyard came into view his speed slowed. As he came closer, Thurga could see a man standing next to a table with two chairs. Gently floating now, his feet touched the ground and he found himself face to face with the Mage, and what a face it was. While Thurga had seen the man a number of times in passing, viewing the scarring up close made him wince. He quickly tried to control his expression but not before the Mage noticed it causing a brief smile to crease the horrid face. Truly the man was a riddle.

Rumors spread about the strange mage who wandered the community asking odd questions and watching. Just the other day Marda the washerwoman said the man had asked her what fabric held up the best wash after wash. She claimed the Mage had sat with her for some time listening to her explain the differences in fabric fibers and the dyes that faded and those that kept their colors. This bit of information had raised the mage in Thurga's esteem since

Marda's sons had left on a merchant vessel to find work and she was starved for conversation.

With a wave of his hand, the Mage motioned for Thurga to sit. Quietly taking his seat, Thurga saw the table was prepared for breakfast. Eggs, honey cakes, and peeled fruit made his mouth water. Thurga rarely had breakfast but the fare in front of him was not to be ignored.

"Please Master Thurga, enjoy yourself. I have been told on great authority that the honey cakes are not to be wasted."

Taking a plate the mage began to help himself. After a moment's hesitation Thurga heaped a plate of cakes and fruit and began enjoying the meal. For several moments the two men simply enjoyed the good food in early morning air. After indicating that Thurga should keep eating, the Mage reached under the table and produced the missing sack. Pushing his plate aside, the Mage removed the item from the sack and placed it on the table. For a long moment he simply stared at it.

Truly, Orkus was a genius of sorts when it came to inventions and gadgetry. Made out of dark treated wood and grey marble, it was pleasing to the eye. The clock face would change from polished gold to a pale blue ceramic indicating day and night. The gears had taken weeks of constant experimentation so that they moved nearly soundlessly. He watched as the mage opened the glass face case and moved the hands. A moment later a soft chime indicated the hour. In silence the two men listened to the chimes. Leaning back in his chair, the Mage looked up with a smile.

"It is a wonder, Master Thurga. Your friend Orkus is remarkable. Truly."

Thurga swallowed his mouth full and he chose his next words carefully, "The lady had commissioned the clock several weeks ago. Orkus came to me then and admitted he was a bit intimidated by the project, but I could tell he loved the challenge. He is a strange, solitary man, but a true craftsman."

Chuckling, the Mage replied, "A minor deception. I commissioned the piece as a surprise for 'the lady.' You came highly recommended as someone who would know where to find a clock maker, Master Thurga. I wanted to see what skill could be used without magic to create a piece like this. Without you worrying what the evil Mage might do if he were displeased with the work. He is not. Displeased that is."

Thurga turned his head toward his plate trying to hide the relieved look that had traveled across his face. In truth he had been uneasy through the meal, fearful of the Mage's reaction to the clock. While he knew it to be fine work, everything he knew about mages indicated that they could be unpredictable. Lost in his thoughts for the moment, he almost missed that he had been asked a question.

"Bigger, did you say, Honored Mage?"

"Yes, could Master Orkus make the clock bigger, say, large enough to fit in the square so that all would be able to view it?"

Thurga shrugged, "If it can be done, Orkus is your man. Why may I ask, would you want such a thing?"

Standing up, the Mage motioned for Thurga to follow him to the edge of the courtyard. Small bushes and trees were arrayed around the space adding to the quaint feeling of comfort and relaxation. When Thurga took his place next to the mage, he whistled in appreciation. From this view, the whole town could be seen.

The masons working on the outer harbor walls looked to be tiny insects scurrying on the stones. To the right could be seen the fields that had been planted the previous year and were actually producing good quality crops for the first time anyone could remember. Volcanic rock had been crushed and mixed with leavings from the fishermen to make a fertilizer. Mixed in with the native dirt it created a topsoil that was foamy and rich.

Shaking his head in wonder Thurga commented, "You have worked wonders with the town, honored mage. It is like magic."

"Yes, like magic, but it is not." Motioning his scarred hand as if to encompass the whole view the Mage continued on,

"All of these accomplishments have been made through the use of hard work and ingenuity. No magic. No rawstones." The man nearly spat when he mentioned the rawstones. His dislike of the stones were legendary.

"However, Spuros brought to my attention that the rawstones did provide power for many necessities, fuel for many of the clocks and time keepers that many here had used, for one. We have had complaints from a number of quarters. Most recently the tanners who claim that their hides need to be treated for a certain period of time before being sold, therefore, we need a system of time keeping that is reliable."

Thurga ran a hand over his chin in thought, thinking out loud he said, "The lady's clock must be wound every day. Such a method would be inefficient for a larger mechanism. Perhaps a clock that needed to be rewound once per week or month would be more realistic. It is a task I am sure Orkus will be excited to take on."

Thurga felt the other man's gaze and turned to meet it. A wide smile graced the unscarred side of the Mage's face.

Placing a hand on Thurga's shoulder he assured, "Tell him to not fear failure. I know his efforts will be his best."

As if realizing that he was being too familiar the Mage dropped his hand. The smile faded a bit as he hesitantly asked, "Unless of course you or Orkus have a problem with the project, or perhaps with who commissioned it?"

Thurga kept the surprise from his face as he pretended to consider the offer. He was amazed at how comfortable he felt in the Mage's presence. The man had vision yet seemed to maintain a humble and approachable attitude. Giving a half smile, Thurga answered, "No, honored mage. I have worked for ugly men before."

The laughter of the two men was halted abruptly at the arrival of the Lady. While Thurga never considered himself a flesh driven man, it was hard not to gaze upon the woman without profound appreciation. Skin that would seem too pale on another woman seemed to almost glow. Red hair like a rope of flame was braided down one side. A simple robe of light green seemed to cling invitingly as she approached. Light blue eyes crinkled slightly as she smiled. The only blemish was a small bruise that appeared on her upper cheek.

Walking forward, the Mage hesitatingly took her hand. With his other hand he gently brushed finger tips across the bruise. Quiet words were exchanged and Thurga felt uncomfortably like an intruder during this almost intimate moment. Hand in hand, the couple approached. Thurga took his seat after the lady was settled.

"Master Thurga. I had forgotten to thank you for the herbals you provided for Sann while the Mage was away. They helped considerably." This brought a slight frown from the Mage. An uncomfortable moment passed. Noticing the clock, she gently picked it up. "My Lord has explained to me his idea concerning the clock. Who made it?"

"Orkus, my Lady."

Putting the clock back on the table, she asked, "The hunchback?" At Thurga's nod, she began to question him about Orkus and what he know about the clock's construction. After a few moments, the Mage excused himself and walked back into the manse, leaving the two to their discussion.

Slowly the Mage drifted through the manse. Servants quietly stepped out of his way and nodded respectfully since he had forbidden bowing or any kind of groveling. He moved down the hallway and gently opened the door at the end. After a moment of hesitation, he slipped inside. Satisfied that the door would remain closed, the Mage looked down on the bed's occupant.

Sann was a good looking boy which was not surprising given who his mother was. His father must have had a darker complexion because Sann's skin would turn a darker brown in the sun as opposed to his mother who often burned. Usually after the sickness took him, Sann would sleep half a day and wake up fit and full of energy. This time was different. The Mage had not been here when the seizures had begun and Sann had lain on death's door for almost two days before Denna had told him. In anger he had struck her before rushing to the boy's side. He winced at the memory.

He had just been back from the most recent foray against the frogs. He had been exhausted and irritable. He had ordered no one to bother him until he had some proper sleep. The Lady had not told him that Sann had an episode. He had learned of it from a servant. It had been a close thing. Sitting down at the edge of the bed, careful not to wake him, the Mage closed his normal hazel eye and gazed at Sann with only his white orb. He still did not understand how he could see in any normal fashion with the cloudy white eye, but he did. And when he used it like this he could view other, more interesting things.

There, he found the lines, or threads he sometimes called them. Dozens flittered out and away from Sann. He did not understand what the lines actually were, only that for some reason he could see them emanating from mundanes and rawstones. Most simply faded into nothingness while others were more pronounced and held their shape. Very like the threads that connected Sann to Denna. It was how he had known for some time that Sann was her son and not just her personal page boy.

Sann's threads were different than other mundanes that he had viewed. The boy's lines were stronger in their color definitions and seemed more substantive and real. He had seen only one other mundane who had similar threads; his own.

Sann suffered from the Mund Fever. He hated the word 'Mund' but that is what everyone called it. Mostly it struck children shortly after birth and there was no known treatment. He had been told that few children were afflicted at a much older age like Sann. Cases like Sann's were rare but not unheard of. Shortly after the Mage had come to his agreement with Spuros, Sann had suffered an episode. He had immediately seen that what was happening to the boy was not natural. Unlike his own threads, Sann's turned darker the closer they were to his body. Where they touched his skin, they were almost black. The mage's own threads held no such discoloration. Something was happening with Sann's threads, something that would surely kill him.

Last year, when Sann had again been afflicted, the Mage acted. With Cinder and Aeris, he had been able to detect a power surge of some kind coming from Sann that was blocked by something in the boy's threads. Unable to leave Sann's body, the power was reflected back into him thus creating the seizures. The surge was identical to that of his own threads when he used his magic. So he had carefully manipulated Sann's threads and created the smallest of breaches allowing the power to filter out of the boy before hitting the block.

This served two purposes; first it allowed Sann to survive and second it recharged his own powers. The second benefit was unlooked for. His intention had been to only save the boy. The fact that he could fill his own reserves of power had been an unintended boon that he felt guilty to partake of when Sann was ill.

He sat quietly looking at the sleeping boy. Sann had always seemed a familiar name, like a familiar memory yet a bit . . . off. When he looked at the boy he always thought the hair should be darker in color and his eyes brown, not green. Sometimes he felt that his inability to remember would drive him crazy. Shaking his head, he turned at the door opening. Denna quietly entered. He put a finger to his lips and motioned for her to accompany him out the door. Hand in hand, they walked back to their rooms.

CHAPTER FIVE

Spuros sat quietly as they waited for the mage. He leaned back slightly in his chair, eyes closed, listening quietly to the harbor waters lapping against the side of the ship. They usually met in his captain's cabin. While he was now a very wealthy man, his cabin was somewhat simple. A cot that folded out from the wall, a table with four chairs, a liquor cabinet in the corner and a chest for his clothes and maps filled the small space. All were made of solid, if slightly used wood. Spuros disliked conducting business on shore unless absolutely necessary. He felt more in control on the *Spite* than in any dockside tavern. Even with his eyes closed he could sense his guest's unease.

Hett was a Riskh. A green skinned people who had been conquered by the Mok's thousands of years ago. While the two races shared a skin color and an affinity for water, that seemed to be the end to the similarities. Mok's were large sometimes pudgy looking creatures, while the Riskh were small and slight. Their faces were narrow and pointed in contrast to the Mok's broad almost fishlike features. Many Riskh served as servants to the wealthier

Mok broods, often alongside mund slaves. The race had few magic users because, Hett always claimed, the Mok's fished out and killed any Riskh who exhibited the talent. It was a story that the old sailor could believe given the Mok's superiority complex that permeated their culture.

Magical abilities or no, if the Riskh as a race excelled at one thing it was the gathering of information. The fact that most races overlooked them as being insignificant allowed Hett and his people to observe and gather information in the most unlikely of places. Much of the illegal activities in the Mok Empire occurred right under the Empress' nose due to these unobtrusive people.

Hett was a member of a gang of Riskh who operated mostly in the dockyards of the empire. They worked with numerous members of the underworld; mostly thieves, smugglers, the occasional assassin. Spuros had a history of dealing with Hett and his people and had been paying them considerable sums to stay informed as to the movements of the Mok naval command.

Just as Spuros was going to offer the nervous Hett something to drink, the Mage quietly entered. Closing the door behind him, the man sat down in the chair next to Spuros. A grey hooded cloak covered his features.

At a gesture from Spuros, Hett cleared a nervous throat and spoke, "Captain, Honored Mage, as you are aware, I was given instructions to keep a look out for any unusual developments. While these instructions were a bit vague, the amounts that you are paying to employ a number of my agents outweighed any questions I might have for clarification. However, I think that we may have found something that might be of interest to you."

Hett waited for nods from the two men before he continued, "As you are aware the Empire's rawstone production had come to an almost complete halt at the beginning of the conflict with the Mages Council. That is, until recently." This got the attention of both men, as they turned to each other. It had long been assumed that the Mages Council alone controlled the secrets of creating the rawstones. The idea that the Empress may have discovered a method of producing her own rawstones could be disastrous for the Corsairs. As of yet, the Moks had kept a tight rein on using their rawstone powered weaponry against them. That could drastically change if the Moks could produce the stones.

After pausing a moment to let his employers soak in the ramifications of his words, Hett continued, "At this time, we have confirmed that the Empress has only one rawstone production facility in operation. We do not know why she is limited to this one facility, but whether this is due to the materials necessary in the process of production or that the Empire has been unable to refine their technique is unclear. What is clear is that they are producing rawstones, albeit at a very slow rate. It is also clear, that the number of munds used in this facility are . . . excessive."

The Mage leaned forward in his seat, placing a scarred hand on the table between them and asked, "What do you mean, excessive?"

Hett swallowed as he mentally prepared his words. The Mage had never spoken directly to him before, and the anger he sensed behind the question was a bit unnerving. Hett's instincts screamed for caution and he chose his next words carefully.

"Perhaps, excessive is not a good choice of words, Honored Mage. Brutal might be a better description. Most people know that the mages employ munds in their process in producing the rawstones. Whatever the process entails, it often involves harm to the mund via loss of weight, sickness, and in some cases addiction of some kind. We have harbored a suspicion for years that many munds do not survive the process, though we have no proof of this, very few mund owners have ever complained of a mund failing to return from a rawstone facility. We believe this to be the case because the Mage Council pays for any death or damage to a mund used for this purpose, thus giving the former owner nothing to complain about." Somewhat lost in his explanation, Hett did not notice that the wooden table under the Mage's hand had begun to smolder as he continued his report.

"In this case the numbers of munds that have been recorded to enter the facility are somewhat large. Several hundred a week have been reported to be transported to the location. While it is unsure what use they are being put to, we have been able to discover how they are being disposed of . . . ." The table suddenly burst into flame. Hett squealed in surprise as he fell back in the chair away from the flames. At a gesture from the Mage, the flames disappeared leaving only smoke and burnt wood testifying to their destructive power.

Bare feet pounded on the wooden deck as sailors rushed to the source of the now extinct fire. Spuros walked to the door and bellowed out that all was well. Closing the door he walked over and helped the wide eyed Hett to his slightly charred chair. The Mage simply sat motionless, watching the pair. The hooded features gave no indication if another demonstration would be forthcoming. Reclaiming his own seat, Spuros ignored the Mage and asked, "You mentioned that the munds were being disposed of, my friend. How so?"

Licking his lips, Hett found he could not look at the mage and put together a coherent thought due to the terror that was coursing through his veins, "Captain, given the most recent, ah, reaction I hesitate to continue on without some assurances."

Forcing a laugh and waiving his hand as if nothing out of the ordinary had just happened Spuros assured him, "Fear not, friend Hett. We mean you no harm. In fact, we are so impressed with your continued endeavors on our behalf that a bonus to your usually high fees is in order. Please, continue."

Hett slowly nodded, thinking, *What good is a bonus if I am charred to the bone?* "Yes, well, our reports are that large numbers of bodies are being burned at the location. While we have viewed this only from a distance, we are fairly sure they are the same munds who had been brought to the facility. Also, there is some indication that these bodies have been maimed or tortured in some fashion. Whether this was before or after death is unclear."

After a few preliminary questions, Spuros thanked Hett and walked him to the cabin door. Shutting the door, he turned and walked to the liquor cabinet and filled two small cups with whiskey. Handing one to the mage, he took a moment to enjoy the burn of the brew as it slid down his throat. Sitting back down, he put his legs up on a fire blackened table board.

"So, when do we head out?"

Looking down at the cup in his hand, the Mage threw back its contents and handed it empty back to the captain. Standing up, he answered, "Now."

HETT WAS not a happy man as he stepped onto the island of Yeg. First he was almost burnt to a crisp by mage fire then packed up into the hold of the *Spite* to accompany the Corsairs on what was most likely a suicide mission. Add to all that the fact that the Corsair fleet approached the island in the full light of day under what the Mage called a 'concealment' of some kind. The large weight of his recently acquired bonus gave him no feeling of assurance as he did not believe that he would be alive to spend it.

The island of Yeg had a dark reputation. Used by the Empress for years as a prison for those who had especially displeased her, it was a place many had visited but few had returned. The Mage had insisted that Hett accompany him to the island and spent the two day voyage interrogating the frightened Riskh on every detail he knew about the island's defenses.

Hett had never seen the Corsairs in action and was impressed. In a matter of hours the Mok's had been over run and the island secured. Somehow every rawstone, and every rawstone weapon, on the island had been disabled. The nearly defenseless guards had been little of a challenge to the ruthless pirates. Hett picked one of the darkened stones up from the body of a Mok guardsman. The stone was still hard but cool to the touch, a small crack marred the otherwise perfect surface. He pocketed the stone before he headed on.

Hett now walked escorted by two large Corsairs through what had been the main courtyard of the prison. The formidable walls seemed to be in denial of the destruction of its protectors. Everywhere, green Mok bodies littered the dusty grounds. Here and there small groups of Corsairs wrapped the bodies of fallen comrades in pieces of ship sail, before the return voyage the dead would be dropped over side weighed down with heavy bits of plunder to ensure a safe trip to the bottom; it was their way.

Hett was ushered towards two long one story buildings that appeared to be of newer construction than the other structures in the compound. They approached the doorway to the first building where a strange chemical smell filled the air. As the door was shut behind him, it took a moment for his eyes to adjust to the dim light. He was standing in a large room filled with beds or cots of some kind. Many had been knocked over and some were damaged, Hett assumed during the invasion of the island. The wall closest to him was covered with some kind of decorations. As he moved closer he could see that what he had taken for decorations were instead metal masks of some kind. Hundreds of masks covered the wall, seeming to gaze at him in emotionless metallic judgment. Hett shuddered and looked at the rest of the room.

A thin layer of dust clung to the room. The place had the feeling of recent neglect as if its purpose had simply ceased to be important. Hett guessed that the place had been abandoned for only a few months.

At a grunt from one of his two keepers, he advanced toward the other side of the room where Spuros and the hooded Mage were quietly talking. The two men stood next to a table that had seen some very recent use. The table ran the length of the wall and was covered with various glass and metal canisters. Several glass vials still bubbled and steamed with the distinctive smell of rawstones. Two large wooden bowls were set off to the side, one held small fingernail sized crystals, the other a fine red sand. Seeing his approach, the Mage waved him closer to the bowls.

Handing Hett one of the small crystals, the Mage explained, "This is called Crystal Meth, or methamphetamine, crank, or just crystal. It allows the transfer of the victim's life essence into the rawstones." The voice seemed to speak ominously from beneath the hood. Placing his hand in the other bowl, he showed Hett the red sand-like substance, "This is called red sand. It somehow sedates the victim and ensures that they remain paralyzed during the process. It could be days, or even weeks at a time."

Rubbing the fine sand through his fingers Hett took another look around the room. The need for the beds became obvious; the munds had to be placed on something while being force fed the meth. Without the masks the room looked like some sort of Medica of some kind.

Putting the bowl down, the Mage picked up one of the masks. Upon closer examination a hollowed out rut was visible just over the eyes slits on the forehead and tubes that led from the nose holes could also be seen. Removing a darkened rawstone from his pocket the Mage explained, "The inactive stone is placed in the indenture over the eyes, the meth is placed in a vial and pumped through one nose hole; a second vial pumps the red sand into the other; thus immobilizing the victim and allowing the stone to be charged almost simultaneously."

Hett quietly digested this new information. His people had tried for years to obtain knowledge connected to the creation of the rawstones. The mages had guarded their secret with tenacious fortitude. Yet, here was this mund, albeit a mage mund, who was simply giving Hett information as if it were general knowledge free for all. Brushing the red sand from his fingers, Hett paused before asking, "Then what changed?"

Spuros motioned the two guardsmen away and began to give orders in a quiet voice. The Mage waited in hooded silence until the three Corsairs were out of ear shot before he spoke.

"What are your observations, Hett?

Hett was being tested, he knew. While his dealings with Spuros had dated back years, the Corsairs were now a power, albeit a small power, but a power nonetheless. This mund, this mage, was the cornerstone, the foundation of the Corsairs continued rise. It was vitally important that he impress this man. Hett took a small breath before speaking, "This facility is very similar to a Medica; if not for the masks and what you just told me I would expect to see healers and their assistants scurrying around attending their patients. I would assume if we had been able to see it in operation, each cot would have been occupied by a mundane and someone, or some ones, charged with monitoring the rawstone process. This was a decent sized operation; just over one hundred beds, probably a dozen individuals working here to maintain it. That number is just an estimate since I have no information to draw on concerning the charging of the rawstones."

Hett glanced around the room before saying, "Something changed. Something made the Mok's abandon this operation. It wasn't at the outbreak of the war; this building was abandoned only months ago. No, it was even more more recent than that. So, what happened?"

Turning back to the Mage, Hett tried to discern the hooded face that considered his words so thoughtfully. Another moment of reflection, and the mage suddenly was striding away, motioning for Hett to follow. As they exited the building Spuros and his two escorts joined them as they made their way to the other building.

A muggy stench came from the doorway and Hett hastily put a cloth to his face. Overpowering, the smell was familiar but he could not place it. Inside he found the mage and Spuros had stopped and stood side by side.

The building seemed to be one big hall with no windows. Small flames that floated in the air gave light to the otherwise darkened place. Hett noticed that rawstone lamp holders lined the walls but their stones were as dead as the one in his pocket. The place gave off the feeling of an oversized coffin and Hett shuddered.

Overhead thick wooden beams supported a vaulted ceiling. From the beams hung metal chains that dropped towards the floor, swinging from the chains like giant pendants were wheels of some kind. On each wheel, stuck to the surface like some horrible ornament was a body. A mund body.

Hett's earlier meal rose up then and he retched onto the ground. Falling to one knee he wiped his mouth with a shaking hand. Looking up, he saw a mund child looking at him with death's stare. Her blond curls seemed clean as if someone had recently washed them. The hair belied the state of her corpse. Long jagged rents had been made to her legs and the skin peeled back showing the bones in perfect detail. The rest of her body was untouched as if the torturer wished to emphasize the damage already done.

"Stone."

The Mage's voice broke the silent gloom of the place. At Hett's questioning look, the Mage turned to face him, "The wheels are made of some kind of stone." Hett recoiled involuntarily. The Mage had his hood thrown back and for the first time Hett saw the scar savaged face; a mundane face. The milky eye gazed at him as if accusing Hett of some terrible crime. The other eye was swollen red as if from too many tears. Turing back, the Mage walked down the row of stones. Spuros motioned for Hett to follow and the Corsair Captain took up the rear. There was no sign of Hett's two escorts.

Must have taken leave as soon as possible. Smart.

Hett followed the mage through the hanging wheels and the stench got stronger, thicker. Closer now, he noticed that under each wheel was a grate, like those used to drain rain water from a street. Stopping for a moment he stepped a bit closer. A red sticky sludge seemed to be congealed at the lip of the grate.

He stepped back quickly as he recalled where he had smelled something similar before; a butchery. In the Empire where you could get almost any item from around the world butcheries were common. Large scale butcher shops where fresh meat could be bought, sold, cured, or stored. Butcheries were usually restricted to certain areas of the city because of the stench that came with their operation.

Lost in his horrible thoughts, Hett did not notice that the Mage had stopped until he nearly collided with the man. They had come to what looked to be the center of the large hall. A bulky stone block rose out of the floor. Steps carved into the block lead to a platform where four tall backed chairs were placed around an oval table. The remains of a meal were slowly rotting amid the glitter of golden plates and goblets. The Mage ignored this scene and instead stepped towards the base of the block where a bundle of rags lay in a haphazard heap. As they approached Hett saw that a long skinny arm stuck out of the pile and was attached to a manacle. Directly in front of the pile hung another wheel, this one held the body of an older mund male. All the fingers and toes had been removed from the body and the face was stuck in a gaze that suggested endless pleading. On the man's cheek was a spiral tattoo of some kind.

Approaching the rags the mage gave it a hard kick and barked, "Get up."

Hett jumped back and Spuros drew his dagger as a series of hisses issued forth. Another kick and another command by the mage caused the thing to stand. 'Thing' was all that Hett could think to call it. Tall and hunched over, the attempt by the creature to cover itself with the insignificant rags could not hide the grey scales beneath. The arm attached to the manacle ended in long grey fingers and the face was like a reptile's but almost man shaped. Where ears should be were instead two tiny holes. Two large bi-pupiled eyes gazed at the three men with an expression that could only be considered alien. The thing had obviously been tortured as well and the hunched shoulder seemed to be broken and the other arm ended in a stump at the elbow. Hett could not help to think that this is what a snake would look like with legs and arms.

The mage stepped closer to the creature and asked, "Who are you?"

A momentary pause, and then numerous hisses and strange noises followed. The Mage stood there listening and finally nodded. Out of the air appeared two apparitions; one a fiery nightmare the other an elegant wisp of some kind. A blast of heat freed the creature's arm and then it was whisked away out of the doorway. Even as its feet left the floor the creature's alien gaze was fixed on the Mage.

Hours later Hett watched from the ship as the island of Yeg burned. Not just the buildings but the entire island. The Mage had set up a blaze whose heat could be felt even from this distance out on the open water. From his perch, Hett thought he could see two figures flying to and fro among the flames. It was an impressive monument to the munds tortured there. The whole island would be scorched to the bare rocks. Nothing would grow or take purchase in the flame charred soil for years, even decades. It was all impressive, horribly impressive.

The creature looked much better since their first meeting, Hett thought. Completely covered in two sailor's cloaks, it sat on the wooden floor boards, its back resting against the corner walls. An empty plate was testimonial to the fact that the creature required sustenance. Hett had to admit that he found that reassuring for some reason. He had been called by the Mage into Spuros' cabin, but for what he had no idea. For the past several minutes the Mage had been asking questions and the creature had been answering in its strange hissing dialect.

Hett had dealt with numerous different peoples in his lifetime. Each race had its own look, color, even smells. But this creature was the first one that Hett would ever consider almost alien; like it did not belong here. It was other. It was a feeling he could not shake.

Spuros entered the cabin and quietly shut the door. In his hands he held a small wooden box. Handing it to the mage, the captain silently took a seat. For a few moments the Mage sat and looked at the box in his lap. More glared at the thing, Hett thought. With a grimace of distaste the mage opened the box and withdrew a rawstone. The stone was a blue color and sparkled in the cabin's light. After another pause, he handed the stone to the creature.

Taking the stone, the creature pushed open a section of the rough clothing and exposed a grey scale covered throat. From Hett's seat he could see that there was some sort of indent or opening of some kind worked into the grey skin. Gently, the creature placed the rawstone into the opening and quickly recovered its chest. Leaning back against the wall, it seemed to almost sigh in relief.

"Better?" asked the Mage.

"Yes, thank you honored mage." The creature answered. The voice still added a slight hiss to the words but they were understandable. Hett almost let out a grunt of surprise. Spuros kept his face impassive but seemed to bore his gaze into the creature. Sitting back in his chair, the mage nearly spat,

"You have no idea how repulsive that is to me. If I did not think it necessary for my companions here to hear your words I would have had you thrown into the sea for your request."

Nodding, the creature said, "Yes Honored Mage, I can sense your dislike for me. Your anger. But I doubt you would have thrown me over the side."

Crossing his arms the mage now gave the creature a darker glare and asked in a quiet, cold voice, "Are you so sure?"

Nodding the creature continued as if the anger of the mage had held no danger, "Yes. If you truly had any wish to harm me, I would have sensed it. I feel nothing from you now except what might be considered curiosity. Is that correct?"

For a moment, the Mage's face got darker, almost thunderous. Then, as if by magic, the frown melted away and a wry smile gave way to a soft chuckle, "Now that is a talent that I would very much like to have. I would give you my name, but I don't recall it; literally. Most simply refer to me as 'Mage.' To my right is Spuros. This is his ship and if he decides you are a danger to us, have no doubt that *he* will throw you over. To my left is Hett. What should we call you?"

Nodding to both Hett and Spuros in turn the creature said, "Those not of my kind call me Liss." Nodding in return, the Mage said, "Well, Liss. You were correct that I am curious about something; however it is not about you necessarily. The man who had been put on the stone wheel that hung in front of you; did you know him?"

The Mage had definitely caught Liss off guard with his question. Putting a hand to its face, the creature covered its eyes; it looked to almost be grieving. With a small sigh, it answered, "He was my *tal*, a servant of sorts. I was made to watch while they tortured him."

"They?" Spuros' tone was anything but approving. He had wished to let Liss burn with the rest of the island. This creature was something outside of his experience and gave him the jitters.

"The S'Ahas." Liss let the words die. It leaned back against the wall, letting the hand fall but keeping eyes closed and continued, "They thought that if I were forced to watch all of the *tal-mak*, the marked ones, tortured that I would reveal secrets to them."

"What kind of secrets?" Hett could not help himself. Secrets were his stock and trade. With his eyes still on Liss, the creature began to speak.

The three men sat in the hold of the ship. Spuros had ordered the place cleared except for three stools and a lantern. Outside the darkening sky blanketed the moon and the ship skimmed through the calm waters. The only sound was the scratch of Hett's pen as he tried to make sense of his notes. After a few more moments, the Mage asked, "Well?"

Hett looked up from his work. A small smudge of ink marred his light green face. With a sigh he answered, "It is an amazing tale."

"We know that, Hett. Is it believable?" Spuros' voice sounded strained. The old sea dog was a creature of habit and routine. Liss's story added new dimensions to their conflict filled world that were hard to comprehend.

"Well, the creature seemed genuine. I did not detect any change in its voice patterns that would indicate a lie. What it told us, it truly believes."

"All of it? All this nonsense about Great Mothers and Sky Fathers? Of hollowed out mountains and . . ."

"Spuros." The Mage's voice was not angry nor was he chastising Spuros, the man simply wished to speak. The Corsair clamped his mouth shut. With a small nod of thanks, the mage spoke,

"I have dealt with these dark ones, these S'Ahas, before. As usual, my recollections are hazy and confusing." He said the last with a rueful smile. From what Hett could gather from Spuros and the rest of the crew, the Mage remembered nothing about his life until his joining with the Corsairs. This reference to other memories was interesting, very interesting.

The Mage continued on, "The important part of Liss's story, is that it explains how the Empress was able to begin the manufacture of rawstones again. We had always thought that the mages held the secrets to their creation. Therefore, the Empire's stockpiles of stones were all they had to draw on. But according to our strange new friend, these Orda held the key to the stones. Now, these 'S'Ahas' show up and are able to create their own versions of the stones.

Our main strategy here in the Isles was to become too costly for the Mok's to use their limited supply of rawstones on us and instead concentrate on their conflict with Hyberan. If they can create their own stones, then we have no chance. The Empress can just grind us down."

The Mage lapsed into silence. Spuros took out a striker and lit his pipe. Hett put down his papers and took turns looking at both men. The continued silence was driving the green man crazy. Finally he asked, "Well, what do we do?"

CHAPTER SIX

We are truly and utterly fucked. Tyrell thought as he watched as Grach was roughly carried away. He sat in a circle with the other prisoners, all chained together like a strange dysfunctional family. Black skinned Tuak, blue Ferrekei, and numerous others made a dull rainbow of colored misery. Over all of them loomed the green Moks, most armed with rawstone weapons of one sort or another. Many also had the long wicked knives that the Empire's marines favored. Tyrell watched impassively as the green bastards hoisted Grach up onto a sharpened stake and slowly lowered his friend onto the deadly thing.

How did things go so wrong, so quickly?

It had been decided that the group would be a small one in an attempt to avoid undue attention. So, Grach, himself, the mage Fenn, and three Gurachi guardsmen had begun the journey. For the most part the trip had been uneventful. They had crossed the mountains back into Hyberan where they had been booked on a ship to the Lost Isles.

They had sighted other ships only three times, which their vessel easily avoided. They landed ahead of schedule at the port town of Nurn, a community located on an island on the far south western tip of the Mok Empire. It served unofficially as the illegal market place for the Empire's elites and the fact that the Empire was currently at war with the mages paled in comparison to well placed bribes. It was the perfect place for the group to make contact with their agent who was to slip them into regions controlled by the Corsairs.

The party was hustled before the local magistrate upon making port. The Mok official was ugly even for his own kind. He put on a show of throwing them into the gallows until Fenn produced some paperwork and a considerable bribe was exchanged. Fenn had then settled them down in a comfortable if rundown inn while he tracked down said agent. Yes, the plan thus far had gone smoothly.

Fenn had been gone for two days. This did not concern anyone since he told them to expect him gone for at least three. The group had enjoyed two days of travel free rest and relaxation, far removed from the war and fighting. Then the fighting found them.

A Mok war galley had limped into port. The ship looked like a giant child had set fire to it, then used it as a chew toy and thrown it away. Huge charred rents lined the hull and the crew continued to bail water even as she docked. It's crew looked pissed as hell and looking for a fight. The Mok's swarmed off their ship and began ransacking the town and confiscating all the rawstones they could find.

Word eventually leaked out that a Mok fleet had been destroyed by the newly emerged Corsairs. This ship and crew had been the only to escape to tell the tale and the survivors were determined to find Corsair agents to vent their fury upon. The theory they acted upon was a simple one: anyone not a Mok was deemed to be in collaboration with the Corsairs unless proven otherwise. The Mok magistrate had made some feeble protest at the treatment of some of the wealthier citizenry but he had been easily shouldered aside. He was now hunkered down in the local barracks with Fenn's bribe money under his pillow no doubt.

The first act by the crew had been to target all of the Gurachii in the town. In all fifteen Gurachii, most of them slaves, which included three women and one child were executed in front of the frightened onlookers, their heads stacked up like wood as a gruesome lesson. Tyrell's three companions were among those killed in the first few hours of occupation. The rest of the non-Mok residents were rounded up and confined to their makeshift prison.

The first day of interrogations had not been as fruitful as the captain of the ship had hoped. In an attempt to show the eventual repercussions of aiding or hiding a Corsair, he had a line of twenty spikes driven into the ground in the town square. It was well known that the Empress was fond of having her enemies spiked and this method of death was standard issue for her armies.

On the second day, twenty munds were spiked. Women, children, and old men; screaming, kicking, and begging they all met a horrible fate. The entire town was ordered out to watch the spectacle under the frowning presence of heavily armed marines. Tyrell could not help the tears that flowed down his cheeks.

Before meeting Jonathan Champion, the scene would not have affected him in such a way. Of course the cruelty and barbarity of it would have offended him. He had thought of munds just like any beast of burden. They should be cared for but they were not 'real' people. But now, he thought of his friend and knew what such a thing would cause Champion to do. He wiped the tears away quickly before his captors notices his grief.

It had now been three days since their incarceration and no sign of Fenn. Tyrell hoped the Air Mage had read things correctly and was holed up somewhere. Grach had overheard the guards say that an example had to be set for the prisoners in order to ferret out the true traitors. Grach, heroic Grach, had taken it upon himself to make a spectacle of attacking one of the guards in order to draw attention to himself and potentially save a fellow prisoner, and he was now paying for it.

Tyrell was relieved that these sailors were not familiar with the Molden or they would have known to burn or hack him to bits. Since he did not have any vital organs to damage, a spike through Grach's body would do nothing but provide an uncomfortable evening for the rotund warrior. When the dark of night fell, Grach would 'un-spike' himself then the two hoped to get free and make for a better port and find Fenn. Not a perfect plan, but it was what they had to work with.

WE ARE *truly and utterly fucked*, Fenn thought to himself. This whole trip had turned into a nightmare virtually overnight. Hours after making arrangements with his agent for transport to the Lost Isles he had been informed that a Mok vessel had appeared in port and taken control of the whole town. Needless to say his agent made an immediate exit and rescinded the agreement. Fenn then was forced to make his way back to Nurn on foot from the other side of the Island.

Luckily the rolling, hilly region was prone to mists which Fenn was able to use as significant cover with little use of his magic. It took less effort to deepen the mist covering a ravine rather than try to make it from scratch. Fenn had spent the last three days skirting Mok search parties and had finally made it to the outskirts of the town. He was hungry, wet, and scared to the point he almost felt numb.

He had decided the night before that attempting to slip into town was the only way to learn what happened to his companions. If they were dead, he could try to continue onward with the mission. If they were alive and captive, then he would need to try to free them. As the last golden sliver of sunshine slipped behind the horizon, he squared his shoulders, called the wind, and swept toward the town.

Staying as high as he could, Fenn approached a tall plain looking building. He had chosen the warehouse more for the large flat roof than for any other tactical reason, the flatter the roof the easier the landing. With a quiet grunt he landed and quickly surveyed his surroundings.

From his vantage point he could see those portions of the town that torch light allowed. The stakes in the square were horrible to view in the flickering flames. Groups of Mok sailors and marines wandered throughout the town, going from inn to inn, commandeering ale and food stuffs. To the left of the square, a newly erected palisade housed the incarcerated citizenry. He just hoped that Tyrell and the others had managed to stay alive.

Fenn put his hands on the roofs railings and looked down. This would be a tricky piece of air magic. He had to float quickly to the ground and then make his way to the palisade on the ground. Flying over the well-lit town center would only bring attention to himself. Taking a deep breath, he leapt over the railing and began to concentrate an air flow to glide to the street below.

His concentration was so intense that he screamed when he felt a pair of hands grip him under the arm pits. A gust of wind attached to his face and drowned any further sound as he watched the ground below him get smaller and smaller, and the air got lighter and lighter. A voice chuckled next to his ear,

"Mageling, you do show up in the strangest places. I have a most august personage that is going to be excited to see you again." Fenn's attempt to respond was lost in the clouds as he was swept away.

GRACH had decided hours ago that being spiked was something he would try to avoid in the future. While the pain and discomfort of having a sharp wooden shaft pierced through his body was bearable, the fact that the Mok's insisted on spiking their victims upside down was annoying. He had waited until the night darkness had deepened before beginning the hard process of pushing himself off the spike.

The wood had been smoothed and hardened by fire and long practice by the marines. He had to jiggle himself a bit loose before he completely freed himself. Halfway through the process a lone guard had walked drunkenly up to one of the mund corpses and pissed on it, as if the act could degrade the already dead soul any more. Grach had stayed silent and hoped the Mok moved on quickly.

After the guard had lurched out of sight, Grach freed himself with a slight pop. Hugging himself until the pain receded, he felt his body slowly repairing itself until he could stand. As quietly as he could make his large body move, he made his way through the forest of stakes. He tried to avoid looking at the decomposing bodies but it was difficult. Most of these munds had been attached as workers to the dockside warehouses. They had no idea why they were being herded into the square or what fate lay in store for them.

Approaching the palisade, he saw that two guards were stationed at the entrance. A haphazard door had been constructed across the gateway. From observations he and Tyrell had made, pairs of guards would be stationed at regular intervals around the perimeter of the palisade; about thirty in all. Each pair was armed with one rawstone weapon, the other with a long blade. Why this crew was so short on rawstones was a mystery. The plan was simple; Grach would kill the two guards at the gate, Tyrell would bolt through, and the two would flee away into the night. Tyrell had argued that the guards would be mostly expecting trouble from the thirty prisoners rather than anything from outside.

Grach crept closer slowly, trying to stay out of the light of the line of torches that ringed the palisade. He decided to take out the guard with the rawstone weapon first. He was able to get close enough to the guard that he could whiff the bitter smell of an unwashed Mok body. Closer . . . closer . . . he waited until the guard turned away to say something to his companion, then . . . he exploded. The guard exploded, with bits of green blood and gore covering the skulking Molden.

All around the compound similar explosions followed. Cries of pain and fear filled the once quiet night. Somehow the gate had caught fire and the other guard was momentarily shocked motionless as bits and pieces of his companion littered the ground. Grach moved quickly against the shocked guard and pounded his stone like fists into the green face until bones shattered and all breathing had stopped. From within the palisade cries of fear pierced the night as the fire caught more of the wood works alight.

From within he heard Tyrell calling for his name. With a roar, Grach covered his face and charged through the burning gateway.

Shards of burning wood scattered as he collided with the flaming doorframe. Grach bellowed in pain as fire burned his arms and legs and charred his flesh. The few moments felt like a burning eternity until he stumbled and rolled through the now broken entry. A cold douse of water hit his body like a soothing blanket, then another. Soon the flames were out and he was helped onto unsteady feet.

"I thought you mushrooms hated fire." A familiar voice asked over the noise.

"Almost as much as we hate blue skinned smart asses." Grach grunted. With a laugh, Tyrell gave his shoulder a squeeze and helped his burnt friend out of the now doused gateway. The quiet night had turned into chaos. Some of the newly freed prisoners had overpowered the few guards that remained and were now armed. Off in the town, scattered explosions could be heard.

Just as Tyrell thought they had a chance to make an escape, Grach stumbled. With a groan, the Molden tried to stand. Bits of grey skin had shriveled on his large frame and his breathing became ragged and slow. Tyrell cried out in frustration as a group of Mok marines jogged into view. The other prisoners turned to flee, but Tyrell continued to try to get Grach to his feet.

Almost as one the marines stopped and lined up into a firing formation. Tyrell's heart sank as he saw they were all armed with rawstone weapons. Long barreled black metal tubes with a wooden shoulder handle, the glow of different colored raw stones made it look like the Mok's held miniature rainbows. A shouted order and twenty barrels were focused on the two friends and the fleeing prisoners. With a huge heave Tyrell got Grach to his feet. The pair stared with wide eyes as the order to fire was given. An explosion lit through the night, as the marines were themselves suddenly engulfed in flames. Tyrell and Grach were thrown through the air and landed in a painful tangle of arms and legs.

Tyrell opened his eyes and knew he had lost track of time. The dark night sky was giving way to early morning. Grach lay next to him, his skin coloring looking much better as his body slowly healed itself. Tyrell knew that the Molden would need a few days to fully recuperate from the ordeal of fire. He tried standing up and gasped at the pain. Feeling down his leg, he could feel fragments sticking out of his ankle. As if his brain just became aware of the injury, Tyrell nearly gagged at the waves of pain that ran up through his leg. Pulling the leg around he saw that the fragments were actually pieces of his ankle sticking through the skin and his foot was at an odd angle to the rest of the leg. Lying back, he nearly passed out until he heard his named called.

A moment later a familiar face bobbed over him. Through gritted teeth Tyrell asked, "Where the hell have you been?"

"You wouldn't believe me if I told you." Fenn answered.

CHAPTER SEVEN

The Mage looked at the two men with a wooden, expressionless face. He sat in a camp chair in what had been the local barracks. On his left Aeris watched with interest while on his right Cinder silently fumed. The two were old friends of his. Or rather, they claimed to be old friends of his. They had given him a name; Jonathan Champion. It rang familiar in his mind, as if it were a bell in the distance that could almost be heard. Hett, Spuros and three Corsair guardsmen regarded the two men with open hostility.

It had been a lucky break that the Mok ship had ventured to Nurn. If the Captain had been a better sailor he would have known to have tried sailing east instead of west. Hett had been able to learn where the ship had found safe harbor. Now, half the Corsair fleet had berthed in Nurn and had begun to somewhat peacefully loot the community.

With the Empress's new rawstone supply now coming into play, Spuros had counseled that they needed to intercept the ship that had been allowed to survive the battle several weeks earlier. The less the Empress knew about them the better. It was amazing that the Mok's had survived that long at sea. The crew had to have been half dead by the time they arrived in Nurn. Now, they were all dead.

It had been a simple thing to arrive almost unnoticed into the harbor. A mage mist had concealed the long boat crews until they were almost at the docks. Once the alarm was sounded, the mage had simply begun to destroy every rawstone he could identify; which explained how Grach and Tyrell had survived. The explosions had also rocked the Mok vessel to its foundations and now the ship rested in the deeper waters at the end of the harbor.

The Mage focused his attention back to his new guests, his old friends if they were to be believed. That the pair were glad to see him was obvious. The Ferrekei yelled something about a feast brother and had run and hugged him before the Corsair guards could intercede while the Molden had simply looked at him with a huge half burned smile on his face. He could not remember if he had ever met these two before, but there was no doubt he felt relaxed and content in their company. The other mage Fenn, had objected to being excluded from this meeting but had grudgingly accepted his lot when he realized he had no choice.

Neither Cinder nor Aeris had refuted the pair's claim of friendship. The two elemental creatures, or manifestations as Fenn called them, had held to a code of rigid silence since the destruction of the Mok's ship and crew. The Mage decided to break the uncomfortable silence.

"How is your leg?" The Ferrekei grimaced a bit and shrugged as he answered, "One of the Corsairs gave me something for the pain, so now it just feels like a small fire instead of a raging inferno."

"You had called me, Feast Brother. Why was that?"

The question made the blue man pause before saying, "It means you are considered kin to me. You, Grach, and I have been through . . . much together."

Slowly nodding as if mentally chewing on Tyrell's words the mage turned to the Molden, "And you, are you a feast brother as well?" Grach looked from the mage and back to Tyrell. The moment of silence seemed to drag on. Then Grach tilted his head back and laughed, no guffawed. It was a loud, thundering, sound that startled the others present. Only a sharp command from Spuros kept the Corsairs from drawing their weapons.

Wiping his eyes, Grach gazed back at the mage, "Ah, friend Champion, you fill my days with humor; even when you don't know yourself. But no, my kind do not have 'feast brothers.'" Grach then leaned forward and pointed a thick finger at the Mage, "But know this, I would go through fire and oblivion to help you. Indeed, Tyrell and I already have. We came looking for you not because the mages wanted us to, but because we are your friends. To me, that is reason enough." Putting his hands in his lap, the large warrior leaned back in his chair. The Corsairs seemed impressed by this candid speech. Even Spuros gave a small grimace of approval.

Nodding the Mage said, "You two and your companion mage are now our guests, for how long will depend on many things that we don't have time to discuss. We leave when Captain Spuros gives the word. We will talk more when we reach home."

Tyrell and Grach were led from the room. A short while later, the mage Fenn was brought in. Giving a slight nod, Spuros and the Corsairs left the room. A moment later, Aeris and Cinder left as well, albeit a bit more slowly than the Corsairs, leaving the two mages alone. Fenn sat at the edge of his seat, his back rigid as if he expected an attack at any moment.

He asked his new captor, "Should I thank you for saving us? Or have we gone from one danger to another?" Fenn tried to put as much angry courage as he could into his voice, but the words still sounded frail to his ears.

"Well, you have no danger of being put on a sharp stick. Does that reassure you?" While lightly spoken, the words barely masked a deep seeded fury. Fenn had seen what remained of the mundanes who had been so cruelly spiked by the Moks. He could not repress a slight shudder at the mental picture.

"That was unfair, Mage Fenn. I am not fun to talk too after I see the how the Moks treat the weak and innocent. Sorry." Fenn gave a cautious nod in acceptance of the apology before changing the subject,

"So, should I call you Jonathan Champion, or do you prefer some other title or name?" The man tilted his head slightly as he considered Fenn's words before answering,

"That name seems to ring true for me. It is definitely better than simply being called 'Mage' or 'Sir.' Plus, with you being with us for the foreseeable future it would be a bit confusing for us both to be called 'The Mage.'" Fenn did not get a chance to address that last sentence before the now named Jonathan Champion continued on, "I have some questions about magic. Can you answer them?"

The request caught Fenn off guard for a moment. He tried to put it out of his mind that the two men were sitting in a town which had been terrorized by the Moks, was currently being looted by the Corsairs, and he was now going to have a question and answer session with him on the answer side of it. The Ferrekei mage considered what he might be asked to reveal before answering, "I will answer what I can."

Champion shrugged, "Fair enough. First question: How does magic work?"

Fenn waited for the question to be narrowed down a bit. When no further words from Champion were forthcoming, he licked suddenly dry lips as he tried to mentally organize a response to the difficult question. "You ask a question that mages and scholars have been asking for centuries upon centuries. But, I see that you are serious, so I will do my best."

Sitting further back in his chair, the mage's voice took on a lecturing tone, "Magic can best be understood by talking about life force. All people have a life force, unique to each individual. It connects us to the world we live in and it grows at our birth, and is developed and influenced by the world we live in. Some of us have a life force that is subtly different, that allows us to exert some control over our environment that manifests itself elementally; fire, earth, water, air. These people are mages.

The one trait that all mages have in common, no matter their power, is the ability to speak and understand languages. It is widely held that this is also related to our unique life force in allowing such a broad power of communication. This makes it easy for adolescent mages to be identified early on. This ability can be greater or lesser depending on the mage. For instance, some very powerful mages have been known to be able to communicate not just with people, but animals as well depending on their elementals. Examples: Earth mages with mammals, water mages with certain sea creatures, air mages with birds, etc . . ."

Fenn paused for a moment to see if his words were sinking in, at Champion's nod, he went on, "Different races seem to be attuned to certain types of magical abilities in line with their life forces. An example would be the Moks. Due to their swampy origins, they tend to produce a disproportionate amount of water mages. Some races are also more prone to producing mages than others. The Tuaks have very few mages while the Ferrekei produce dozens each year. Until recently, only one race had never produced a mage." Fenn spoke that last sentence delicately. He did not want to use the word 'mund' in front of this man given the reaction it had produced on their first visit. Fenn still had vivid dreams about being held upside down and forced to face the scarred mund.

Champion sat motionless as he considered Fenn's words. The explanation had been incredibly basic but Fenn felt that given the fact that the Corsairs would be departing soon, a simple, direct definition would be a better idea. The loud sound of breaking glass invaded the quiet moment and Champion gave a rueful smile. Leaning over, he grasped Fenn's hand and said, "I look forward to having more of these conversations, Mage Fenn."

Hours later Grach, Tyrell and Fenn shared a small cabin on Captain Spuros' ship. The three had just finished a meal of hard cheese and bread. Fenn had demanded that they share with him everything from their meeting with Jonathan Champion. Now, the blue skinned mage sat in silence digesting what he had learned.

Grach cleared his throat and interrupted the quie, "These two creatures . . ."

"Manifestations." Fenn quietly corrected him.

"Manifestations, whatever they are, they look like Champion."

Grach waited and indicated with a slight gesture toward Fenn that he needed more information. Nodding Fenn said, "Yes, that is most unusual. The histories tell stories of powerful mages who had been able to make similar creations. But nothing like these two beings. And the fact that they can communicate and appear to have personalities separate from their creator is all very interesting."

Tyrell stretched his leg out. It was still very painful and any movement made him wince. Through a small spasm of pain, he asked, "But what are they? Are they good or evil? Is it a sign of some sickness that Jonathan has been stricken with?"

Fenn snorted at that and answered, "They are fucking incredible is what they are."

"I like the mageling's answer myself." The voice, which spoke just above their heads, startled the three men. Slowly floating down from the ceiling, the air manifestation glimmered into view. When it reached the floor, Aeris crossed its legs and sat next to Tyrell as if it was the most natural thing in the world. Slowly rubbing its hands together, Aeris chuckled, "What a fine group of trouble makers you three are! I am so glad you are here to liven things up. It gets so dull when all we have to waste our time with is taking on the Mok Empress and her hordes of frogeyes."

"Trouble makers! Hah, we should just burn them to ash and be done with them." The fire manifestation made no secret of his entrance. Flames and smoke billowed from under the door way and Cinder appeared arms crossed looming over the group.

Aeris sighed, "Excuse my friend. His pleasures are limited to burning things up."

Tyrell's eyes had gotten very large as he took in Cinder's scowling scarred visage. He scooted a bit closer to Grach. Holding up two pale hands, Aeris said reassuringly, "Now, Now. You are honored guests of the master. You have nothing to fear from us. Right Cinder?" Aeris gave the other a stern look cusing Cinder gruffly take a few steps back from the three companions and it seemed that his flames burned just a little lower.

Nodding, Aeris said, "Yes. Now isn't that better? The big nasty fire man won't do any harm to you three."

"What do you want?" Fenn asked. He looked at Aeris as if trying to peer through the creature, as if he stared long enough he could understand how the manifestation worked.

Aeris snapped its fingers, "Excellent question. What do we want? Why, nothing of course. Or rather, we want you three to *do* nothing that is, or as little as possible." Aeris said this last as he absently looked over his finger nails.

"What do you mean? Speak plainly creature!" Grach now stood and faced the two beings. Hands on his hips he jutted his chin out at a stubborn angle. "We came here for Jonathan Champion. Our friend. What business of it is yours?"

"Why, it is our business, my stout fellow." As he spoke Aeris rose to his feet. Joining Cinder, he folded his hands together and continued, "You are under the impression that our mage, our *master*, is Jonathan Champion. I can assure you, he is not."

Grach scowled. Aeris continued on before a reply could be voiced, "He may have been Jonathan Champion at one time. He may have been your friend, he may be your friend again. But he is not the same man."

Tyrell had risen with a helpful arm from Grach before speaking, "It was important that we know he lived, surely you can understand that? We had to know. We had to find him. Whether he remembers us or not, whether he remembers himself or not."

Aeris waved another hand, "We know my sincere fellow why you two are here. It is the motivations of your companion that we find suspect."

Fenn had tried to shrink in the background during this conversation. At being singled out, he stood cautiously and hoped his voice did not shake and break, "The Mage Counsel concerns themselves with all things of the Art. We cannot have mages running around without the guidance of the council. A wild mage is always a danger to the world at large."

Aeris made a delicate sound that might have been his version of a snort, "Come now mageling that is such a boring by the book stock answer! Surely you can do better than that?"

Fenn's face took on a closed and defensive look, "I don't understand your meaning. I . . ." His response was interrupted by Cinder's approach. While the fires did not glow any hotter, they did take on an ominous darker red color before the creature spoke.

"What we mean, boy, is that we can understand why the feast brother and the friendly fungus are both here. But why are you here? The Master hates your council. He would never agree to come back with you, even at the behest of your two buddies here. And why would he come back? So you sick shits could take him apart to see what makes him tick? Or to hide him away somewhere so that you're fucked up notions of mund inferiority can't be challenged? Here he is needed. Here he is a man of respect and power. He would be nothing less than a freak back in your clean cut world. Why would he go back? Tell me!"

Fenn realized that Cinder had backed him up to the ship's wooden wall. Sweat had begun to slide down his forehead. Glancing over Cinder's smoking shoulder he could see the three others looking at him and waiting for an answer. He swallowed in a suddenly dry throat before answering, "Because, Jonathan Champion has a son."

CHAPTER EIGHT

S he was right, but he would never admit it. Sweat beaded on Mosha's forehead as he continued his walk. Though walk was not really a proper description for what he was making his body do at the moment. More like a fast paced jaunt. With the light of the new sun just peering over the horizon he lowered his head and concentrated on his task.

That woman was right, and she knew she was right. Gritting his teeth, he buried the annoying thought as he pushed his legs into an almost run. Last year at this time he never would have been able to keep such a pace. He never would have set himself the daunting task of climbing the steep incline of the northwestern slopes.

She did this to him. Always challenging him; always arguing with him on nearly any topic. Arguing! With him! Like she did not know he remembered everything that she had ever said. Every utterance from those sweet, pouty lips . . . .

He pushed his legs harder; willing all thoughts of the infuriating creature from his mind. Several yards ahead he could see his destination; the shrine seemed to beckon him as the first glimmers of sunlight reflected off its white surface. Breathing hard now, he grunted with effort. Cresting the hill he placed his out stretched hand towards the shrine, fingers touching the cool surface just as the first rays of the sun poured through the building's pillars.

He had never done something so strenuous. His lungs burned and his legs trembled and shook so much that he had to lean against a pillar. Looking up, he felt the sun's early morning warmth against his face. Grinning in spite of the pain, he felt a deep seeded satisfaction.

"Ah yes, you beat the sun. Good for you."

He whirled around. Sitting in the center of the shrine was a wizened old woman. Wrinkled tan fingers clutched a thin length of wood that scratched idly in the dirt. A strange assortment of mismatched cloths and threads seemed to form a colorful mess of a dress of some kind. Black hair without a single grey strand was wound in a lopsided pile on her head. Bright blue eyes and a shiny white toothed smile sparkled up at him.

She sat with her back against the large statue of a woman done all in white marble. Here and there, green veins marred the stone and seemed to provide the stone lady with almost magical shading that seemed more lifelike. Approaching the statue he stopped a few feet in front of its base. Looking down on this uninvited guest, he pursed his lips in thought. Though he had never met the woman before, he recognized her immediately.

"Terra."

The white smile got wider. With a cackle of glee the woman motioned him closer. His legs still trembling, he stiffly walked forward. Grunting, he lowered himself so he sat with his back against the statute. With a quiet apologetic glance at the shrine's stone patroness, he settled his considerable backside next to this strange morning visitor. She had given her attention back to her stick scratching and seemed content to ignore him. Too tired to care, he leaned back against the statue's base and closed his eyes.

"I knew her you know." The words had their desired effect and he opened one eye. Still she scratched.

"Your wonderful Lady. Yes, I knew her well."

With both eyes open, Mosha frowned, "If you mean to call the Eldest Sister my lady, then by all means please do so with a little more . . ."

A snort of laughter paused the stick scratching for a moment, "Not your trollope, dear Mosha, this one." She flicked her stick firmly against the base of the statue with a loud crack. Mosha's face turned a bit red at the 'trollope' comment.

"What do you mean you knew her? Knew who you crazed old thing?"

Then he stopped, his mind processing her words. He looked up and took in the statue and then dropped his gaze to the creature in front of him. The black hair bobbed as her head nodded at the unasked question.

"Oh yes. The precious White Lady. I knew her well." A tired sigh escaped her lips before saying, "And I suppose I owe her an apology of sorts. She was always so damned smug in her looks. Damned woman always got her way just by batting her eyes or shaking her ass in someone's face. But, in the end she had a difficult task." The stick stopped and the old face took on a look of distant sorrow, "Yes, perhaps the most difficult task. An impossible task." The words were spoken so soft that Mosha was not sure he was meant to hear.

He leaned his head back against the cool marble and recalled the conversation where he had first learned of Terra from Jonathan Champion. The man's face came easily to mind. Not a face easily forgotten; horribly scarred yet there was something about the man that made him approachable. He had spent two days with Jonathan Champion that had changed his life. Turned it upside down in fact. In moments he had revisited that conversation and identified the information concerning the old woman. He turned back to find that she was looking him over with a practiced eye.

"You get a faraway look when you access that brain of yours. Kinda cute, in fact. I bet your trollope gets all hot and bothered by that stare." Chuckling she bent back to her scratching.

He gave her a hard glare. By his brain she meant his memory of course. Which was nothing to joke about; though Mosha was sure that there was not much this old hag would not make fun of as long as she knew it would annoy him. His memory was colossal. He had built his entire ego around it, his entire personality. He remembered everything; his first steps as a child, every conversation and person he had ever met. And the books; he could repeat verbatim every word he had ever read.

His love of books was central to his enjoyment of life. Thus his work as a librarian at the Great Library. The obsession with books and the knowledge they held was also the main part of his current predicament. He closed his eyes briefly and pictured the book he had found. A mystery that haunted him sometimes was hidden in its simple pages. He had only managed to translate a small portion of the frustrating rune like writing; and most of that was pure guess work.

He opened his eyes again. He was not sure what Terra was; mundane, mage, spirit? Champion had no idea when he had questioned him. She had appeared twice to help the scarred man and disappeared just as suddenly. Mosha knew he would have to tread carefully with her. Collecting his thoughts he paused to glance at the woman's dirt scratching. For a moment nothing registered, then he exclaimed in surprise.

Looking up with a clever smile, Terra asked, "Looks familiar big brain?"

Staring at him from the freshly scraped mud were four perfect runes; his runes! Immediately he calculated that these three runes where repeated one hundred and twenty seven times in his book. They were also etched into the ax blade and helmet that Champion had left behind when he was captured.

She reached up and gently touched his cheek, "Dear Mosha, I have a bargain to make with you. I have lost my Champion and he is lost without me. I must find him before, he . . ." The hand dropped carefully back into her lap but she held his gaze.

"Before what?" Mosha whispered.

"Why, before he destroys us all, my Mosha." And she put her head in both hands and wept. Mosha was not good with emotions; and definitely not adept at consoling those who were suffering from an emotional episode. Feeling completely out of his depth, Mosha reached over and gave the woman a small clumsy pat on the back. Suddenly, Terra reached over and grabbed a handful of Mosha's blue librarian's robe. Before he could object, she put the material up to her face and blew her nose loudly. Grimacing in disgust, Mosha got to his feet, a long green slimy trail marring his robe.

Looking down on the now tearless woman, Mosha withheld the impulse to wipe his snot soaked robe on her smug face. Trying to save what little remained of his dignity,

Mosha ignored his soiled clothing and asked, "What do you need from me?"

"A bargain is what I offer, big brain."

"What type of bargain?"

Chuckling Terra bent back to her dirty scribbling before saying, "I will show you the secret of these curious runes, and you will deliver a message for me."

The runes in his book had consumed him like no other riddle had in his entire life. He felt a giddy feeling of excitement run through his body at the idea of being able to read his mysterious tome. Mosha took a calming breathe, before asking,

"A message to whom?"

Smiling a cat like smile, Terra answered, "You will know her, when you see her. Now for the message. Repeat after me, 'Dear Fat Cow . . .'"

THE SOUND of water dripping was a constant in this damp world. Trickles of brown city sludge mingled with rain water to create a dark place of moist grossness. The whole underdark smelled like an old turd. Nah, an old turd would smell better than this, Nook thought to himself.

He pressed the rag tighter against his mouth and nose. The lumps of garlic and cider beans did a good job of taking the putrid sting out of the nasty air, but could not completely dispel the smell. They had needed to stop while the fat man spewed up his lunch, adding his own stink to the stench of the place.

In truth, Nook had not yet made up his mind about his current employer. Though fat, the man seemed to have the wind to keep up the pace. Though what they were looking for, Nook could only guess.

Only a fool or a crazed one would think anything of value could be found in the underdark. The name was one the poorer inhabitants of the old quarter gave to the vast sewer system that spread underneath the city of Hyberan. Used mostly by thieves and runaway munds, the place had an unsavory reputation. It had taken three silver bars for Nook to agree to serve as a guide to the librarian.

He felt the weight of the bars in his pocket and suddenly the stench seemed more bearable. He thought of the surprise on his Ma's face when he brought the money home. She would insist on giving one bar to the Sublime Sisters of course since they had cured little Alia of her infection the year before and Ma was a stickler for paying her debts. The other two bars would keep them fed for months to come.

Until your father comes back, she would say. If he did not have the cloth over his mouth he would have spit. The bastard is never coming back, and Nook knew it.

Tough enough being a mund in the Shinning City, but a mund mother with two kids to take care of was near misery. Ma worked her fingers to the bone stitching sails down at the docks and some nights she stole away to pleasure some sailors for a couple of copper bars. The silver would let her rest for a bit and get some of her pride back.

"I swear I have never considered where my shit goes after using the privy. Gods below! This place is a stench filled hell." Groaning the fat man righted himself. Wiping a sleeve across his mouth, he put the cloth back up to cover his nose. Waving to Nook to continue, the pair marched on.

Should have charged him another silver for the face cloth, Nook thought as the pair made their way through the dark. Alia had told Nook that she had heard the fat man asking around the quarter for someone who could take him beneath the city. Nook was a bit surprised that the man turned out to be a librarian; and suspicious. As soon as Nook made it clear he was not one of the 'bottom boys' who sold his ass for a copper a poke, the two had struck a bargain; and here they were.

The man wanted to get to the center of the old city, nearly under the Sisters Temple. It was a crazy idea. The fumes in the underdark were enough to addle your brains. No torch could be brought because it might set the air on fire and no rawstone could be found because the Mages were using them all for the war, so the two walked in near darkness.

Hours later the duo stopped for a breather; Nook took the risk of removing his cloth and wiped the sweat from his brow. The fat man stood on unsteady feet; the only sound being the wheezing of his breath. Seeing that the man would not be ready any time soon, the boy sat down on a moldy rock and waited.

"So, Rook, is it? How on earth do you know about this place?"

The boy grimaced, "The name's Nook, big man. And why do you want to know?"

"Ah yes. Sorry boy. Nook. Fascinating name. Did your mother perhaps play a joke on you with a name like that?" The man asked the question in a mildly curious tone. The boy's grimace became a slight smile.

"Nah. Ma doesn't have a joking bone in her body. But then, I know who my Ma is. Can ye say the same?"

A moment of quiet, then a slight chuckle, "I suppose I earned that, young man. My name is Mosha."

"Mosha? Is that a kind of wet turd? You should be right at home down here then."

Waving his hand as if to brush off the rebuke, Mosha said, "Doubly earned then, young Nook. You may regale me with your gutter trash wit as long as you like if you would but tell me how long until we get to our destination."

Now Nook smiled. This fat man was funny.

"Another hour or so and we will get to the 'armpit'; the king of all cesspits. Make your eyes melt and your nose hairs burn. After that, we will drop down a bit and the air will clear up. But walkin' is slower, as the path we walk won't be like good stone." For emphasis he slapped his hand against the cement path the two stood on.

"But, we can light a torch down there; no fear of burning air. So it is not so bad."

Nodding, Mosha motioned him forward and they started off.

Mosha woke to the smell of smoke. Groaning, he sat up to see the small fire Nook had made. The boy sat silently watching him. He rolled his tongue around his mouth and grimaced at the taste of fresh vomit. The 'armpit' had been just as terrible as the boy had described. It was in fact a huge underwater lake of sludge and slime. Green mist hung over the noxious expanse and watered the eyes making it impossible to go quickly past. Minutes had seemed like hours and he recalled Nook had to help the last few yards. How the boy bore any of his weight was a mystery.

Feeling now obligated for his assistance, Mosha took a moment to look closer at his young guide. Nook appeared to be a typical lower class mund; brown hair, brown eyes, skin that looked like it needed a good washing. A small but wicked scar traced its way over one ear and disappeared into the boy's hair line. The spotted green shirt was complimented by dull brown trousers held together with a rope belt. Small bare feet were covered in calluses from hard use.

Rising to his feet, Mosha removed the pack he had hidden under his blue librarian's cloak. Approaching the fire, he sat down with a slight grunt that made the boy start. Slowly opening the pack, Mosha removed a loaf of bread, cheese, and some dry cured beef. Ripping the loaf in half, he handed a portion to the boy; after a moment's hesitation Nook took the offering but waited for Mosha to take a bite of his first before tearing into the moist bread.

Several moments later, after the cheese and beef were devoured, the two odd companions stared at each other across the dwindling flames. Clearing his throat, Mosha broke the silence by saying, "Thank you, Nook. For your help back there. I swear I was going to faint and fall into that filthy lake."

No response.

"Thank you also for not . . . taking advantage of me while I was passed out. You could have taken the pack and left me here."

That got a blink and a scowl, "We made a deal? Yeah? I ain't no word breaker, see? You paid me an'I aim to come through. We from the quarter keep to a deal till it's done. Thanks for the food, though."

The last was said a bit grudgingly and Mosha nodded in acknowledgment. Taking a skin of water from the pack, he took a long drink. Handing it over to the boy, Mosha waited until he swallowed to speak, "What will we find further down, Nook?"

Wiping a grimy hand across his mouth, the boy handed the skin back, "Some strange looking buildings, some half sunk into'th ground. Nothing like gold or copper or worth nothing. Maybe these shiny worms, glowing like little lights. Strange pictures or writing; the smell is not so bad . . ."

"Writing? What type of writing?" Mosha's voice sounded eager and the big man leaned closer.

Nook looked a bit startled at the interruption. He shrugged his small shoulders, "Dunno. Can't read a lick. Just looks like it."

"Can you show me when we get there? Where the writing is?"

At the boy's nod, the fat man smiled.

Mosha and Nook walked through the streets of a strange metropolis. The librarian had thought that they would find a few buildings from the Shinning City's early years. Never did he imagine an entire city beneath the City. Avenues and side streets went off in all directions. The buildings that had not fallen down were in different stages of decay. A grey moss covered most of the stone surfaces making them crumbly to the touch. Lifting his torch up, he tried to make out strange markings near the top of one of the structures but could not.

Nook walked close by him as if reassured by the big man's presence. The sounds of his small bare feet and Mosha's sandals made a quiet noise in the oppressive silence. Mosha felt the boy's hand snake into his own; they both felt reassured by the touch.

The place was dead. Not a whisper of movement, no sounds of animals of any kind penetrated the dense quiet dark. Not just dead; this place was forgotten. Left to die alone and unremembered.

Hand in hand they walked for some time in silence, past strangely slanted buildings and fallen domes. The torch flames cast a light that seemed to be unwelcome. As if the buildings did not want to be reminded of what they had become.

Mosha stopped next to a structure that at one time had held a dome. Upon closer inspection the lower part of the building seemed to be made of a lighter stone. Taking a hand, he rubbed at the near white stone and was surprised at the gritty feel. Between his fingers he could feel the hard grainy stuff break apart. On impulse he placed a bit on his tongue and quickly spit it out, "Salt." He said surprised.

Walking to the next building he observed the same condition. Obviously whatever had happened to this city the ocean had played a part. Mosha shuddered at the thought of watery tombs for the inhabitants.

Finally, they came to a tall monolith set into the middle of a circular courtyard surrounded on all sides by pillars. While it was ancient, it appeared to have weathered time better than its other stone brethren. About four stories in height, it loomed over the pair. Walking, and partially dragging a reluctant Nook, Mosha came to the base of the stone monster. Like the other buildings, a film of salt covered the lower half of the structure.

Beneath the salty crust he could see slight indents just lower than eye level. Gently letting go of the boy's hand, Mosha removed a small pen knife from his pack. He scraped until he could begin to see the smooth stone beneath. Slowly, a rune appeared, and then another. Across the smooth stone crude lettering had been chiseled across the surface; familiar lettering. His arm soon ached but he could not remove the smile from his face.

Two hours later, Mosha sat by a small fire and tried to ignore his aching arms. Sweat lathered his clothing and gave his hair a greasy feel. Taking a spare sip from the water skin, he thought back on Terra's instructions:

I know that she was under siege. She would have left something in the way of a record. She was a librarian of sorts so you should understand that, big man. What's left of the old city is under the poor quarter. Find it, and then find the Lore. It was not used outside of certain circles unless necessary so it should jump out at you.

The alphabet is an ancient one. Twenty-seven runes make up the entire vocabulary. Placing the runes together, and sometimes on top of, or within each other, makes up unique wordings . . . .

Mosha stood and rolled his shoulders. He recalled every word of Terra's instructions concerning the rune language; or Lore as she called it. The Lore was a surprisingly simple language once the basics were explained. However, the runes that had been placed on the monolith had been done in obvious haste and were hard to read. He had stood there for several hours before sitting down with Nook to eat sparingly of their meager rations.

Mosha had not meant to be gone from aboveground for so long, in fact, Terre had said he should be able to find the runes and fulfill his errand and return back at his leisure. He noted to himself that any future information from the strange woman needed to be taken with a grain of salt. However, after the difficulty of the journey, and his nagging curiosity, Mosha had decided to stay as long as possible.

Nook seemed a bit bored. He had totally disregarded Mosha's warning to stay close and had spent hours searching the surrounding buildings. Through their strange bonding in the dark, Nook had opened up a bit more. He had confessed that he had never been to the strange city before, but had been going off of information from his father. Asking about his father had resulted in an uncomfortable silence which ended in Mosha turning his attention back to the monolith and Nook disappearing on another adventure.

Mosha had left the black book back in his rooms at the Sisters Temple. He feared damaging the tome while searching in the sewers. In truth, he did not need it for a reference at all. He turned his attention back to the stone's newly revealed runes:

Trust lost
Trust betrayed
My children's lives could not be saved

I wait beyond the spirit gate
I wait for those who come too late
I wait because it is my fate

With bloody hands I implore
My Children use the ancient Lore
To step beyond the stone closed door

He leaned his head against the cool stone. "A riddle. A fucking riddle here in the shit smelling dark. Nook my boy, are you there? We have a riddle here but my stomach says it might be time to go back into the sunshine and find some food. Nook?"

Cursing under his breath, Mosha grabbed a torch from the dwindling fire and marched in the direction he had seen the boy disappear, "Nook! Nook! Boy, I am done here for now! I am hungry for some real food! What say you to that? Something warm and greasy?!"

No answer. He paused. The boy should be able to hear him; could he be playing some childish game? Hide and seek in this god's forsaken place?

Turning a corner, he came to an amazed stop. Before him, covering an entire stone wall, were hundreds of silver lights. No, not lights. Worms. The strange creatures pulsed with an ethereal glow. At the base of the wall a small pool of water glimmered with the same light. Near the pool he saw a small form sitting with his feet in the water. Mosha sighed in relief, "Nook. There you are. Found your worms did you? You were right, or at least your father was."

As he approached, Mosha noticed that the boy was not sitting upright but slouched over, leaning against a salt covered bench. His head was rolled to the side and he had not acknowledged Mosha's greeting. Placing a hand on a small shoulder, Mosha shook gently, "Nook?" No response.

Settling down next to him, Mosha followed his small companion's gaze into the water. More worms. Their glowing forms making silver currents in the water, sliding back and forth.

"Much livelier in the water aren't they boy? Hey now, you have a few that seem to like you." Three wiggling forms seemed to be hovering near Nook's right foot that was dangling in the water. No, not hovering . . . stuck to the boys toes, almost like . . .

"Forgotten Gods! Get up boy . . . up!"

Grabbing Nook's shoulders he dragged him away from the pool. Attached to his feet were three long worms, their forms thrashing about as they followed their prey from the water. Mosha gripped one and tried to rip it from Nook's big toe. The slick body was hard to hold but he felt a satisfying crunch as he squeezed. With a wet slurping sound, the worm let go of its purchase on Nook's foot and fell to the ground. Small sharp teeth in a circular mouth were exposed as the thing whipped back and forth on the ground in its death throes. Moments later, two other worms joined their now dead companion.

Laying Nook gently down, Mosha took stock of his condition. Small silver lines branched out from the boy's foot where the worms had been attached. Nook groaned quietly; placing a hand on his head Mosha could feel that a fever had set in.

"Damn me, boy. I am a librarian, not a healer." Mosha calculated that it would take him at least a day and a half to get back to the surface and that took into account carrying the now limp Nook. Idly he scratched his leg as he knelt next to Nook.

"Ow! Burn me!"

Looking down he saw a worm sucking on his hand. With a curse, he smashed the thing against the hard ground. He noticed the circular puncture marks on his palm slowly oozed red blood mixed with a white glowing substance. Looking up, he saw that the once near motionless worms on the wall were now dropping into the water. The pond quickly became a writhing mass of glowing silver bodies. With a shiver of fear, Mosha got to his feet and picked up the unconscious Nook.

Backing up slowly, Mosha never took his eyes off the now churning waters. The creatures seemed to be massing together, their soft bodies melding into each other. Almost sickened with fear, Mosha barely avoided gagging and hoisted the boy's limp body onto his shoulder and stumbled away from the pool. Abruptly, the worms' cozy glow went out and the place was flooded in darkness. Closing his eyes, Mosha began to retrace his steps.

Adjusting Nook's weight on his shoulders, Mosha began a steady jog in the dark, his only thoughts to retrace his steps out of the city. Behind him he could hear the movement of something large scraping itself across the ground. He refused to look back knowing his courage was held together by the thinnest of threads.

Turning a corner, he made out the monolith in front of him. The giant stone loomed over head as Mosha trudged toward it. Laying Nook down against the stone giant, Mosha scrabbled in his pack. With a cry of triumph he found the wooden torch and turned to face his fear. Striking his flint against the stone monolith, the torch caught fire and Mosha raised it toward the sound of his pursuer.

A nightmare come to life. A huge creature lurched in between two pillars. While the opening appeared to be too small at first, the giant monster simply seemed to ooze through it. A thousand tiny mouths with razor sharp teeth alternately closed and opened as if tasting the air. Pausing for a moment, the thing seemed to get its bearing and surged toward the two companions.

Mosha's mind was flooded with fear. Dropping his torch, he picked up the unconscious boy in one arm. Never a brave man, he turned his back on the monstrous death that was heading toward them. Placing his bloodied hand upon the stone, he slowly traced the runes and quietly spoke them under his breath. With a sigh, he slowly lowered himself to his knees, his head resting against the salty stone. A mystery that he would never solve; knowledge literally at his fingertips forever lost to him. His last thought was that he wished he could simply pass out to avoid the painful death that was assuredly coming for him. Then, darkness.

"And then Mosha here called my name, but I could'na answer though I could hear him; like my body was asleep but I was awake. He come up to me and pulled me out of the water and squished those li'll buggers."

"The worms must have some sort of venom that incapacitates their victims, dear Nook. For reference, 'could'na and li'll' are not proper words to use; 'could not' and 'little' in the future please." The voice was definitely female and sultry in a way that reminded him of the Eldest Sister.

He seemed to be lying on something soft but firm. Without moving his hand, Mosha used a finger to gently brush what appeared to be a soft blanket covering him. His eye lids seemed to be made of led as he tried to open them. At first his efforts only rewarded him with a dull sludgy light. After a few moments his eyes adjusted and he took in his new environment.

A spacious room surrounded him. Large couches with no backs on them surrounded a small fountain of grey stone that bubbled quietly. Sitting up he realized that he occupied one of those very same couches. Off to the left and right corridors exited to places unknown. All around the place a cozy yellow glow filled the air; it was both calming and relaxing.

"Well, I see our valiant librarian is awake." That voice again, this time ripe with wry amusement. Shifting, Mosha turned to see Nook sharing a couch with a . . . . Goddess. That was the only thing that he could come up with. When you see someone who has been enshrined in a temple, her likeness put on statues, and she suddenly shows up in front of you like some spectral dream, what else can you call her?

Through a mouth suddenly dry he croaked out," The White Lady." And darkness claimed him . . . again.

CHAPTER NINE

It was a glorious morning. Sunlight shone through the tall marble pillars. It was a warm day that held no mugginess in the air. From the streets the first sounds of the city could be heard as early morning merchants called out their wares. This wonderful mood was totally lost on Sister Kitla as she walked quickly down the hallway glancing down to make sure she was following the trail.

Little shit! He has only been walking for a few months! How did he get out the damn window?

Near the conclusion of her pregnancy Kitla had been reassigned a room on the first floor of the temple. With a window that looked out upon one of the three gardens housed within the complex, she had been grateful to be able to avoid traveling down the flights of stairs with a newborn in tow as she carried out her temple duties. Looking back, being on the first floor also assured that her son did not fall out of the third story windows in her old quarters. Instead of a broken neck, the boy only suffered from a set of very muddy feet. Making him at least easy to follow on the white marble flooring.

Hustling around a corner she collided with a green glad guardsman. Grimacing as the man stepped on her foot,

Kitla's apology was nearly out of her mouth when the guard greeted her, "Such haste Sister. It's almost as if you have lost something?"

Kitla could not help the wry smile that came to her lips. She could always recognize Gam's voice through the mesh guard's mask. She knew it was better to play along with his game or he would become insufferable.

"Why yes, honored warrior. I have lost a precious, but dirty, thing that escaped my rooms but a few moments ago."

Nodding gravely, Gam offered her an arm and began to escort her down the hallway she had been following, "Indeed, I may have certain knowledge of your charge. However, I must warn you that he has been involved with an incident that touches upon temple security. The Captain has requested your presence." Barely stifling a groan, Kitla allowed herself to be led towards the guard's mess hall.

Unlike many military orders, the Green Guard did not have an official barracks. Instead, each guard had a room to himself or shared one with a fellow guardsman. Locating men around the temple complex increased the chance that a Guardsman was nearby to deal with any trouble.

But the guardsmen needed a place to train and socialize. So the mess hall and the training yard were built. In these two places the guards could train and build that type of camaraderie that is required of a fighting force. Here the men need not wear their green mesh guards masks and could somewhat relax in an almost public setting.

Approaching the mess hall front gate, Gam led her to a side corridor that was little more than a narrow tunnel. The two walked in silence as they approached a wooden door that was partially open allowing an obviously irritated voice to drift down the hall.

"No, young sir, do not put that in your mouth. By the dead gods, you are sticking to everything! Ahhhh, my report, ruined! Please, just follow orders and . . . ."

Kitla could almost feel Gam's smile through the mask as he hesitantly pushed the door open. Thinking that she was ready for anything, Kitla followed through the open door. At the sight in front of her, she could not quite stifle the laugh before she covered her mouth.

The Captain was strange looking for a Gurashi. A large belly protruded from a thin frame attached to a pair of stick like legs. Skinny arms which were often held clasped behind his back when he addressed his men were now desperately clutching a pile of papers. Plump almost sinuous lips protruded from a large bald head that seemed to bob up and down on its own. Standing now, the Captain was backed into a corner trying to stay as far from his assailant as possible. It was hard to imagine that this man would be so feared and respected by a group as hard bitten and tough as the Green Guard.

The 'assailant' was a small chubby boy. The fact that he was a boy was without question as the little creature was bare naked and dirty as all hell. As Kitla approached she could see that dirt, leaves, feathers, and bits of paper covered the little body. Sensing her approach, the escapee turned around to face her. Standing before him, Kilta frowned for a moment before sweeping him off his dirty feet into her arms.

With a contented sigh, Kitla felt the relief of finding her son safe; if not in a bit of trouble. She rested her cheek on the top of his head and held him for a quiet moment. Gam moved a chair closer and gently whispered for her to sit. It was after she was seated that she noticed the boy was covered in . . . something.

A sticky sweetness clawed at her nose as the little body squirmed in her lap. Kitla's green robe quickly became grimy with sticky filth. Vainly attempting to make the child sit, Kitla gave the Captain a questioning look. He answered the unspoken question simply.

"Honey."

Kitla looked down at the now motionless child who was looking at the Captain as if trying to decide how to bother the poor man again. She was constantly amazed when she looked at her son. He was an almost miracle; literally.

As a Sublime Sister, Kitla had certain responsibilities to serve in the pleasure houses, or Green Inns as they are commonly known, operated by the Sisterhood. As things usually go in these types of practices, pregnancies can be a burden to a Sister who has not served out her number of years at the Green Inns. Thus, all Sisters of serviceable ages are administered a birth control tonic. The elixir in no way damages a woman's ability to have children later in life and is simply considered one of the requirements of Sisterhood.

Kitla had always taken the elixir routinely once per month at the beginning of her cycles. It was administered and monitored by the healers within the Sisterhood. Which is why the fact that she became pregnant at all was such a surprise; which was an understatement. The Healers had been thrown into a furor of activity to determine whether the elixir had been somehow compromised or if Kitla's pregnancy was simply a single glitch on its effectiveness. Before any further inquiry could be made Eldest Sister had stepped in and put an end to the discussion. Sister Kitla was pregnant; the elixir was still viable; discussion closed. Eldest Sister rarely used her iron fist of authority, but when she did, the Sisterhood as a whole hopped too.

The Captain's voice interrupted her reminiscence. "Yes, Sister Kitla, honey."

The Captain had seated himself and now glared at her across from the large wooden table. The office was a small, almost cramped room. The table took up almost the entire space and the polished wood surface gleamed in the morning light. The contents of the table were an epitome of organized obsession. Pens and stacks of papers were all properly coordinated into place. Small jars of ink lined one side of the table, perfectly spaced as if they were soldiers at parade rest. The walls of the room were covered, nearly from top to bottom, by shelving of different sizes and shapes. Each shelf was color coordinated to correspond to different types of reports and guard business. Yes, the Captain had created a very ordered and quiet world; albeit a cramped one.

Enter into this organized utopia a honey covered child. A dirty, unclean thing that refuses to take orders and whose only purpose was to pack in as much chaos and destruction in between nap times. Yes, the Captain would be beyond annoyed.

Giving her charge a little squeeze, she asked, "Honey? How?"

Taking up the pile of honey drenched papers that he had attempted to save, the Captain barked, "Gam!"

Straightening his back even further, Gam gave a quick salute and began to report, "Apparently the boy, . . ."

"Perpetrator" The Captain interrupted without looking up from his sticky pages as Gam continued.

"Yes Sir! The Perpetrator made his way into the mess hall where he made the acquaintance of certain guardsmen. There were still men eating breakfast who had just gotten off night duty and there were pots of honey on the table. The Perpetrator then . . . ."

An hour later Kitla was sitting in the courtyard watching 'The Perpetrator' play with some other young children. The pepper spiced bath that she had given him had removed much of the honey though there was still a slight stickiness on his chubby toes. Her moment of calm reflection did not last long as a shy yellow haired acolyte approached and softly whispered a summons from the Eldest Sister. With a sigh, Kitla left her son under the protective care of the other sisters and quietly followed the young girl down the hallway wondering what the rest of the day would bring.

CHAPTER TEN

Kitla looked up at the tall obelisk and then gave an irritated glare to the librarian. "You want me to do what?" She was not happy. Her meeting with Eldest Sister had been short and abrupt. Mosha had found something. He needed her assistance. Put on a warm cloak and some boots as she might get muddy.

Muddy. Eldest Sister should have mentioned the shit, the toxic fumes, and the flesh eating worms. Not that Kitla's trip into the tunnels had been as dangerous as Mosha and his young companion's had been. Her journey had been done under the supervision of the Green Guard and there had been two stops to refresh themselves. She had been given a thick cloth drenched in perfume to keep most of the stink from clogging her nostrils and the worms had subsided to their more comatose state in the wading pool but were still constantly monitored by the guards for any signs of aggression.

Giving her a somewhat apologetic smile, the fat man assured her, "The knife is sharp and clean, Sister. You just need enough blood to make a hand print on the surface of the stone." He gestured toward the monolith, "Please Kitla."

In resignation, she took the knife and placed it against her palm. Taking a quick breathe she sliced a small cut at the base of her hand, hoping that no one noticed that the other shook slightly. The blood oozed quickly over her skin making her fingers sticky. Seeing that Nook and Mosha had done the same to their hands, she followed suit and placed her palm against the stone. She felt a slight vibrating under her finger tips, and then her world grew dark.

"Yes Mosha, be gentle with her now. She needs to be sitting up in order to drink. You should have asked her if her moon cycle was upon her before allowing her to enter the portal." A woman's sultry voice chided. A reply was somewhat muffled as a pair of sweaty fat hands gently eased her into a sitting position. A moment later a cup was put to her lips. Taking a long drink of the cool water, Kilta opened her bleary eyes.

She was sitting on a low couch of some sort with her back supported by Mosha. Sitting next to her was a striking vision of a woman. Lush black hair flowed just past the base of a long neck that rested on a pair of perfect shoulders. A green robe, similar to Kitla's own in color but of a much more archaic style, draped over a pair of large breasts and was cinched at the waist by a brown belt. Brown eyes looked out of a classically beautiful face and a warm sensuous mouth was pouted in a worried expression. With a very motherly move, the woman brushed a few stray strands of Kitla's hair back into place.

"Now my dear. You have had quite a change to your day and I apologize for that. But, you seem to have some answers to questions I have and Mosha here was anxious to return here to my little abode." Taking the cup out of the librarian's hand, Kitla took another sip and took in her new surroundings.

She sat in a circle of wooden couches each covered with color pillows filled the center of an oval room. In the center a marble fountain in the shape of a leaping fish quietly gurgled sparkling water. It all seemed very relaxed until she looked at the walls.

At first glance they appeared to be just grey colored stucco walls. As she peered closer the walls became less substantial; less real. For a moment, pinpoints of light began to show through and the substance of the walls swirled. Kitla became dizzy.

"Tisk, none of that dear. Don't look at the walls." The voice brought Kitla back. She felt dizzy. Taking another sip, she looked at the woman before her again. With an apologetic shrug the beauty added, "I have been here for so long I forget the difficulties visitors have. The walls are difficult to accommodate for newcomers. Best if you just concentrate on me, heh?" Another motherly hair flick. Kitla drained the cup and felt much better. Noticing that the strange woman now sat next to her, she wondered where Mosha had gone off too.

Seeing her look, the woman said, "Mosha and Nook have gone back into my library. That man has a hunger for knowledge that I find quite attractive. I made him promise to allow Nook to accompany him. That way you and I have a chance to have a nice girl chat." Standing, the woman helped Kitla to her feet.

"Oh dear, I absolutely love your outfit. Here give me a moment." Stepping back, her robe shimmered into a replica of Kitla's own. The lighter material cling to her body in a nearly indecent way. Kitla exclaimed before she could catch herself.

"With a body like that, I could have any patron in the city. The gold would flow."

With a throaty chuckle, the woman did a small twirl in her new attire. "Such a sweet girl you are. Now, as much as I would love to talk clothes, we need to discuss a few more serious topics. This way child."

Kitla was ushered through a doorway that she had not noticed upon her arrival. Inside was a much smaller chamber dominated by a long strangely shaped table. Along the walls, smokeless torches sputtered silently giving the room an almost gloomy feel. The woman approached the table. Kitla followed slowly and gasped.

Not a table. A map; but a map unlike anything that Kitla had ever seen or even imagined. She could see forests and mountains; seas and rivers. One shining replica of Hyberan glowed golden in the small room; north of the golden city was the great lake evident in such detail she could see storm fronts come and go over the bright blue waters.

Far south of the city the Tuan Straight led to the principalities. Golden pinpoints dotted the far northern Tuan lands. Just south of these points, dark green smudges appeared. Golden and green spread out to make a thin line between them. Kitla's hand moved almost involuntarily to touch the points. The lady gently put a hand over hers.

"The war dear. The gold are the mage's forces and the green those of the empress. But don't touch the construct, please. It is at times a bit unstable."

Kitla nodded and put her arms down to her side. Nodding, her hostess waved her hand and the map shimmered. Suddenly, Kitla was looking at a picture of geography that was unfamiliar. Green smudges covered the lands shown here.

"This is the southern part of the Mok Empire, dear. Several thousand miles from the current conflict. Look here please . . . ." Another wave of the hand the map shifted again. The picture zoomed in on a large group of islands. Very few green smudges were evident. Instead there were red streaks across several of the islands. The woman put her elbows on the edge of the map and peered intently. After a moment, Kitla mimicked her and stepped closer trying to see what so captivated her hostess. After several moments the woman broke the silence.

"He is there, you know." Startled, Kitla glanced up. The look on her face must have portrayed her confusion. Giving her a wry smile the woman said, "Why your champion of course. Jonathan Champion."

Several minutes later the two women were sitting back in the Couch Room, as Kitla now thought of it. She sipped a cup of the bittersweet tea the woman had provided. Having been well versed in the pleasure houses, Kitla could recognize the comforting routine the woman was practicing. She herself had done similar things with nervous patrons who needed to relax before partaking of the pleasures of a Sublime Sister.

"How is the tea, Dear?" Kitla could not shake the soothing sensuality of that voice. This woman was someone who knew how to get what she wanted and used an arsenal of comforting words, sensuality, and kindness to get it; strong stuff.

Kitla smiled, "Excellent, thank you." In fact she was very irritated. First she is forced to follow a fat librarian through the shitty underbelly of the city, then cut herself bloody so she could be transported to some strange private sanctuary of some sort, then to be told that her lover, and father of her child, was alive but had somehow traveled thousands of miles past what many viewed as the civilized world, and the woman wanted to know how the tea was?

Fine bitch, I will play this game. Just tell me what I want to know. "How does one come by tea in a place like this, my dear?" Kitla threw the phrase back at her host. She sipped again.

The lady took another drink before answering, "It's not really tea, my dear. But my memory of it." She set the tea cup down and continued, "Now, as much as I would have enjoyed a good old fashioned bitch fest with you, and oh yes, I could tell your hackles were up my dear, we simply do not have the time. This place was not meant for your kind."

Again, Kitla could not hide her confused look. She was beginning to dislike the uncertainty this woman caused in her. A question was on her lips when the lady abruptly stood up. Kitla watched as her hostess cocked her head to the side as if listening. The beautiful features hardened before she spoke, "Follow me, girl. We have unwanted visitors."

SHIT flows down.

At least that's what Tesh's father always used to say. The guardsman sighed at his current experience of the literal truth of that statement. Escorting the Sister to the very bowels of the city had at first been an exciting adventure; until the smells of the shit strewn underground had invaded the senses.

Since joining the Green Guard he had spent hours each day training with his fellows. He had put up with some of the comments of being one of the few black skinned Tuak among the guard. He had almost adapted to the food served in the mess hall. He felt as though he had found a place.

It was only quiet times like this when he missed home. He leaned slightly against the salty covered column that towered overhead and wondered if his brothers prospered. If his father knew that his third son still lived and had found a place of honor. He brought to mind the old man's wrinkled face and imagined it smiling with approval. This was Tesh's last thought before a black clawed hand reached from the darkness and ripped his face off.

Mosha, Nook, and Kitla walked back through the obelisk in the midst of chaos. The bodies of two guardsmen lay nearby, the fine green fabric of their cloaks contrasting with the pools of red blood that spread from their mangled forms. The sounds of fighting could be heard close by but torches that had been placed around the large courtyard seemed to only deepen the shadows instead of banish them.

Nook moved first. The boy quickly ran to the edge of the torch light and fell to his knees. Removing a grey stone from his pocket, he began digging furiously with his tool.

Nook's actions seemed to free Mosha and Kitla from their shocked standstill. Both followed Nook's lead, but ran different directions from the obelisk. Soon three holes had been dug and the grey stones deposited into the holes. Quickly the dirt was covered back over the stones. Nook finished his first stone before his two elders and ran to the opposite side of the courtyard. Though Kitla had objected to requiring him to take two of the stones, the Lady had stated in a firm voice that the boy was the fastest and the most able of the three to form the grid.

The grid. A square of four stones in fact, with the monolith in the middle. Why the Lady referred to it as a grid was unclear but a lengthy explanation was not possible given the circumstances. Nook's hands were damp with fear and the stone slipped from his fingers. Cursing he bent down to pick it up when a black nightmare separated from the shadows.

Tall and lean, the creature moved with an alien sinuous grace to stand in front of the boy. Black scales covered long arms that ended in jagged claws which dripped with new blood. A set of shiny black armor covered its chest that gave off a sickly glow in the torch light. The face that stared down on Nook was like nothing he had even seen. Instead of a nose, two thin slits came together at a point. Plump lips formed an almost sensuous mouth; almost, if you could get passed the fangs that jutted from its mouth like oversized needles out of a pincushion. Dark eyes could just be seen through the thing's helmet that was in the shape of a large snake. A clawed hand reached up and idly drummed on its armored chest as if lost in thought as it contemplated the boy.

In his life on the streets, fear was something Nook dealt with on a daily basis. Fear of going hungry, fear of the mages, fear of losing his mother and sister; all these fears could be dealt with through the street tough attitude of survival that he had used ever since he could remember. But this was different. This was a fear of a new degree, a new scale of dread, that visited him as this strange thing looked down at him. As he met its dark gaze, Nook somehow knew that this creature could visit such pain and suffering upon him and his family that was almost beyond understanding. This was not fear, it was terror. The type of terror that left one numb and useless; like a statue unable to move out of the way of impending doom.

In his current state of terror Nook could only clutch the stone in his hand and watch as the dark one stepped closer. He closed his eyes as a sharp clawed hand almost gently touched his hair. A sigh filled with wistful anticipation came from black plump lips.

"Yesssss, little one. You wish to please me I can see. The things I could show you . . . yessss. You have no idea how much pain such a small form like yours can take. But I can show you. Oh yessss . . . I can . . . ."

"Noooooook!!!!"

With a snarl, the creature removed its hand and turned toward the voice. The thing was fast, ungodly fast. But it could not quite get out of the way of a heavy set librarian once he had his large form moving in one direction. Brandishing his pen knife, Mosha swept onto the scene with a howl that was filled half with fear and half hysterical courage. Fat man and dark nightmare went down in a swirl of hissing and cursing.

Mosha let out a cry of triumph as he drove the silver blade into a scale covered thigh. The victory was shorted lived as the creature flung the large man off. Landing on his side Mosha felt the breath rush from his body. Gasping weakly, the large man tried to gain his feet as black scaled death stalked him.

Seeing Mosha scrambling on hands and knees broke the terror filled spell. Nook grasped the stone tighter and threw himself to the ground. In a few moments the stone was covered with dirt. Nook jumped to his feet yelling, "Lady, it's done!"

Turning, Nook saw that the creature had Mosha by the neck. The librarian struggled helplessly as clawed hands slowly squeezed the life from him. So intent on its victim, the creature did not notice the slight rumbling at its feet.

Shooting out of the ground, a thin root wrapped round a black scaled ankle. Hissing in surprise, the creature kicked backward ripping the root from the ground. Instead of loosening, the root seemed to tighten its hold as soon as it was free from the earth. Little popping sounds filled the air as other roots shot up quickly wrapping both legs of the creature in a rope like cocoon. Hissing louder now, black talons released Mosha who fell with a grunt and lay still.

Turning clawed hands to the roots, the creature tried to slash it's way free. For every root cut, three more seemed to joined in the fun. Soon, only a dark scaled head could be seen over a writhing cocoon of roots. As if by some unspoken command, a hole in the cavern floor rumbled open and the dark one disappeared in a tangle of hissing, roots and dirt.

A bright light seared the darkness. Nooked cried out as he covered his eyes. Stumbling in momentary blindness, he tried to reach where he thought Mosha had fallen. His legs bumped into something solid that gave a disagreeable grunt. Kneeling down, keeping his eyes still shut, Nook felt for a pulse on the large man. Satisfied that Mosha would live for the moment, Nook slowly pried his own eyes open.

Either the bright light had dimmed a bit or his eyes had quickly become accustomed to it. The source of the illumination was the monolith. The cold dull stone of the structure was replaced by a pillar of bright white light. In the area where he and his companions had buried the stones the chaos of the fighting has ceased. A number of circular holes indicated where other black scaled attackers had been dragged beneath the ground. Nook shuddered at the thought of a dirt filled death.

"Well, my two handsome heroes. Well done!"

Nook looked up to see the White Lady herself approaching the pair. Tussling Nook's hair as she passed the lady knelt down to examine Mosha. The librarian was already trying to sit up but at a word from the lady he laid back down. Placing a hand on the large man's neck she closed her perfect eyes and seemed to concentrate. After a moment, Mosha began to cough and then retched out a glob of red and pink gunk. Handing Mosha a cloth to wipe his mouth, she brushed off the big man's apology.

"Hush, sweet man. I have seen more unseemly things in my time. I am glad that the claws of that vile thing did not pierce your skin. Otherwise, we would have been dealing with nasty venom instead of just some damaged tissue. Nook, be so good to help Mosha here closer to the monolith while I check on the others."

Helping the librarian to his feet, Nook carefully guided the big man to the steps at the base of the monolith. The pair observed the Lady and Sister Kitla overseeing the wounded. Slowly, the panic and chaos of the attack lost some its bite as the company was busied with routine chores. Of the twenty guards that had escorted the group, seven were dead and four missing. Three young acolytes, four servants and two Sublime Sisters were also killed. Nook swallowed a lump in his throat as he saw a boy his own age covered in blood; his sightless eyes staring upwards as an attendant covered him with a woolen blanket.

Turning his gaze from the dead boy, he looked out beyond the safety of the lighted monolith. Out in the dark were four missing guards and Nook was just glad he was not one of them. He felt a pang of guilt for feeling that way, for surviving when others had died. His thoughts turned back to the feeling of dreaded fear as the black scaled terror had touched him and promised him pain and agony. He shuddered.

"Now, what is this, my Nook? Why such a long face?" The Lady sat down next to him and placed an arm around his thin shoulders. She smelled of fresh blood, medicine, and those scents only a woman exuded; the types of smells that spoke of love, gentle understanding, and comfort.

Thinking at that moment that he missed his mother, Nook turned his head into a soft female shoulder and cried. Bringing him into a full embrace, the Lady hugged him and whispered, "Nook, my sweet Nook. You were so brave. Don't worry my dear boy. All will be well."

SOME mages on the High Council approached the material world with a stoic attitude. Relishing in the comforts and pleasures that the power of their positions afforded them was something to be wary of. Such luxuries should be avoided as they often distracted from the focus that their craft required and at times led a mage astray in his or her duties. Gazelle did not suffer from that stoic belief.

Her living quarters in the citadel were plush to the point of being garish. Floors made up of polished golden cedar wood covered five large rooms. Vases and art works from around the world filled niches, shelves, and side tables; all gifts from those who had gained the High Mage's favor, or hoped too. Large over stuffed pillows covered couches and chairs giving any visitor a chance to sit and bask in the wonders of the place from any angle. Gazelle had made her living quarters a testament to the power of the Bright City, and herself.

Having just arrived from the war front, the High Mage had wished to enjoy a warm bath and the attention of her servants. Instead, hours after arriving she had a strange party demanding her immediate attention. Tired, irritable, and denied her bath, the three members of this group did nothing to improve her mood. Sitting at her desk, a huge marble affair with intricately carved vines and flowers around its sides, Gazelle drummed her fingers on the cool smooth stone as she considered those before her.

Gazelle noted with a wry grin that the fat librarian had managed a bath before invading her quiet sanctuary. While freshly bathed, the large man still had a faint putrid odor about him. His eyes darted around the room as if refusing to rest his gaze on the mage.

Sitting next to him, the head of the Sublime Sisters held the fat man's hand as if to sooth a skittish animal. The Dryan woman held her years well as all of her race did. While more grey hairs were evident in the intricately bound braid that seemed to weave down her back, Eldest Sister's face seemed to refuse the sagging of age. The woman calmly returned Gazelle's stare, waiting silently.

Finally, Gazelle turned to the last member of this strange trio, Sister Kitla. The Sublime Sister sat quietly reminding Gazelle of a rabbit trying to avoid being spotted by a predator bird. She kept her eyes lowered and held a small bag tightly in her hands. The Sisterhood had often been looked down upon by the mages council for their willingness to allow mundanes into their ranks. However, the Sisters held a special place in the heart of the general populace and interfering with their charitable exploits could cause problems and so such practices went largely ignored.

A grey clad servant came in and offered the guests tea. When all had been served, the servant bowed and exited the room. Gazelle held the warm tea cup up to her nose and breathed in the comforting fumes before taking a sip. She closed her eyes as she felt the warm liquid slide down her throat. Nothing like a good cup of tea to welcome one home.

Eldest Sister cleared her throat. Snapping her eyes open, Gazelle speared the annoying woman with a hard stare that would have had most shivering in fear. The other woman matched her gaze for several moments as the two held each eyes; hard, flinty, unbending. Eldest Sister then bowed her head respectfully, breaking the silent test of wills without admitting defeat.

Nodding her head in return, Gazelle spoke, "So, I understand that you have something of utmost importance to tell me. The last time we were all together was just after this city had successfully fought off an invasion force and scores of mages had died in the process. I do hope that you are not involved in something like that again." The last comment was unfair, and Gazelle knew it. Eldest Sister sat up straighter in her chair but kept silent refusing to rise to the bait. Enjoying the other woman's discomfort, Gazelle was about to add more fuel to the fire when she was interrupted.

"We were told to warn the Mages. That's why we are here, Ma'am." Kitla's voice was quiet and hesitant as she raised her eyes to look at Gazelle as if it was hardest thing she had ever done. Rising, she approached the mage and placed the small bag she had been holding on the desk.

"I was told that you might not like what you see, Ma'am, but that the discomfort is necessary for the message."

Irritation now flooded Gazelle's tired body. Deep down she was mostly annoyed that the seemingly docile mund would have the gall to address her at all. She let her annoyance show through her next words, "Who told you what, girl? If you had not noticed we are in the middle of a damned war of survival against the Empress . . ."

The words shut off as soon as Kitla removed a small stone from the bag. Gazelle's mage senses flared in warning. In a matter of moments, she had pushed her chair up against the back wall, as far from the offensive thing as possible. Her hand glowed with warmth as she instinctually called fire.

The source of her actions was a small, lumpy piece of brown-grey stone. About the size of her fist, the thing rested on her desk as if it were the most inoffensive thing in the world. Her guests wide eyed stare at her reaction gave proof that they felt no ill effects.

For Gazelle the stone seemed to exude an almost greasy feeling of sullied unease. Her mage senses seemed to take offense at the mere idea that the stone existed, let alone that it was on her desk top. Gazelle could not put to words what it was about the stone that made her want to burn it to cinders, except that it did not feel right. Feel was a weak word, but in her current state of mind Gazelle could not think of a better one.

Suddenly the stone blurred. Slowly bending back and forth, the thing began taking a longer shape. Limbs formed, then a head, face, mouth lips. In a few moments, a small figure of a woman faced Gazelle. The woman was dressed in the green robe of a Sublime Sister and was lushly beautiful. Still the feeling of wrongness persisted and Gazelle gathered her will, calling fire and prepared to protect herself.

"Aren't you a little old to be wearing your hair down, dear?"

Gazelle gave out a squawk of surprise. The small figure, its hands now on its hips, smiled up at her. Without releasing her hold on fire, Gazelle unconsciously flipped her long hair over a shoulder. Most elderly Ferrekei women would have their hair cut shorter or in a braided style. But Gazelle allowed her hair to grow out and free as if she were a younger woman. Most had noticed this hair style preference but no one dared to make a comment in her presence. Her three guests looked from the statue to the High Mage, holding their collective breathes.

The brown-grey woman slowly marched across the desk and sat daintily with her little legs dangling over the edge. Crossing her arms, she advised, "I suggest you release the flame, dear. It should make things better."

It took a moment for the words to make sense to Gazelle. Her entire focus was on the small woman, or rather the abhorrent substance that she was made of. Slowly, she eased her will, and let go of fire. As the woman had said, the moment she had released fire her uneasiness lessened; it did not disappear entirely but seemed to fade to a level where it was tolerable for the moment.

Taking a deep, shaking breathe, Gazelle said, "What by the cursed and forgotten gods are you?"

The little woman tilted her head back and laughed before answering, "Well, I am definitely a little diminished so far from my lair, dear. But I needed to talk with you and I fear you would have been most uncomfortable in my home; yes, most uncomfortable."

Gazelle scooted her chair closer to the desk and reclaimed her tea cup. Taking a sip of the now lukewarm liquid, she collected her thoughts. Another sip and she felt back in control of herself.

"What do you want to talk about, you little thing?"

MOSHA and the two Sisters sat on a bench just outside the doorway to High Mage Gazelle's residence. Kitla and Eldest Sister had spent the time in quiet murmured conversation. Mosha was exhausted. The aftermath of the battle in the underground city had resulted in the decision that the mage council had to be alerted to the danger of the snake like creatures. Mosha, Sister Kitla, Nook, and a small group of guardsmen were charged by the Lady to bring a piece of the strange material that made up her magical domicile to Mage Gazelle. First the group had returned to the Great Temple to report to Eldest Sister. Leaving Nook in the safety of the Great Temple, a freshly washed Mosha accompanied Kitla and Eldest Sister to the mage's Citadel.

After Gazelle got over her initial shock of meeting the White Lady, Mosha and the two Sisters were shooed from the room and instructed to sit and wait. The door was then shut, not directly in their faces but close enough. That was almost an hour ago.

Mosha felt slighted to be excluded from the conversation in in the High Mage's apartments. He had walked through a shit filled hell, literally, nearing getting himself killed twice. When he had awoken from his first step through the obelisk, he attempted to give his very important message to the Lady but she had only wanted a summary. Terra had been very explicit in her instructions; he was to deliver her message exactly as instructed. Exactly! Or horrible things would befall his most important person! Horrible things!

Standing up from the bench, he rolled sore neck muscles and took a few steps toward the shut door. Being a large man, it was nearly impossible for him to sneak up on anyone; or to walk softly. But he simply had to know what was being divulged behind that door! Clasping his hands behind his back, he minced his way forward. The closer he got, the better he could hear muffled voices having a heated conversation. The two Sisters had stopped their quiet conversation, watching him; neither woman objected to his action. Putting his ear carefully against the door served to remove the muffle.

". . . . impossible!" Gazelle exclaimed. Mosha grinned to himself, feeling rather sneaky in a self-satisfied way.

"Not impossible." The White Lady's voice answered. The furious tone in both women's voices made Mosha glad that he had a door between himself and the conversation.

Gazelle continued, "The city would be thrown into the chaos! Sanitation and lighting would be all fouled up. Transportation would almost cease, the . . ."

The Lady's voice cut in, "The stones have become an abomination! They were never supposed to be used this way. Lives destroyed so you can keep your cities clean and fight your damned wars? A vile . . ."

Suddenly, the conversation went quiet. Mosha pressed his ear closer, trying to hear, when suddenly both voices yelled in unison, "Mosha!! Get away from the door!!"

He leaped away from the door as if it were a hot iron. Backing up hastily, he resumed his seat next to Eldest Sister who gave him a rueful chuckle and patted his hand. A few moments later, the trio was ushered back into Gazelle's presence. The small version of the Lady sat demurely on an upturned tea cup and watched as the three re-took their seats.

Looking up at Gazelle, the Lady asked, "May I?" At Gazelle's nod, she continued, "We have much to do, my dears. But first, Mosha I would like to hear the message my sweet colleague asked that you give to me." The little woman's eyes almost glowed in anticipation.

Mosha licked his lips nervously. Clearing his throat he said, "You already have the important part of the communication, my Lady."

"But did not sweet Terra require you to give me the message in its entire? As she dictated it? I am sure she threatened some unpleasantness if you did not follow her instructions to the letter."

"Here? Lady? Shouldn't we go somewhere private? Some of the word usage in your colleague's message is . . . ." Mosha waved a hand helplessly as if mentally searching for the right word. He was not used to this verbal stumbling; far from it, usually at some point in a conversation people wanted him to shut up.

"The entire message, please, dear Mosha." The Lady and Gazelle leaned forward. The two Sisters also leaned forward with curious anticipation glinting in their eyes. *Why do women so enjoy conversations like this?*

Closing his eyes, he began, "Dear Fat Cow . . . ."

THE RAIN made the shrine seem a sad place. Mosha shrugged away that thought. Adding water to a place should not make it happy or sad; simply wetter. But still . . . .

He forced his thoughts from sad rain drops to the events of the past few days. He had walked through a nightmare of a shit filled underground, been attacked by a large worm, and nearly killed by a black scaled horror. Yet the unease he had felt in relaying Terra's message to the White Lady had been terror on a totally different scale.

While he had repeated the message verbatim, the Lady had paced back and forth on the desk, her arms crossed. The other three women watched the small lady with expectant expressions; almost like they knew what would happen but that knowledge did not lessen their interest. Back and forth, back and forth.

When Mosha had finished speaking, the Lady stopped pacing next to a small bottle of ink. Idly she put a small foot against the glass bottle; a moment of quiet passed. Then suddenly, she pulled the foot back and kicked the bottle from its berth. Then a profanity laced tirade spewed from her tiny lips.

The small woman then stomped across the desk flinging her fists into the air as if she fought an invisible adversary. The other three women watched this as if it were the most normal thing in the world. Mosha eyed the woman as if she were a dangerous animal that needed to be watched closely; small albeit but lethal. The offensive bottle had spilled its inky contents across the table and small foot prints now dotted the desk top from the Lady's stomping.

Suddenly, as if a light were turned off, the tirade stopped; the Lady reclaimed her seat on the desk and appeared calm and composed. Giving Mosha a flashy smile she purred, "Thank you, Mosha. Your services as a messenger are much appreciated; especially when you are required to be associated with a person of such ugly demeanor." Mosha was fairly sure the Lady was not referring to herself.

Cocking her head as if carefully considering her next words, she continued, "I have a reply to my sweet colleague, and you will deliver my message completely with no deviation, is that understood?" At his nod, she began in that same purring voice, to dictate her response.

A sudden easing of the rain brought Mosha back to his present wet situation. Trying to ignore the soggy feel of wet clothing, he mentally went through the message he was to deliver in his mind and shook his head in self-pity. What he had done to deserve to be the messenger boy between these two strange, powerful, and sometimes cranky women he could not answer. But, the fact that he was in a position to help Jonathan Champion was important. The strange man had touched Mosha's life very briefly two years ago but with resounding consequences for the librarian. Lost in thought he did not notice that he had a visitor until she was nearly underfoot; or rather, until she had stepped on his foot.

Giving the fat man a sweet smile, Terra gave his foot an extra little stomp before saying, "Well, well, Mr., Big Brain. I thought maybe you had forgotten about me. Did I not make a good first impression?"

Mosha looked down his nose at the irritating woman but the rain running down his face made it difficult to maintain the haughty expression he was going for, "Have you ever made a good first impression, Ma'am?"

Terra gave a snort and gave him an almost gentle tap with her stick. She looked exactly like she had on their first meeting; dark black hair in a jumbled bob, strange multi colored dress that covered what looked to be a dumpy form, and bright blue eyes that regarded Mosha with an irritating humor.

Giving him another stick tap, this time a bit harder as if to assure she had his attention, she spoke, "So, my big friend, I sent you on a little mission. Were you successful?"

At his nod, Terra gave a loud sigh of relief. "Excellent. And how was my initial inquiry taken?"

"Taken, Ma'am?"

"How did my dear colleague take my message? You did repeat it exactly as I had instructed did you not?" On the last word she took a threatening step toward him, raising her stick a fraction.

Holding his hands up as if to hold off some harm, Mosha said hastily, "Yes, Yes. Exactly as you had instructed, Ma'am."

Smiling Terra asked, "And?"

"And?" Mosha repeated dumbly.

"And how did she take it, you dense fool of a man?"

"Take it?" Mosha felt a moment true panic. What the hell was this crazed woman talking about? Terra stepped right up to him and placed her stick in the middle of his impressive belly. Each of her next words was emphasized with a little sharp and painful poke, "Listen carefully, Mosha. You will relate to me exactly how that fat cow responded to my message. Every little miniscule flutter of her fat eyelids, every little frown of her slutty lips, everything! Then, you will give me her reply, understood?"

Swallowing, Mosha could only nod. Stepping back, Terra waved her stick for him to begin. So, he began his account. Initially, Terra held his gaze as he spoke but after a few minutes she began to walk back and forth across the open grass of the shrine, humming quietly to herself. Back and forth, back and forth. As he spoke, Mosha noticed that the rain seemed not to bother the strange woman; a halo of dry air hovered over her head providing a heated covering. When he finished with relating the tiny woman's tantrum on Gazelle's desk, Terra gave a satisfied chuckle and turned back toward him.

"Ahhhh, I wish I had been there, Mosha. I truly do. And her response?"

Women truly are a crazed and unreasonable gender. Closing his eyes, Mosha began, "Dear Flat Chested Imp, as usual, I find myself in the position of picking up the pieces of your idiotic mistakes and trying to put things right. Your Champion is in the Lost Isles, or at least he was at the time I am dictating you this message. There is something strange going on with him; I detect three distinct mage signatures but they all have nearly the same aura, as if they were three parts of the same mage which makes little sense.

I am sure this strange anomaly surrounding your Champion is due to your ineptness at preparing him for his role. Only one untrained mage and you still can't call him to heel? I should not be surprised at your near complete failure in this regard. He is a man after all. Men are definitely not your strong suit, especially keeping them interested long enough to get what you need out of them. If you are able to rope him in again, I suggest you send him my way as I am sure I can keep him occupied.

The snakes are awake. They attacked us under the city and we were able to fight them off. There were no magic users among this lot but I can report that I sense their evil magic somewhere to the far south, south of the Mok Empire. Those are desert lands that I am sure are to their liking.

I have demanded that all cooperation in the production of the rawstones be stopped for the time being. You can imagine how well that went over. I have not seen any grey skinned Orda about, but can feel their presence in the Citadel. I am sure that they continue in their creation of new rawstones but I am in no position to do anything except shout and threaten at this point. I understand your Champion put the fear of Fire and Air in them when he learned about the stones. I suppose you may not have completely failed in his instruction.

That is all I know for now. As usual, you need to rely on me to put you on the proper path and save you from your own twisted incompetence. I do hope the years have been kind to you as they definitely could not have been any crueler to you unless you still have that dreadful haircut and short, dumpy stature. I wish I was there to give you this message in person, you slutty tart."

As Mosha finished the message, he opened his eyes. Terra had stopped her pacing and was now looking up at the statue of the White Lady. Her eyes blazed with anger as she raised her stick high over her head. Mosha thought the woman might call down some sort of curse on the statue but instead she brought the stick down on a marble foot. Over and over the stick came down with loud cracks as Terra grumbled obscenities to herself.

Eventually, her stick broke and Terra stood there glaring at the statue as if daring it to object to the harsh beating it just received. Without removing her gaze from the statue, Terra whispered harshly, "Thank you Mosha. You are more than a competent messenger. I will have another message for you when I return." With that, she disappeared. With a sigh of relief, Mosha took in the quiet safety of the shrine. Thinking to himself that being wet was much preferable to being in the middle of this female word feud, he began to trudge his way back down the hill.

CHAPTER ELEVEN

F enn walked the streets of Haven enjoying the morning sunshine. He knew that his two Corsair guardsmen were somewhere behind him, but they rarely intruded on his privacy. He had been given unlimited access to the community by the Mage. Everyone in town referred to Jonathan Champion as the Mage and Fenn grimaced a bit as he found himself thinking of the strange mund in that light.

Looking around at the shops and residents Haven had the feel of bustling prosperity of a growing community. The deep harbor allowed the Corsairs to dock their ever growing fleet with little difficulty. Merchant vessels were allowed to unload their wares and items for sale at the modest sized market located near the docks and warehouses. Yes, everything in the town seemed very familiar except for the Munds.

These were not Munds who followed the normal roles that Fenn was accustomed too. No one wore a *bacha*, or service collar of any kind. Munds did not follow their Masters bidding or meekly keep their eyes averted downward to avoid making offensive eye contact. Munds did not take on the normal meek, submissive demeanor that Fenn associated with the normal way of things.

In truth, Fenn thought, they did not act like Munds at all and they were everywhere in the community. Setting aside the numbers who filled the ranks of the Corsairs, Munds owned shops, were tailors and craftsmen, haggled with other races at the market on equal footings, and even married, maintained households, and had families.

While the Munds new found roles in this strange place did make him feel a bit out of place there was another factor that bothered him even more as he continued his walk. His entire life he had been taught, and firmly believed, that Magic was the glue that held society together. That without the order and peace that Hyberan, The Bright City, provided by the strength of her magical rulers, society would quickly turn to destruction and ruin. It was the bright magic of the mages that stood between the darkness of the world and utter chaos.

Yet now he was forced to reconsider that belief which had been a cornerstone of comfort his entire life. Because here was a community, a group of nearly two thousand people, who seemed to prosper, were content, and happy without the daily presence of Magic. It challenged Fenn's once firm sense of order. How could this be?

Case in point, he thought as he passed a group of workers lifting a large pedestal into place in the town square. Off to the right, was the large face of a clock. Fenn had been told that a local craftsman had made the clock at the request of the Mage. The contraption supposedly only had to be wound once per every thirty days and kept perfect time. No Magic. No rawstones. Amazing!

As if the routine of the town were not enough to make his head spin, Fenn had the pleasure of conversations with the Mage himself most mornings over breakfast. One sided conversations where he was to answer questions and forbidden to make his own inquiries. While the tones of the conversations were mild and even friendly, afterward Fenn always felt like a damp rag that had been squeezed for every ounce of water he held. The Mage's topics of conversation were as diverse as the town he had established. Fenn had been asked about his early experiences as a mage. Who his teachers and mentors were and how young mages were taught in the Bright City. The fact that Fenn was a historian made the Mage almost clap his hands in glee and he had spent three straight mornings grilling Fenn about mage history. The man's interests were wide and varied. The only time when Fenn seemed to have failed as an interesting breakfast companion was his apparent lack of knowledge about the rawstones. *Don't you know what they are? Don't you care?* He remembered the Mage asking. Knowing the man's feelings towards the stones, Fenn had wisely remained silent.

One morning Fenn had bit into a spicy egg omelet which made him exclaim out loud, *Cursed Gods!* From there, an hour long discussion had ensued about gods and religion. The Mage seemed amazed that Fenn, and most mages, held little belief in anything more powerful than their own magic. Fenn had explained that many races held traditional beliefs in higher beings, he used his own Ferreki people's worship of forest spirits as an example. But while the mages tolerated these belief systems in others, they themselves did not support or encourage any religion.

While he mused over his former talks with the Mage, Fenn walked past the square and took a right and approached his destination for this morning. A large grey stone building that had no adornment except for a large iron bound wooden door. A guard leaning against the side of the building barely stifled a yawn as he motioned Fenn past. His two guardians stopped outside the door and Fenn was alone as he entered the building.

Inside, windows were covered by thin veils of curtains that took that harsh glare out of the morning sunshine and allowed a gentle, dim light to permeate the place. Fenn found himself in a long room. Dozens of beds lined each side of the room making a narrow aisle down the center which allowed green attired attendants to see to their charges. Today, almost every bed was filled. Fenn slowly made his way to the other end of the room, careful to avoid bumping into any of the attendants. He approached a table which ran the width of the room and at which a green cloaked figure sat quietly humming to herself.

Sister Ella was a dark skinned Tuak. Like all Tuak, her nose and lips seemed a bit too large for the rest of her face. That face was now bent over a small wooden bowl; a concentrating frown marred her face as she carefully crushed a yellow flower into a paste. As a Sublime Sister, Sister Ella wore a form fitting green gown. The practical garment was comfortable and allowed her to perform her duties as a healer and at the same time remind those around her that she did not forget the Sisterhood's erotic licenses. Not wishing to cause undue surprise, Fenn approached and stood quietly until he was noticed. Putting her bowl aside, Sister Ella motioned for Fenn to sit.

"You sent for me Sister?"

Fenn's voice was carefully respectful. While some mages held the Sisterhood in low regard, he was very conscious of the good works that the Sisters provided to the poorer underclasses. Also, Sister Ella was a very valued and respected member of the Haven community. It would be a potentially dangerous error to needlessly offend her.

The Sister cocked her head to the side slightly, looking him up and down before replying, "No, Honored Mage. I did not send for you. The Mage asked that I enlighten you on a few new developments." As she spoke, Sister Ella placed her right hand on the table and began drumming her fingers in thought. Fenn could not help staring.

Noticing his interest, she smiled. Lifting her hand up for his examination she explained, "When I was just initiated as a Sister, a few of us had the dream of coming to the isles to open a charter house to bring our teachings to this part of the world. The Mok's boarded our ship and entertained themselves with me and my fellow sisters before dumping us over the side. I washed ashore in Haven. I was lucky."

Fenn simply nodded as he studied what was before his eyes. The Sister's arm was long and lean. A thin, delicate wrist seemed a bit too small to adequately hold up the large hand. The palm was a bit lighter in color than the rest of the hand, giving it a dark tan color in contrast to the black skin. Past the palm the fingers followed but then simply stopped. Jagged scaring was evident of a very violent and brutal incident where Sister Elle had her fingers cut off. Fenn would have shuddered at the pain involved in losing all of the fingers on one hand. But what drew his attention was what had replaced the fingers.

Beautifully crafted brass appendages had been attached to each missing finger. Each piece had been detailed and measured to look exactly like a finger. At Sister Ella's nod, Fenn reached forward and gently ran his fingers down the length of the brass wonders. The metal felt almost soft and in place of knuckles, small metal gears served to bring the fingers closer together when Sister Ella closed her palm. Fenn saw that someone had even detailed the fingers with golden finger nails. After a few moments, the Sister gently reclaimed her hand from Fenn.

"Master Orkus is truly a clever man. And by clever, I mean genius."

Fenn smiled ruefully before saying, "Another Master Orkus invention? Is he not responsible for the amazing clock going up in the town square? I have asked to meet this most interesting man, but alas no luck."

Sister Ella's laugh cut through the quiet of the long room with an almost erotic twist to it. "Oh, Master Orkus is a bit on the peculiar side, Honored Mage. Plus, he has little love for mages. Though, he and the Mage have come to an accord of sorts."

Standing up, she motioned for him to follow. In silence, the pair left the long room by an entrance off to the left. Down a darkened hallway that was lit intermittently by oil lamps. Not rawstone lamps. Not in the Mages Haven.

A flight of steps took them down into the cellar of the building. A door at the bottom was slightly cracked open and a dim light outlined a wooden frame. Fenn's ears picked up noises that made the hair on the back of his neck stand on end. With a brave breathe he followed the Sister through the doorway.

Like the room above, the space that Fenn entered was a long space, but that is where the similarities ended. Instead of beds the whole room had been draped in padded materials of various colors. Against the walls, figures huddled. Some were quiet as if in sleep, others moaned and groaned as if suffering some quiet pain. Green clad attendants softly shuffled between the figures, speaking quietly and tending to various needs.

Sister Elle motioned for him to join her in a far corner. At his questioning look, she leaned close and whispered, "The Corsairs boarded a ship three days ago. The hold was filled with munds, stacked on top of each other like cords of wood. Most were dead. The Moks on board fought to the death so no explanation was forthcoming. These were the few who survived the voyage to Haven. The Corsairs thought that it was some kind of plague and so did little to help the poor creatures for fear of catching it."

She moved quietly toward a figure on the floor. What looked to be an adolescent girl was lying asleep in a soft pile of blankets. Small thin fingers clutched a crude cuddle toy made from faded red material. Fenn knelt down and gently brushed aside blond hair to reveal a thin, gaunt face. Dark blue circles under the closed eyes looked almost like bruises. At his touch the girl clutched the toy tighter and sighed in her sleep.

Sister Elle whispered quietly, "She hasn't let go of that since she arrived here. Even to eat. I think it is her protector of sorts."

Fenn stood, still looking down at the girl. Glancing around the room, he noted the number of figures being tended before asking quietly, "How many were in the ship?"

Before answering, Sister Elle motioned him to follow her back through the door. After softly closing the door she spoke, still keeping her voice low, "Hundreds of munds were in the hold. These few were all that survived." She turned and began ascending the steps.

Fenn was stunned. It was well known that the Mok Empire treated their Munds like chattel. But still, even chattel deserved some sort of decent treatment. The conditions on the ship indicated something horrible going on in the Empire. He followed the Sister up the stairs as she continued to speak.

"The Mage was furious when he learned that the Corsairs had done nothing to aid the poor souls until reaching port. Spuros thought the whole crew was going to get burned to cinders. It has happened before when Munds have been misused."

Thinking back to his first meeting with the powerful mage on the *Swift* he said, "He doesn't like the word Mund."

Fenn's comment caused the Sister to stop and meet his eyes over her shoulder, "I do not use that word in the Mage's presence. You should do the same."

FENN paused a moment to catch his breathe. The long hike up past the outskirts of Haven into the foothills was tiring but physically exhilarating. The sunny day and the fresh air almost made him forget that he was a prisoner. His two Corsair 'companions' had instructed him that the Mage wished for a special meeting. He was given directions on where the meeting would take place and wished a grim good luck.

As he walked he mentally chewed on what Sister Elle had revealed. The good Sister refused to provide any further information concerning the munds under her care. Her instructions had been to show him the poor creatures and answer a few rudimentary questions, but any additional information was to come from the Mage. Period.

Stopping for a moment, he took in the surroundings. From where he stood miles of ocean could be seen in every direction. In the hustle and bustle of Haven, it was easy to forget that he was on an island. At this higher elevation the island's isolated location was evident. Miles of solid blue surrounded him. It would have been a beautiful sight if there wasn't so much of it. Repressing the image of what all that salt water could do to his forest born skin made him shudder. Keeping his head focused straight ahead, he walked on.

Several minutes later, Fenn looked up at his destination; a high, jagged spear of rock that stuck out of the foothills like some sort of infected needle. Where the foothills were filled with the warm browns and greens of wavy tall grasses, short trees and bushes, the crag was a thing of pitch black ugliness. While many rock formations had stringy trees or grasses growing from them, this stone was utterly devoid of vegetation. It looked like a rotted out stone tree that refused to fall down. In testament to the islands volcanic origins, its surface was pock marked with jagged clumps of sharp black rock. Smooth stone vied with rough volcanic rock to dominate the hill formation.

Local lore held that a dark creature had lived in the crag and the Mage had driven it out, or imprisoned it, and taken the lair for himself. Many of the children claim that some nights the wind brings the soft hissing sound of the fell beast to sensitive ears. Whatever the case, Fenn would conserve his strength for the upcoming test.

For it was a test; a test of his magical abilities and perhaps his resolve. As an Air Mage he was the only other person on the island who could access the mysterious Jonathan Champion's private sanctuary. The trail he was on wound in almost dreamy curves until it reached the base of the steep rock and then ended. No trail wound upwards on the formation. No steps or handholds had been chiseled to allow any access from the ground. Only abilities beyond walking or climbing would allow Fenn his much awaited meeting.

Closing his eyes, he concentrated on feeling the air currents above him. 'Feeling' was not really a good description of what mages do with their elements. 'Super Sensitively Charged Awareness' would actually be more accurate. When a mage felt for their element, it was as if they were reconnecting to another part of themselves.

With his eyes still closed, Fenn mentally mapped a path to the upper parts of the crag. Near the top, he felt the currents enter the formation instead of swirling around its surface. This indicated that there was an opening, probably a cave, most likely the Mage's hideout. Silently, Fenn thanked the strange mage for having the meeting on such a clear windless day. Almost any amount of wind would have made the currents dangerously unstable at such a height. Taking a deep breathe, Fenn opened his eyes as he called Air and began to gently rise towards his destination.

As he rose, Fenn kept his eyes squarely on the spot of the rock spire where he felt the cave to be. From the edges of his sight, the view of the ocean seemed to get larger, like an immense bright blue blanket spread out to cover the entire earth. He knew that if his concentration strayed then the Air he had called may also lose its potency. During his training as a younger mage, he had suffered two broken arms while embarking on just such an exercise. The key was focus; keeping your will focused on the task at hand kept Air under control. Mentally blocking out the bright blue, he continued on his way.

Coming closer to his destination, he saw a ledge jutting out from the rock face. With a deep breath, he exerted his will towards the ledge. As expected, Air resisted. Unlike Fire, which enjoyed being directed as long as it involved burning something, Air was resistant to being manipulated. Air was elusive and hard to get a firm grip of at times. It wanted to follow its currents and was not agreeable to being directed. Hardening his will, Fenn slowly won the battle as his feet gently touched the rocky ledge. Once settled, he released Air and took in his surroundings.

The ledge where he was standing was like the point of a spear; wide at one end and narrow at the other. Standing on the narrow edge, Fenn took a few steps forward to put some distance between himself and a long fall. Ahead of him yawned a dark opening in the rock pierced by a small warm glow. On either side of the opening, the two manifestations waited silently.

Cinder stood with its feet spread, arms crossed, and stared flame filled daggers at the Air Mage. Aeris sat nonchalantly, in midair, as if bored by the whole procedure. As Fenn approached Aeris began clapping silently; Cinder's flames seemed to darken to a blood red blackness that reminded him of charred flesh. Watching both creatures warily, he entered the cave.

Cozy. That was the first word that came to mind. The floor gave way to a thick red rug. Rugs in a cave, Fenn mused as he gingerly stepped on the soft material. A large table held books of various shapes and colors. Most had been opened to specific pages and looked like large leather-bound butterflies resting on the table. Along one wall the rock had been chiseled away to form a crude book shelf filled with more tomes. To one side of the table, a large chair had been placed. Small pillows had been stacked onto the chair into a haphazard pile. Nestled on this pile of comfort stretched the Mage.

Long arms were crossed as the strange mund studied Fenn. The one eyed white stare seemed to look right through him. Loose fitting blue garments seemed bright in comparison to the imposing grey colors the man usually wore. In contrast to Fenn's now almost defensive posture, the Mage looked relaxed and laid back.

Resisting the urge to swallow, Fenn turned his eyes to the walls of the cave which was the source of the warm glow that filled the place. Glancing passed the table he saw the cave continued on to what looked like a corridor disappearing around a dark corner. His eyes turning back to the wall he reached out a hand to touch the softly glowing surface.

"It's a fungus."

The words stopped Fenn's hand. Stretching to his feet, the Mage joined Fenn. At a reassuring nod from his host, Fenn ran a hand against the wall. A slippery, bumpy texture greeted his touch. Looking at his hands he saw small spongy particles sticking to his fingers. Almost immediately, the particles on his skin began to lose their glow. Looking back to the wall, small black streaks were evidence of where his fingers had touched.

"In a day or so, the black marks will be gone. The stuff grows back quickly. But for some reason will only grow on the inside of this damn fortress of solitude. I had hopes that we could replace Haven's oil lamps with the fungus; at least at night. But no such luck. Oil is becoming a hard commodity to come by in the isles."

Fenn simply nodded. The obvious answer would be to make use of rawstones. But that was an option not to be voiced; not to this man. The Mage extended an arm toward the chair and Fenn found himself seated in the chair his host had recently exited. For himself, the Mage sat on the edge of the table, paused for a moment as if collecting his thoughts before speaking.

"Thank you for meeting with me here, Fenn. I trust that during your stay in Haven you have been treated well?" At Fenn's nod, he continued.

"I am going to begin speaking. I know that some of the things I am going to say will make little sense to you. But, please don't interrupt me. Even for clarification. I am not sure how much I will be allowed to divulge to you."

Fenn tried to stop the look of confusion that attempted to spread across his face. Giving the Mage another slow nod, he sat further back in the pillows. Patiently attentive.

Clearing his throat the Mage began, "Where I am from there are no Mages. There is no Magic. There are only my people. No Ferrekei, no damned Moks, no Tuak, no Gurashii, no Molden, only my people."

Fenn bit his tongue as questions leapt to his lips. His fingers itched to have a paper and quill to write this down. Oblivious to his guest's inner struggle, the Mage continued.

"While there was no Magic, we still had amazing creations. We could fly; build cities, and buildings that nearly touched the clouds. All with no Magic. That's what you see in Haven. My attempt to show people that survival and prosperity is possible without Magic. Without the mages. Without the rawstones." He spat these last words, as if trying to get rid of a foul taste is his mouth.

"Not to say that we were perfect. We had wars. We had our tyrants. Our calamities. We created wonderful things that made our lives better. We also created horrible things. Horrible, horrible, things; like Meth."

From within the folds of his shirt, the Mage removed a small glass vial and tossed it to Fenn. Catching it, Fenn saw that the vial held a number of small crystals. Very small.

"That is Meth. It is a drug that is very addictive. Very destructive. I have known people who have sold their souls just to get more of that stuff. My job was to track down those who made and sold this shit. Track them down and bring them to justice.

I can't remember any specifics you understand? I can't remember names or dates; times or places. I can see in my mind's eye faces of people; people I knew and worked with. People I loved and hated. Sometimes I dream. I have strange dreams."

Fenn was now sitting at the edge of the chair, the comfort of the pillows forgotten. As the Mage spoke he looked off down the darkness of the farther corridor; as if he were trying to mentally catch his forgotten memories. Fenn was entranced.

"When your two companions named me Jonathan Champion it rang true. Seeing Tyrell and Grach also brought back memories, shades of times spent with them. Their words also ring true. This worries the happy couple out front."

The Mage nodded toward the cave entrance. Following his nod, Fenn saw the two manifestations standing in the entrance. Both held themselves in place with rigid stances; arms at their sides. Both stared at Fenn and the Mage. Fenn shuddered slightly under their attention as he turned back to his host.

Chuckling at his fear, the Mage said, "Oh yes. They do not like you. Or rather, they don't like your presence here. They fear that if I remember too much, that I will revert back to that other person. And by doing that, that they may cease to exist; they may be right."

Giving a noncommittal shrug, the Mage began to pace slowly before speaking, "I got off subject. I do that sometimes. We were talking of Meth. Or white tar as it is known here in this world. I discovered while in your Bright City, that there is a connection between Meth and your rawstones. A very direct connection. In fact, the stones cannot be created without Meth.

It involves the torture of thousands of my people. Torture Fenn. Torture. My people strapped down and force fed Meth; forced addiction. Being forced to lay for days, months, years? Years Fenn? Years while this shit is pumped into them.

The Mok's are even worse. They have developed some kind of new method to create rawstones; fucking horrendous. You visited Sister Elle? You saw? You saw what was done to them? The children? *Children!*"

The last word was shouted and Fenn's hands were clasped together to keep them from shaking. The tone in the Mage's voice had become a bit hysterical and dangerous. The tall man's strides became longer as he paced and Fenn leaned further back in the chair trying to place a few extra inches of safety between himself and the overwrought mage.

"Meth destroys the body, Fenn. Many of the people in Sister Elle's care have no teeth because they rotted out. It's called Meth Mouth. Basically the teeth simply decay to the point that they look like they are rotten and eroding. Almost every one of the good Sisters patients had to have their teeth pulled.

I remember seeing a woman with Meth Mouth in your precious Citadel. She was hooked up to some sort of contraption with a hot metal mask over her face with a rawstone sucking the life out just as the meth was pumped into her. The metal mask was so hot it burned my fingers when I touched it. That's why so many rawstone victims have had burned faces. That's why people thought I had burned my face in a rawstone accident. The common knowledge is out there that the rawstone process mutilates people but the actual 'how' of it all is a mystery. Don't they care? Didn't you ever wonder why that was, Fenn? Why people were scarred and mutilated by burning? Don't answer that. Any answer you give is going to piss me off." A few moments of quiet, the determined stride of the pacing man the only sound.

Then, as if to himself in a musing tone, "Mages or Mok's. Who is worse? I have to choose. Too many enemies. But I have chosen. But, the mages must pay too. They all must *pay*."

This last word was hissed at Fenn. The Mage stopped his pacing and turned. Fenn was ready for some sort of angry outburst; some sort of accusation. Instead the Mage stood there, shaking. The skin of his face had turned white and his lips trembled. With one hand he braced himself against the cavern wall; the other he brought to his face and pinched his nose between two fingers as if experiencing a severe headache.

Stumbling a bit, the tall man reached the stone book shelf and fumbled for something behind a large brown tome. Suddenly, his knees buckled and the Mage fell, with the brown book and a small red bag joining him on the floor. Fenn sprang to his feet and took a step to help the man, when a loud hissing sound came from the darkened corridor stopping him in his tracks.

A grey figure rushed out of the darkness. Quickly it leaned down next to the Mage. A strange clanking sound accompanied its movements as it helped the Mage to sit up. Long grey fingers opened the red bag and removed a small clay jug. Breaking the wax stopper, the jar was held to trembling lips and its contents poured into his mouth. The Mage weakly gulped the liquid down, and rested against the figure's shoulder. Fenn watched in stunned silence at the strange pair. After a few moments, the Mage stood, bracing himself up against a stone wall, his hands leaving darkened streaks on its glowing surface.

Giving the grey figure a gentle shove, the Mage stood on his own wobbly legs. After a few moments, like a thin tree after a strong wind has passed, the shaking ceased and the man stood, facing Fenn, a wry grin on his face.

"I told you I was not sure how much I could share."

Turning to the grey figure, which now stood quietly to one side, the Mage gave a slight dip of his head, "Thank you Liss."

The figure gave a silent nod in reply and Fenn had the chance to see that it was covered from head to foot in grey cloth, even its head and feet. Long grey fingers, now clasped patiently together, and a pair of black on black eyes were the only glimpses of identity. After a few moments of sharing a stare with the Mage, the creature gave another slight nod before backing away into the darkened corridor. Fenn could now see that the source of the clanking sound was a thin metal chain that had been attached to a manacle on the figures right ankle. Soon, both grey clad stranger and the sound of its passing faded into the darkness.

From somewhere the Mage had produced two flagons and handed one to Fenn. A careful sip revealed a slightly watered down wine; tasty but not too strong to invite drunken chatter.

Reclaiming his seat on the table, the Mage took a long drink before saying, "That has been long overdue. It always comes on when I have been overly active in using my energies. The Mok's have been very busy lately, so that means I have been using my powers. Tiring business. You may ask questions now, if you wish. I am usually better able to answer right after I take the tonic."

Holding the flagon in both hands, Fenn took a moment to collect his thoughts. After taking another drink, for courage, he asked, "You mentioned that you had made a choice? May I know what that refers to?"

"Of course. You came here to obtain my aid against the Mok Empire. Your masters are too savvy to think I would ever return with you and place myself in their power. Even the knowledge that I have a son in your city will not get me to go with you; knowledge that I cannot verify unless I return with you. I assume the boy is well? He is unharmed?"

Letting the flagon rest in his lap, Fenn held up his hands in a placating gesture. "Your son is well. He lives under the care of the Sublime Sisters and his mother, Kitla. Do you remember Kitla?"

The Mage cocked his head to the side as if mentally sifting through his memories before answering. "A vague image of a sexy woman in a green dress, a very sexy bath scene . . ." He chuckled quietly, closing his eyes for a moment. Shrugging, he stood and turned, motioning Fenn to follow.

Quietly, the pair walked toward the darkened corridor in the back of the cave. Fenn noticed that the strange glowing fungus was absent from this part of the Mage's quarters, making the cave walls dark and ominous. The Mage lifted his arm and a soft light emanated from his scarred flesh. To the left a small room had been hollowed out. The strange grey figure sat within with its back to a stone wall, watching them pass. Long grey fingers idly played with the chain.

"Liss hates the wall fungus. Says it smells bad. I think it's kind may have additional senses the rest of us don's have, because I smell nothing. It also has amazing self-healing abilities. When we first met Liss had lost a hand and had a horribly broken shoulder. The hand grew back and the shoulder repaired itself.

Spuros insists that Liss be chained. The Captain is not the trusting sort. I don't think he had such a long length of chain in mind to allow Liss free reign in my cave. But, Liss's confinement will soon be over. Careful, now." The Mage stopped and put his unscarred arm out to stop Fenn's progress. Looking down, the mage's light showed a large hole the dropped off into the darkness. With a quick grin, the Mage stepped off and slowly started to float down. Swallowing his fear, Fenn called Air and followed.

The hole widened out as the duo quietly descended. More of the glowing fungus appeared on the dark stone walls and the Mage extinguished his light. After what seemed like an eternity of quiet, Fenn began to hear faint sounds. As they continued to go further down, the smell of the sea permeated the air and the sounds grew louder. By the time that the pair finally rested their feet onto a solid floor, the glowing walls revealed the sounds to be the crashing of low waves on a rock lined shore.

Fenn hesitantly followed the Mage to the edge of what was a small underground lake. The smell of salt was heavy and Fenn thought that at high tide this cavern may well be filled with water. Approaching the waterline, he saw that the shore was littered with small bones and animal skeletons. Before Fenn could comment on this a large dose of sea water drenched his face. Coughing and sputtering, wiping the stinging salt from his eyes, Fenn fell back from the waters edge and landed on this his back.

Behind him, the Mage gave a rueful chuckle, "Waven, that was not very hospitable. We are your guests."

Helping Fenn to his feet, the Mage stepped closer to the water's edge. Folding his arms together, the tall man addressed the water, "Waven." The word held a slightly disapproving tone.

"*Not guests. Meat!*" The voice sounded as if it were under the water. Like the speaker was trying to talk and gurgle at the same time.

The Mage gave out a bark of laughter. "Our hides are much too tough for an old sea cow like you, Waven. Let's skip the trading of insults and threats. I have a friend I would like you to meet."

On the surface of the water, a small shape appeared. Two arms and two legs, with an oval shaped head. The thing began dancing around on the watery surface. Looking closer at the strange dancer, Fenn gasped.

"Manifestation!"

As if in response to his voice, the strange thing danced closer to the waiting men. Water. They were watching a creature made entirely of water. Compared to Cinder or Aeris, this manifestation appeared crude; almost like a child had put it together using watery clay. Ready this time, Fenn dodged the splash of water that was aimed at his head.

The Mage allowed the dance to continue for a few more moments before speaking. "Stop showing off, Waven. You have made your point. We have business to discuss."

Suddenly, the water sprite disappeared beneath the water. "*What do you want?*"

Stepping closer to the water's edge, the Mage sat on a damp stone. Settling himself, he motioned for Fenn to join him before he answered, "We have an agreement. This one here will allow us to fulfill our goal. I wanted you to meet him since he will guard what you and I hold dear."

A few moments of silence. Then, "*Don't want to go. Too far. Too boring.*"

"We agreed, Waven. We must do this. Don't make me threaten you again." The Mage's voice was sharp; as if the words were lined in steel.

Again, silence. Then the waters began to churn and boil. Fenn stepped back from his place beside the Mage as a large form revealed itself. A huge sluggish body surrounded by waving tentacles breached the surface of the water. A beak like mouth filled with jagged teeth snapped at the air. A dozen large red eyes blazed blood lusting hatred as they stared at the two men.

Waiting calmly on his rock, the Mage sat with an unconcerned wry smile. Meeting the red stare, he began to speak in a quiet, steady voice. Slowly, the waters stopped churning. The water bound horror seemed to calm and listen. The red eyes lost their blood lust and turned thoughtful as the creature listened.

Hours later, the two men were back in the silent comfort of the Mages cave. Sipping quietly on warmed wine watching as the Mage flip idly through a book, Fenn was the first to break the silence.

"You know what it is don't you?"

The scarred man ignored him and continued leafing through pages.

Refusing to be put off, Fenn continued. "A Kraken. A cursed gods Kraken. One with mage like ability. That's your guest in the cellar."

Not looking up from his book, the Mage answered. "He has been here far longer than I, good Fenn. If anything, we are his guests. The people of Haven think he is a local protective spirit of some kind; though none have ever seen him. Many leave offerings of food and wine hoping that he will continue to protect them. Even Spuros pours an offering of strong whiskey into the harbor before leaving port."

Putting his cup down, Fenn asked, "And is he a protective spirit?"

Shutting the book, the Mage locked eyes with Fenn, giving him a measuring stare before answering. "Good question. Waven has spent quite some time using its abilities to modify the water currents, to ensure that those in search of the island do not find it. I think it looks upon Haven's residents as its children; sort of. I am not an expert on Waven's kind but I can imagine that perhaps it got lonely and allowed Haven to be established."

Fenn sat for a moment, and digested this before saying, "And now you and this Kraken are leaving. Going on some mysterious little errand and you expect me to stay here? To protect these . . . these . . . people?"

Nodding, the Mage stood up, grabbed the wine jug and re-filled Fenn's cup. "That is exactly it, my dear Fenn. And I promise you that your Masters will approve of my little 'errand' as you put it. You stay here and protect Haven until my return and I agree to an alliance with the Mage Council. Think of all the praise you will receive; your Masters hearts will lift at the mere mention of their sweet Fenn."

Putting the jug down, the Mage sat at the edge of the table, waiting for Fenn's reply. Draining the wine in one swig, Fenn put the cup down and snorted. "What choice do I have?"

Smiling, the Mage reached over to refill his own cup, "None what so ever, Fenn. But you don't have to pout about it."

THE MAGE was leaving. Where? He won't say. For how long? He can't be sure, maybe a month, maybe a year. Why? He has an errand to run. What kind of errand? He won't say. The angry words between them had gone round and round her chamber until they could almost be felt in the tension filled air. They both lay in her bed, naked but not touching.

"What if the Mok's come?"

"Then you must all defend Haven. Protect the children."

The Mage's voice had a slight hitch to it when he said the word 'children.' Denna had come to the conclusion early on that at one time the man had had a family. The way he interacted with Sann, even though the boy was not his, and the way he seemed to fall into an almost domestic routine when he returned from his exploits pointed to a man who was used to family life. The high priced whore and the scarred freak had created a warm household based on caring and affection. Even love? Denna mentally shied away from contemplating that.

The fact that Fenn had brought to light another son, one of the Mage's body if not his heart, did not seem to have the effect that the Mage Council had anticipated. After confirming that the boy was well and properly taken care of, the Mage stopped asking questions. Instead, he had closed himself away with Fenn's two companions, Grach and Tyrell, and hatched some sort of plan. That Riskh Hett was also involved somehow. The four of them had been thick as thieves for weeks. The fact that she had been kept in the dark about their plans irritated her.

Well, if she was going to be irritated she might as well milk it for all it was worth. She rolled over and ordered in a haughty voice, "Do be a good man and get the oil from that stand in the corner. Rub it into my back before we fall asleep. My skin is terribly dry."

With a chuckle, the Mage obeyed, and poured some of the oil onto his hand. The smell of mint and berries greeted his nose as he began to rub. Slowly, gently he continued to massage the oil into her skin. Across her shoulder blades and then her lower back . . . then lower still.

After a time she said,

"You have a very interesting idea of where my back is."

Her breathe caught sharply,

"That is definitely not my back."

"Do you want me to stop?" His fingers slowed.

"No. Oh no. Put another finger in me. Yes, there . . . deeper. Oh, cursed gods, yesssss."

She moaned. The Mage rubbed oil on his cock, rose to his knees, slipped the pillow from her head, rolled it into a cylinder and slipped it just under her pelvis. He moved between her thighs as she opened them. Gripping her ass with his hands he held her in place. He caressed her sex with the head of his cock, once, twice, three times, and then slipped it slowly inside.

"There," He whispered. "Do you want me there?"

"Yes!" Her voice louder now. "Yes. There. In me. Now, damn you, now!"

Forgotten was the prior argument; gone were the cares and concerns of the world. For now, two bodies rocked back and forth in a dance as ancient as time itself. For the moment, only they mattered; only they existed.

Later that night, Denna watched as the ship disappeared. The Mage had wanted few to know of his departure and so had left before sun rise. Spuros stood to her left; on her right the mage Fenn. Behind the three, the creature Liss, newly released from its chain, waited quietly.

The first sounds of Haven awakening could be heard; fishermen calling to each other, bakers firing up their ovens, mothers waking sleeping children. Yesterday these people knew their Mage was here, protecting them. How will they feel when they know he is gone?

CHAPTER TWELVE

He lived in a watery existence. The water was sludge like and heavy, yet his small slick body slid easily through it as he explored. His brood kin swam back and forth, testing the waters, exploring like himself. Suddenly, one of the larger ones attacked a smaller one. He and the others made a quiet circle around the battle; it was brutal and short with the victor eating the defeated. This changed things. It added caution to their world.

His memory blurred and he was still in the water. Except his body was bigger, he had arms and legs instead of the sleek thin form that had so easily navigated the water. Now he struggled to gain control of these new appendages. There were fewer brood kin now. Many had been eaten; others had simply disappeared. He was not the largest, but he was quick and constantly watched those around him. He was cautious yet took his opportunities to feed when they arose.

He felt something strange in the water. It smelled similar to the brood, but different. Curious, he swam toward it. It did not move like a brood brother. He swam closer and nudged the thing. Suddenly, he was grabbed. He struggled. He bit, clawed, almost *he wriggled free, but the thing got a better grip and pulled him from the heavy water, from the brood kin, to a bright light . . . .*

The scene changed. He was in a great room filled with his fellow brood siblings. They all had grown, losing the tadpole like tales. Crudely tailored coarse brown robes now covered them all with yellow cords serving as belts. Sunlight came in through large green glassed windows bathing the whole place in emerald.

They all sat at long tables eating their mid-day meal. Soon, Adults in the black and white of Brood Clond would arrive for their lessons. Language, Reading and writing and of course teachings that emphasized the Brood Clans devotion to the holy Empress. But for now, they ate.

Meals were the most dangerous times. Here, the strong ate, and the weak went hungry. He was not the weakest male in the group and the larger predators had left him alone, until now. The largest of the females approached him. He knew she had already eaten her food and that she was looking for more.

"Give me your food, squirt." As she reached for his plate, he dropped his hand to his belt, removing the wooden stake he had there. In a flash he struck, pinning the female's hand to the table. Crying in pain, she tried to fall back but her hand remained stuck to the table, stopping her flight. He then climbed up onto the table so that he was eye to eye with his new enemy and began to punch her in the face until she was unconscious. Breathing heavily, he clambered down off the table as the others watched with calculating eyes, grabbed his plate and moved off to an empty table. He did not want anyone to see how badly his hands shook so he quickly finished the meal.

After his last bite, a voice startled him, "How did you get that weapon?"

Peering around, he tried to find the owner of the voice. A slight chuckle revealed an average sized Mok watching from a shadow drenched corner. The Mok's clothing was dark blue and black, making him blend in easily with the shadows.

The first and harshest rule the young ones had been taught was that a question asked by an adult was to be answered immediately, but still he paused before answering, choosing his words carefully, "A few days ago, a fight broke a wooden chair. A piece flew near me and I grabbed it. It had a sharp end that I liked."

Nodding as if that were the most reasonable explanation in the world, the adult said, "Very resourceful. My name is Deski, I think you have certain attributes that could be useful to the Brood Clan."

"Spy Master." A voice broke through the memory. A hand shook his shoulder. His senses spiraled away from Deski, the brood kin, all gone.

"Spy Master, open your eyes." He felt his body resting on a solid form. A bed his memories called it. His hands felt soft fabric and a firm mattress. He was tired, so tired. He wanted to rest, to sleep. But the voice was familiar; annoyingly familiar. Turning toward the voice, he opened his eyes to see a small Mok giving him a sour smile.

The small Mok spoke again, "Welcome back Spy Master. Welcome back to the world of the living."

Hours later Calphan stood in a room that most Mok's would have given everything they owned to enter. Great green root like appendages covered the walls. The floor was also covered in green roots, but these were so thin and packed together that they looked to the unobservant eye like grains in a green colored wood. The air was humid with warm thick moisture that felt almost oppressive even to an amphibian like creature as a Mok. Moisture dripped and dribbled down the walls joining together to make a shallow pool on the floor. The temperature of the water was surprising cool and served to dull a bit of the room's heat.

Only one piece of furniture existed in the room. A large throne that was made up of the same packed green roots that covered the rest of the room. On the throne sat an immense figure. Wide flat, flipper like feet rested firmly on the floor. Rolls of dull green fat covered puffy legs and a huge torso. In contrast, two heavily muscled arms rested lightly on the throne. A huge box like head topped off the figure. Green spots covered ridges that jutted out over the eyes that were now closed as if in sleep.

Calphan tried to ignore the enormity of where he stood and instead studied the Mok to his right. The High Mage, Archen, had not changed much since Calphan had last seen him. Still short, still very intelligent, still annoyingly difficult to deal with. The mage stood there and did little to hide his impatience. While his short stature would usually have had his Brood Mother discard him Archen's mastery of water magic more than made up for his lack of size. The Empress allowed the little mage his minor impertinences due to his importance to the Empire; and Archen knew it.

He thought of himself as Calphan now. The persona of Calphan the Merchant was not one of his favorites. The merchant embodied most of the unpleasant aspects of the Mok people; arrogance, quick to take offense, and so convinced of Mok superiority that the idea that another race might have anything to contribute to the wide world was unthinkable. Still, since his re-awakening, this new life granted to him, he had thought of himself as Calphan. Not Calphan the merchant, but simply Calphan. It was a strange feeling to be so attached to the name.

Thinking of his new life made him think of waking up to Archen's sour smile. Involuntarily he flexed his right hand, which still felt stiff and sore as if it had had little use in a long time. Which, according the mage had been just over two years. Calphan could scarcely believe that all that remained of his body after the explosion had been his right hand. It was amazing that he stood here at all; a testament to the power of the Empress. To be able to restore one of her children by only having his hand to build on was extraordinary to the point of miracle.

His thought's drifted back to his last few memories before his death. He had been on a vessel, a ship of a small armada. The Empresses' plan had failed to take the Bright City, Hyberan. Calphan quickly drove that thought from his mind. The Empress did not fail; ever! Instead it had been her strange black scaled allies that had failed; they had failed to disable the city from inside while the forces of the Empress attacked from outside.

Though the battle had been lost, he had tried to scavenge something from the defeat. So, he had captured the strange mund, Jonathan Champion; a mundane with mage like powers. Calphan had taken the precaution of drugging the mund and having him completely incapacitated for the duration of their journey back to the Empress. Calphan had been in complete control.

Then inexplicably, Champion had worked magic through the effects of the heavy drugs, burned his way through the leather straps that bound him, and gained his freedom. For two hours Calphan and Archen had scoured the ship frantically searching for the dangerous mund. Finally, the search ended in the belly of the ship, in the stone room where the entire ship functioned through the power of the rawstones.

Rawstones. The stones were vitally important to the functioning of the Empire and the war effort. Rawstones. The cornerstone of most of civilization, and Calphan had found Jonathan Champion standing in the stone room of that ship doing something to the stones. Something strange and unusual, something so dangerous and unknown that even High Mage Archen had been frightened.

He had stood before Champion as the mund stared intently at the rawstones; so intently that he seemed oblivious to the fact that the chase was over. Calphan had smiled in triumph and told the tall mund just that. But instead of the look of defeat he had expected the mund had said a name; Breg.

Even now Calphan barely suppressed a shudder at the memories the name brought with it. His servant Breg was a mundane that had been with him for twenty years. The Empresses black scaled allies had taken charge of Breg when Calphan had been absent just before the attack on the mage city. The poor mund had been cut open in an intentionally cruel and bloody ritual. Somehow, through some dark power, Breg had been horribly mutilated but still lived; his pain ongoing though his body cried out silently for the release of death. The black ones claimed that they used Breg as bait to lure Champion to a trap. The careless cruelty of the act had shocked even Calphan; and Champion had thrown it in his face.

His memories after his confrontation with Champion are filled with fire. An immense heat had engulfed him and burned him in a short painful instant that had seemed to last a lifetime. Then nothing; darkness, nothingness, the void of death. Until his resurrection by the Empress.

He had no idea how Archen had survived. The short mage must be powerful indeed to have escaped the fire's wrath. Somehow, as Archen had recently explained, Champion had ignited the rawstones unleashing incredible destruction. The fire had not just been felt on the one ship, but the entire armada had been destroyed. Over one thousand Mok soldiers, sailors and marines had vanished in a brief moment of fire. Even local towns along the shore line had had reports of rawstone explosions causing power outages and fires.

It was in two words, horribly amazing. Horrible to the point that the Empress had initially feared that the Mages had developed some kind of super weapon and would unleash it on the Empire. However, once Archen had made his way back to the Empress and explained the fate of the armada it was clear that there was no such weapon, and that the act was that of a single freakish mund who was most likely killed in the explosion. So the war continued.

For over two years the war had raged while Calphan had sat in oblivion, or his hand had. He remembered nothing of his time in death. He simply had a two year blankness in his memories. He refused to contemplate that; if he thought about it too much it would distract him from his current task.

Well, he assumed it was a task. Why else would the Empress have brought him back to the land of the living? Why else would Archen be here with him now? The little mage who was her most trusted advisor? Calphan turned his gaze back to the figure on the throne.

An objective part of his mind quietly whispered that there was not much beauty to admire. But there was beauty, and there was beauty. Here sat the Mother of his race. A Goddess. Great flabs of dull green flesh covered an immense body. His Empress. She transcended beauty.

Suddenly her eyes opened, large golden eyes. The Empress quietly contemplated the two in front of her. Calphan felt her gaze like a physical thing, looking through him to his soul and innermost thoughts. Though her eyes only rested on him for a few moments, when she turned them to Archen, Calpahn visibly slumped in relief. His body felt like a worn rag recently wrung of all its moisture.

"Archen." The voice was deep. Deep and vibrant; it seemed to reverberate deep within Calphan, making his toes tremble.

"My Empress." Archen's voice held nothing of his usually cocky tone. It was respectful with an underlying note of fear.

"This is the one who you requested I revive? This Spymaster who had failed me?" Calphan barely stopped himself from answering her question. Noticing this, the Empress lifted an ancient hand saying to him, "You would say something, my child?"

Calphan took two steps forward, ignoring the hissed warning of the small mage. Kneeling down in the shallow water, he bowed his head and spoke, "Empress, your children who fought to take the Mage's city should not be blamed for any failure. We succeeded in all the tasks which were allotted to us. Mage Archen was successful in his attack on the Citadel; Admiral Burda began his bombardment of the outer walls according to plan. I arranged to have your allies hidden in the city until they could fulfill their obligation to you. All was prepared, all was ready." He paused, waiting for a response. Calphan knew that contradicting the Empress in such a way was a dangerous gamble. She was not known for her patient understanding ways, especially in light of failure. He waited there, knowing that the consequences of his words could very well result in his second life being a short one.

A sound began to drift to his ears. It was quiet at first, and then grew louder. A beautiful throaty sound that filled the muggy air with mirth. Calphan lifted his head slightly towards the throne.

The Empress was laughing. Her enormous body wiggled and jiggled as her head was thrown back. A musical wonderful sound issued forth from the large form. After a few more moments of this, she brought her head back down. Raising a hand for Calphan to rise, the Empress asked the little Mage, "Archen, are you sure you did not add a bit of your own insubordinate attitude to the Spymaster when you assisted me in his rejuvenation?"

"I assure you Empress, the Spymaster needed nothing from me in that regard. But his attitude does no detriment to his loyalty to you." The mage had taken a few steps forward to stand beside Calphan.

"Indeed, Archen. Indeed." Looking now to Calphan, the Empress said, "You are correct, Spymaster. Our allies did fail us. However, they have provided me with other services since then and are now back in my good graces. But, I did not bring you back to the living to tell me something I already knew. No, we have a new threat to the Empire. A threat which you are most intimately familiar with."

Calphan glanced over at Archen, raising a questioning eye brow. At the Empresses nod, Archen spoke, "We have recently come to the conclusion that you and I were not the only survivors of the armada's destruction." The mage looked at Calphan full in the face as he let the words sink in.

"Who . . . ?" Calphan stopped his words in midsentence, eyes going wide. Taking a few deep breathes, he answered his own question.

"Jonathan Champion."

HE OFTEN had dreams. Most times it was about people and places he did not know or recall, but the images tugged at his memory just the same. This dream was different.

He had been having this dream for the past three days. Every time he closed his eyes it was there, waiting like a visiting relative who refused to leave. A large cavern was open before his eyes; the only sound was of dripping water, drip, drip, drip. Somehow he knew that the cavern was deep underground, under miles of rock that seemed to weigh down on his dream shoulders. The air smelled musty, like water soaked stone. A shimmering hole of some kind had been cut into the back wall of the cavern. Harsh lights glittered at the edges of the hole in a myriad of colors. Glittering lights aside, it was the enormous body that filled the hole that drew his attention.

It laid there unmoving looking like a dark green bloated snake that had just slithered out of the hole. Barely discernible due to the massive form laying on top of them, he could see what looked to be steps that led up to the hole. If the half of the body that was hidden in the hole matched the half he could see, then the creature was an impressive specimen. Further down the steps, a large serpentine head was attached to the body, its eyes closed as if in sleep. At least, the eyes had been closed in all his previous dreams. Now, the giant eye lids trembled as they opened. White orbs the size of truck tires stared sightlessly around the room. Thick puss like fluid dripped onto the cavern floor, giving the eyes a melted look. Somehow, his dream self knew the creature was blind.

A dull red tongue flicked out from the large mouth as if tasting the air. It flicked again. Then suddenly, the giant head swiveled and the white orbs focused on him. Even if this creature were blind, it definitely knew that is was being watched.

"Mage. Human mage. Can you hear me? Do you remember me?" The serpent's mouth did not move, but he knew that it spoke to him. He struggled to answer, but his voice was muted. Then he felt an enormous presence touch his mind briefly, like a gentle flame that knew if it touched the moth too strongly it *would burn. A part of his memories, those that were locked away in some part of his brain, seemed to recognize this presence. He had a flash image of flying through the air . . .*

"Yes, Mage. I brought you here, to this world. With help of course . . . ." A vision of a short woman with bright eyes and a lopsided hairdo invaded his thoughts. He knew this woman, her name was at the tip of his memories, screaming for recognition . . . He tried to cry out . . .

HETT WATCHED the Mage's troubled sleep. The man moaned, shaking his head back and forth on the pillow. The Mage was tired after his workings and needed sleep, even if it was a nightmare filled sleep. He had explained to Hett that using his powers to create an invisibility cloak was subtle stuff but that what he had been doing the past week made the cloak seem clumsy and crude.

Hett and the mage had discussed for some time how to gain an advantage over the Empress. How to impress upon her that the Lost Isles should be left alone? But the Empire did not tolerate competition. This war with Hyberan was case in point of that. While the Mage Council had never made any move to encroach upon the Empresses lands, indeed they had encouraged trade and cultural exchanges, the mere fact that Hyberan existed, had existed for centuries, free of the dominion of the Empire was unacceptable. The history of the Empire was filled with nations and races who had defied the Empress; they were all gone, ground to dust under her will to control. Those that were not annihilated were made into servants, like Hett's own Riskh people.

But Hyberan was not just some other conquest. Indeed, to date it was the only power to ever challenge, and according to the now defunct Treaty of Seven Fires, defeat the Empress; at least for a time. The mages of the Bright City are the Empire's most challenging adversary in its long bloody history.

Back to the question then; how to keep the Isles free of the Empresses designs. The only sure way would be to destroy the Empress; impossible. Gaining access to the Empress through her thousands of subjects would not be just suicidal but sure to fail. Further, the actual location of the Empress was never certain; she had a constant web of smoke and mirrors surrounding her whereabouts at any given time that it was impossible to plan any assassination. The next best option was to hurt her, hurt the Empire, to the point where she would have to choose between her war against the mages or dealing with the Isles; with the hope she would choose to continue against the mages. Not the most honorable course of action by hoping your enemy continues to harm another party, but it was their best option for survival.

It was a suicidal mission. Hett knew it. But there was something about the Mage, this mund, that made Hett want to participate in this mad plan. It was not purely an issue of loyalty for Hett; he was being paid handsomely, three times his normal fee. No, it was that what the Mage planned to do was so amazingly audacious that Hett simply had to be a part of it, a paid part of it of course.

The small company of four shared a cabin together, spacious in ship travel terms. Four bunks took up most of the space, but those could be cleverly folded up into the walls giving the occupants a good sized open room. Now the Mage slept on the only bunk that was free of the wall giving Hett space to sit on the floor and quietly watch over him.

Master Thurga, the mund herbalist in Haven had given explicit instructions concerning the treatment required.

Every other day, the Mage was to consume a frothy brew filled with a hodgepodge of medicinal herbs that were to ensure the man did not suffer from the sudden seizures. His medicine often made the Mage sleepy and he was allowed to sleep as long as one of his companions watched over him, to ensure a seizure did not occur during his slumber.

Grach quietly opened the door, letting a whiff of sea air into the room. He shared a nod of greeting with Hett. Getting to his feet, Hett moved around the hefty warrior and closed the door as he exited the room. The companions had been sharing the duties of 'mage watch' as Tyrell called it.

Walking out on deck, Hett gave a quiet greeting to Captain Dursh as he passed. The large Mok ignored Hett and bent back to his conversation with the ships first mate. Hett had a brief secret smile at the Captain's rudeness. It was expected from a Mok in dealing with an inferior Riskh.

Hett crossed the deck to where Tyrell was busy repairing a pair of boots. The slim blue skinned Ferrekei seemed to be weathering the voyage well considering that most of his people avoid sea travel. Tyrell wore a faded tan servants robe cinched at the waste with a braided rope. Flimsy sandals barely covered blue toes and had to be cold in the brisk sea air. A large leather collar with a metal hoop was the only part of the disguise that seemed to give Tyrell any discomfort. Grach wore one as well; the two friends, along with Hett were the servants of the often sleeping, and grouchy when awake, Master Pulk.

Master Pulk was a dealer in certain specialty items that those of the Broods Royal craved. His current shipment did not include rare items, but instead two very unique specimens; a well-trained Ferrekei male and one of the famed Molden. It was part of the plan that Hett had even impressed himself at his own cleverness.

They had embarked from Haven aboard a Corsair ship which had taken them to the island of Ish. From Ish, Hett had arranged for transport to the former Gurashi city of Guarn. There, the party had purchased passage with Captain Dursh to the Imperial Capital City of her most August Holiness, The Empress.

The guise of a merchant allowed the small band to move in certain social circles that would not raise alarm with the Mok authorities. So, the fact that Master Pulk had obtained two slaves from races currently at war with the Empire did not bring up any questions that a few well-placed bribes could not sufficiently answer. The advantage of being a merchant with two live slaves as cargo allowed their party better mobility than if they had to transport a load of wool or coal for market. Hett again took a moment to mentally bask in his own genius as he approached Tyrell.

For the purposes of their disguise, Hett required that the two 'slaves' be seen doing menial tasks on behalf of their master. Hett served as the 'supervisor' of all of his master's investments and made sure to complain loudly and often to the Mok ship's crew about the inferior performance of the two slaves. Keeping in that role he put his hands on hips and looked with a disgusted face at Tyrell's work.

"Ridiculous! These boots should have been repaired hours ago! Good thing your blue skin is worth something, because your skills are shit! Give them to me and get back to the cabin, Master is waking up soon and needs to be attended."

Swiping the boots from Tyrell Hett thumped the blue man soundly on his head. For a moment, Tyrell's hands tightened into fists, then as Hett glared the blue man simply bowed, keeping his eyes lowered and hurried past to the laughter of Mok sailors. Hett stayed on deck for a while longer pretending to look over the boots, but was in fact taking stock of the effect the little drama had on the crew. After convincing himself that it had been a sufficient performance he wandered back to the cabin.

Once the cabin door was closed, Hett let out a surprised grunt as he was grabbed by the back of the neck. He saw stars as his head was banged repeatedly against the wooden wall of the cabin. One last bang and he bit his tongue and tasted blood in his mouth.

"Listen, here friend Hett." Tyrell hissed. Hett felt strong hands wrap around his throat as the Ferrekei continued saying, "I have had about enough of your show for the Mok's, is that clear? I am sure they get the point now. Agreed?"

Hett felt the hands tighten, making it impossible to speak. At his nod, Tyrell gave a grim smile and released him. After a few gasping breathes, and rubbing at his now sore throat, Hett croaked, "Indeed, my blue skinned friend. I think our farce has been effective. No more such spectacles are necessary."

Tyrell gave a gruff nod and went to sit on his bunk. Grach seemed unfazed by the incident and lay on his bunk with his arms cradling his head. Hett, still rubbing his throat glanced over at the Mage.

The tall man, now awake, watched the trio and the only indication that he had witnessed the incident was a small smile. Stretching for a moment, he flipped long legs over his bunk and stood. Walking over to Hett, he asked, "We land tonight?"

Speaking around a bitten tongue, Hett answered, "Yes. Tonight we arrive at Argat, a small city with a large port. Then, over land for two days travel to the Capital."

Nodding his understanding, the Mage said, "Well, although Tyrell's drama is over, I believe that we should go bother good Captain Dursh, don't you? Master Pulk would not simply allow the captain and crew a day free of his cranky manners and inappropriate observations, would he?"

At Hett's chuckle, the Mage closed his eyes for a moment in concentration. A glow spread over the man, slowly from his feet to his arms, fingers, and head. In a matter of moments the Mage was gone. In his place stood a large Mok dressed in bulky expensive clothing. Wide green cheeks puffed out from a boxy shaped head. Long green arms spread wide as Hett stepped forward with a perfume bottle containing a green liquid. Hett gave four good sprays on the arms and face. The scent was necessary for the Mage to pass as a Mok; each Mok had a peculiar scent that they exuded. Master Pulk had to smell as well as look like a Mok.

The Mage stood still a moment giving the spray time to settle on his skin. Hett put the bottle away and walked to the door. At Master Pulk's nod, Hett opened the door and he and the Mage exited onto the deck.

CHAPTER THIRTEEN

The S'Hael sat on his throne deep in thought. At least that is what he wanted to portray to those who observed him. He had not been S'Hael long by the years of his people, but those he so recently ruled had learned quickly not to interrupt his silences. He sat in the grand hall, at the center of his power, and thought.

The grand hall was a combination of harsh desert light and deep shadows. Hewn from the very desert stone, the small mountain, or the Fastness as his people called it, had been hollowed out for his people's purposes. As was their custom, there were few straight lines in the architecture. Corridors wound round and seemed to slither through the stone. The grand hall followed this example on a larger scale with brightly sunlit alcoves competing with darkened corners.

Above where the S'Hael sat great depictions of the Sky Fathers had been carved into the stone ceiling. The carvings showed the great creatures soaring through time and space, past stars and planets on their endless search for knowledge and the secrets of the cosmos. On the floor, the Great Mothers were depicted, their dark sinuous bodies intertwining as they created the world with their very essences. Further down the great hall, the carvings of the Fathers and Mothers came closer and closer. On the back wall, as if finally reaching the end of a long journey, the Fathers and Mothers were depicted in their first discovery of each other. Somehow, the artist had infused expressions of wonder and happiness on the reptilian faces of the Fathers, the Mothers serpentine features held cautious curiosity as they looked upon these winged travelers.

Below the depiction of this ancient meeting, limp forms hung, motionless. At other various points along the walls of the grand hall, more figures hung. Each was a mundane, gifts from the Empress. Men, women, children, all were guests of the S'Hael. Each 'guest' was held motionless by some invisible force with their wrists and ankles seemingly fused to the stone walls. Even their heads had been set in an upright position so that they had to look straight into their tormentors faces. Most had had their garments removed so their sweet flesh was vulnerable to dark clawed hands. All of the motionless guests had open wounds that dripped blood onto the stone floor.

Even now some of those clawed hands were enjoying themselves in soft flesh. The S'Hael watched with quiet satisfaction as a group of his dark skinned S'Ahas took turns using their craft on one of the newest arrivals. The creature silently screamed in torment, silently because its' vocal chords had been removed. This was a somewhat new innovation, a fad that many of the S'Ahas had adopted since the S'Hael's awakening. It was a wonderfully strange sensation to watch a victim try to scream in pain and terror and have no sound issue from its mouth. The facial expression of a soundless scream was something many seemed to enjoy.

Dozens of the colored rawstones surrounded each wall bound victim. As the S'Ahas practiced their art, at each silent scream and drop of blood, the stones glowed slightly brighter as they were charged. It was a deviation from the Orda's process but one that built on the S'Ahas' skills and interests. Each victim had been given the 'white tar' which increased the potency of the charging.

While the S'Ahas had been able to reproduce the Orda's process, their stones were still not as potent. It most likely had to do with the fact that the S'Ahas were required to use recycled stones that had used up their power. The location and method by which the Orda were able to obtain new stones was still unknown and a point of frustration for the S'Hael. The stones the Orda produced lasted approximately a year before they went dark. The S'Ahas's rawstones lasted a few months at a time, requiring more victims. Still, the S'Ahas's stones were a valuable resource and something their Mok allies coveted.

The S'Hael's eyes moved to the center of the hall where a huge sculpted rendering of a Great Father in flight reared up from the floor. Obsidian black wings ended with tips of midnight blue seemed to exhibit unbelievable strength captured in stone. A long sinuous neck connected to a reptilian head reared back with its mouth opened wide spouting out red jeweled flames. The artist had ingeniously applied red rawstones covering the rendition of fire, giving the sculpture a lifelike quality. Now the glowing stones wafted sultry fumes that floated throughout the great hall.

The S'Ahas referred to the smoke from the rawstones as Fathers Breathe. Somehow, some way, the rawstone smoke was reminiscent of the scent of one of the great reptiles. This was an unlooked for bonus for the S'Hael and his followers. The smoke had a calming euphoric effect on his people.

Even now, when dark worries threatened his confidence, the soothing smoke allowed him to calm and focus his thoughts.

Next his eyes rested on the floor carvings of the Mothers. Like so many times before, the S'Hael wondered about the Mothers. Where were they? Were they hiding? Why? And why had the Orda, the Keepers, turned from them? Turned from the Father's blood? Was such a thing possible? And where were the Fathers? Had they returned? Would they return?

The Fathers and Mothers had birthed their children in their own image. Strong and powerful, the Fathers had gathered the lesser races from the known universe to serve and amuse their children and as gifts for the Mothers. The S'Ahas had basked in the approval of the Fathers, striving against each other and using their slaves in bloody practices to please their creators. The Orda, The Keepers, had embraced the quiet inquisitive nature of the Mothers, always questing for knowledge and secrets. For years beyond counting, the Fathers and Mothers blessed their children.

Then, suddenly, the Fathers had left on a journey, a journey the Mothers said was so important that they had to leave their children. Before their departure, the Fathers had given the S'Ahas power over the dracoth and other lesser beings. For centuries afterward the S'Ahas and the Orda had flourished in the world their creators had made for them.

Then, the world had heaved with rock, fire and destruction. Thousands of Orda and S'Ahas had perished. At this one time of weakness, the Invaders came. They were ugly creatures with weak skin that would sometimes burn dark under the hot sun. But the Invaders were powerful in their ugliness. They commanded the elements, fire, earth, water, and air; mages they called themselves. The S'Ahas fought them, bringing the might of the Fathers fire against these new enemies. The Orda's gentle natures were not compatible with this war of survival and they fled to the deep of the earth seeking the protection of the Mothers.

For centuries the S'Ahas fought the Invaders, even to the point of near extinction for both sides. Then, with bloody victory almost in their grasp, the Mothers called them. Leaving the war, the S'Ahas had let the Orda guide them to the deep of the dark quiet earth where the Mothers waited. The Mothers explained that even with victory the S'Ahas would be too few to protect their world, that only the Fathers return would ensure the safety of their children. With the Mothers power, they would put both S'Ahas and Orda asleep and protect their children as they slept. Then, when the Fathers returned, the children would awake and expel the Invaders with the Fathers power. And, so, in the comfort of the Mothers embrace, their children slept.

When the S'Hael thought of the Mothers the memories of his own awakening came fresh to mind. He had been woken up by a voice, deep and knowing.

"Wake."

The Mothers power still held him in cold slumber. His mind was foggy with sleep, un-clear. Again the voice, this time louder,

"Wake, my child." *The voice seemed to dance with flames now, warming his body by its very words. He struggled, trying to wake, trying to follow the voice. Still, the Mothers power was tempting him with sweet dark sleep.*

"Child! Wake!" *A fire now filled him; a fiery presence spread through his body releasing him from sleeps cold grip. He opened his eyes, gasping for breath. The chamber where he and the other S'Haels slept was cold, almost frigid. He flicked his forked tongue tasting the air for any sign of the Mothers or the Orda. Nothing.*

He slowly clambered off the sleeping pedestal and gained his feet. The nine pedestals were made from the very rock of the Fastness, looking like little more than stone mushrooms growing out of the floor. His legs weak from disuse tottered as he looked at the other eight shapes that lay unmoving. Slowly, he staggered toward the closest pedestal and gripped the shoulder of the sleeping form. Stone. He had pulled his hand back in alarm at first, and then he lightly poked the skin with a talon. He flicked his tongue against the skin. Stone. This S'Hael had turned to stone. As fast as his wobbly legs could carry him he went from pedestal to pedestal poking and tasting each figure. All stone.

Of the nine S'Hael only he was awake. His eight greatest rivals were motionless by the Mothers sleep and their skin turned to stone. Were they alive? He did not know the answer to that question. But he knew he could not stay in this chamber for long. Already the temperature was making his body shudder to give in to the cold slumber. He walked stiffly to the chamber's entrance and waved a clawed hand over the key stone. Light flared over the stone doors, illuminating their edges. A slow rumble sounded and the doors opened and he stepped out into the corridor.

The Mothers had created the catacombs that tunneled beneath the Fastness so their children could sleep and await the return of the Fathers. Nine Sept's had all lain down to sleep at the Mothers call. All of the children had closed their eyes as one. Fathers Blood, Mothers Blood.

The corridor outside the S'Haels chamber was warmer. He tasted the air again and this time sensed Brothers close by. As if on cue, a black skinned S'Ahas turned a corner and came into view running at a fast pace. Skidding to a stop in front of him, he knelt at his feet and bowed a scaled head. The S'Hael could tell that this one was of his own Sept and he struggled through his sleep dampened thoughts for a name.

Finally, the S'Hael said, "Shinal."

At his name, the Brother looked up, relief spreading across his face. "Yes, S'Hael.

"Have the Fathers returned?" He felt stronger now that he was out of the cold chamber and his body warmed. His thoughts became sharper and clear.

"No, S'Hael."

He reached down and grabbed Shinal by the neck, lifting the unlucky messenger almost effortlessly. Like all the S'Hael the Fathers blood ran strongest in his veins and in times of anger their fire gave him strength. He knew that Shinal saw the burning power of the Fathers glow from his S'Hael's eyes and trembled. Squeezing a clawed hand he felt the Brother struggle for the next breathe. The S'Hael enjoyed the fear his strength inspired for a moment, before releasing Shinal who slipped slowly to the floor wheezing and gasping for air.

Giving Shinal time to compose himself and again kneel, the S'Hael ordered, "Explain."

Keeping his eyes lowered, Shinal spoke, "S'Hael, when I awoke some of our Sept were still asleep and many had turned to stone. We waited for you or the Keepers to come for us for many days. When we grew hungry, we began to search for you. We found other Sept's doing the same. We gathered together and came to sit outside your chamber, to wait for the S'Haels to wake. We waited for many days but you did not come out and we did not know how to open the door.

We were hungry and many Brothers went to search for food. Prey was scarce in the tunnels so we journeyed out into the desert and hunted, but still many grew weak from hunger. Hundreds of days passed and still the S'Haels stayed in your chamber and the Keepers never came. Then, the Green Tail Sept attacked one night taking many of us for food. From that day forward, Sept fought Sept, Brother kills Brother to survive.

We have been many years now fighting and hunting each other in the tunnels and desert.

S'Hael, where are the Fathers? Where are the Keepers? What of the Mothers?"

Shinal's voice quieted as the S'Hael took in his words. He did not have answers to the Brother's questions. He needed time to learn what had happened. But, he had to stop the fighting and Brother killings before their people became too weak.

Looking down, he saw Shinal waiting for his master to speak words of wisdom but the S'Hael needed more answers, "Shinal, did those who turned to stone ever wake up?"

"No, S'Hael. They are dead."

Nodding to himself, the S'Hael spent a few quiet moments thinking before he spoke, considering his words carefully for his attentive servant, "Shinal, call the Septs together. Tell them I will bring Father's fire and death down on them if they do not stop the killing and let me speak with them. Go, now!"

With a vicious grin, Shinal bound to his feet to carry out his master's bidding. The S'Hael waited until the Brother had turned the corner and was out of view before returning to the sleeping chamber. He walked slowly around the other S'Hael thinking of what he would do next. He knew that a Father's voice had woken him. The fiery power had burned away the Mothers sleep and brought him back to life. But he could not sense anything of the Father anymore. Nothing.

He continued to circle the stone sleepers deep in thought. The Septs were weak now from the killings. Even if one of his fellow S'Haels somehow survived in their skins of stone, their people could not afford a struggle for power between two of the Fathers blood.

His steps stopped in front of the stone body of the S'Hael of the Green Tail Sept. Since time out of mind, the Green Tail's had been his Sept's enemy. The idea that the Green Tails had *been the first to attack and feed on their own kind angered him. Calling the Father's power he brought a black fiery fist down on the sleeping S'Hael's stone head. Grey bits of rock and dust filled the air. He paused for a moment and relished the feeling of satisfaction in seeing his enemy turned to dust. Even if all the other S'Haels were truly stone dead, he had the make sure.*

Even as he walked from pedestal to pedestal, ensuring the death of his opponents the S'Hael thought of his next moves. Alone, the nine Septs were weak. Weak from years of fighting and feeding on each other, weak from not having the strong handed guidance of the S'Haels. He had to take the Sept's in hand, mold and coax his people back into what they had been before the Mothers slumber.

Days later he learned that the Orda, the Keepers, had all been gone well before the Brothers and the S'Hael awoke. The tunnels where they were to have slept were covered in centuries of undisturbed dust. After getting firm control of the Septs, the S'Hael had spent many years searching alone for the grey skinned Keepers. Finally, he had tracked them down to an island near the Mok Empire. Three Keepers had stood before him silent in the face of his joy of discovery. The Keeper's silence persisted in the face of his questions. The S'Hael was confused at first. Where had the Keepers gone? Why did they leave the S'Haels and the Brothers to die a stone filled sleep? Where were the Mothers? No answers, only silence. Through his confusion his anger grew.

He had lashed out then with the Fathers fury. Two of the Keepers had been engulfed in black flame their cries of anguish broke through their silence. The third, stronger in the Mothers Blood than the other two, survived his attack, but still was easily overcome with his power. He bound the unconscious survivor and contemplated what to do with his grey skinned prisoner. The S'Hael had been unsettled. He had thought that finding the

Keepers would provide him with much needed answers, instead only more questions resulted. Never before had Fathers and Mothers blood contested with each other. Never.

The place where he had found the Keepers was strange. He was in a room filled with occupied beds. Metal masks covered sleepers who seemed to be awake, yet slept. Stones of various colors that seemed to glow with an unknown power were attached to masks. His curiosity made him wish to examine these stones, but Mok guards soon arrived, challenging him. Stepping forward, the S'Hael instinctively put himself between these new arrivals and the unconscious Orda. While he had just killed two of them, still his blood cried for him to protect the grey skinned Keeper. The Guards soon changed their tone after their more aggressive fellows met a fiery end. While the S'Hael did not understand their language, he understood their placating gestures. Please wait. We have others to deal with you.

The Mok's had changed during the S'Hael's slumber. Bigger now, they showed none of the deference and fear that his presence should have inspired. Yes, he had killed some of them, but they appeared more wary than afraid.

A few moments later a Mok in a blue robe entered the room accompanied by more guards. While much shorter than his fellows, this Mok had an authoritative demeanor. Coming before the S'Hael, the short one asked, "Who are you?" The language was his own, which surprised the S'Hael. The short one was a mage. From his experiences before he slept, the Mok's had no mages. Only one race, the damned Invaders, had evidenced such power. The S'Hael regarded the mage for a number of quiet moments. Then the two began a discussion which gave light to what a different world the S'Hael and his people had awoken too.

The S'Hael had learned much from his time with the Moks. He had agreed to meet their Empress and had gone to great lengths to quell his anger at her impertinence in questioning him. The Mok's had not just gotten physically bigger, they had become powerful. They looked upon the S'Hael as a possible tool in their war against the mages. The Empress was concerned that the Orda, would withhold their aid in producing more rawstones and needed to know if he could provide a different alternative.

During his negotiations with the Empress it became very clear that the world he had known was gone. While his people had slept obliviously trusting of the Mothers promises, their world had been taken over by former slaves and lesser beings. He could not crush this green skinned Empress like he wished. He had to practice a more measured strategy, more subtle. Subtlety was not something his people excelled at, but it was necessary in this new world. So, he had agreed to help this Empress, to aid her in her cause against the mages. His people were not strong enough to take back what was theirs, not yet.

He was so deep in memory, that he almost did not observe the Brother who had approached his throne. With a sinuous flip of his head, the S'Hael dispelled the memories and the disturbing internal questioning and took on the stern manner of leader. When he saw who had approached him, he gave what for his people was a greeting smile. Shinal paused in respect waiting for his master to acknowledge him. The S'Hael gave a gracious nod in return and motioned for the Brother to come forward.

Like all the Brothers, Shinal was tall and slim. Harsh desert sun reflected off of black scales making the Brother look like he was covered in shimmering coins. Silver bracelets studded with the greenish black jade that his people prized glittered as Shinal gave a low graceful bow his head almost touching the floor. A white swath of shimmering cloth matching the S'Hael's own, was wrapped around the Brother's black skin, covering his pelvis and torso, identifying him as a member of the S'Hael's own White Claw Sept. Other Brothers strolled through the great hall wearing other colored cloth; red, purple, green, black, yellow, grey, blue, brown. It was a small concession that the S'hael made to allow the Brothers of the other Sept's to wear their Sept colors. As long as they acknowledged his lordship, he cared little.

"What news, Shinal?"

Straightening to his feet, the S'Ahas approached and bent his head close to ensure that his words only reached the S'Hael's ears. As he spoke, Shinal kept his senses keened on the S'Hael for any sign of danger. His message was not a particularly good one, and it was always uncertain how his master would respond to the continuous demands of the green ones. Shinal did not want to be unprepared if his master's anger called upon the Fathers blood and he was the closest target for the fiery wrath.

The S'Hael's irritation grew as Shinal spoke. He could feel the Fathers fire building in his veins with each word. His outward appearance did not change. An observer would think that the S'Hael was calmly listening to his servant, unaware of the fiery inner struggle.

Shinal finished his report and stepped back quickly from the throne. The S'Hael sat still for a breath and then stood, and walked past his servant. At his Master's nod, Shinal followed a few paces back. The pair walked from the great hall and down a dark corridor that snaked around the corner. From the walls hung rawstone lamps, basking the hallway in an orange smoky light.

The S'Hael breathed in the rawstone fumes as he walked. These stones were truly an amazing creation. The stones provided light and powered amazing machines and creations. The mage city was proof of the wonder and potential of the stones. The Moks showed amazing ingenuity in creating rawstone weapons of war and conquest. But with all the potential of the stones, it was the fumes that gave true enjoyment to his people. The smell aroused memories of the long absent Fathers. The Brothers' senses were soothed by the sultry fumes that made smoky trails from the stones, almost a mellow intoxication. Again, the S'Hael's mind went back to the hardest, most disturbing, question.

Why had the Keepers turned from them? He had been able to keep the fact of the Keepers betrayal a closely held secret between himself and a few of the eldest S'Ahas, but that was about to change. The S'Hael's pace suddenly quickened, as if he tried to distance himself from his decision.

The S'Hael led Shinal to an open stairwell guarded by two adolescent Brothers. Too young yet to have developed an awareness of the Fathers blood, these younger Brothers served as guards and soldiers for their elders. Armed with dark grey blades and covered in black scaled armor, the two younglings bowed at the S'Hael's approach. Ignoring their gestures of respect, the S'Hael and Shinal moved down the stairs.

Almost immediately the pair was encased in darkness, but had no need to slow their steps. The S'Ahas, like all the Fathers children, had keen senses and were not constrained by mere sight and sound. Down the two went, deeper and deeper into the bowels of the Fastness.

The S'Hael stopped at a dead end that seemed to end in a seamless face of stone. Waving a clawed hand a door way appeared in front of master and servant. Quickly the pair entered, and the entrance closed behind them.

Inside, a central room held few furnishings. Two tunnels veered off to each side, curving out of sight. A stone table and two chairs held the center of the space. A few bones and a wickedly curved blade showed evidence that the S'Hael sometimes took his meals here. One of the chairs was occupied by another S'Ahas.

Although he was sitting, it was easy to see that this S'Ahas was tall even for their kind. Instead of Sept colors, a black coarse woven fabric was wrapped around the lean body, evidence that he had been out of the Fastness recently on some business of the S'Hael. Shinal recognized him immediately as Hazz, one who was powerful with the Fathers Blood, perhaps second only to the S'Hael, but had not been seen for some time in the Fastness.

With a slight waive of his hand the S'Hael indicated for Shinal to sit as he began to pace. Back and forth the two Brothers watched their Master take measured steps first one way, then turn. Back and forth. Finally, stopping, the S'Hael turned and faced the pair and spoke, "Shinal, you were the first to greet me from the Mothers sleep, the first to kneel and give me homage. For that reason, you are to be trusted with an important secret, one that has been kept between only Hazz and myself." Shinal absorbed these words then nodded, his eyes hooded in thought.

The S'Hael took up pacing again before speaking, "The Keepers have turned from us. Hazz himself fought with an Invader while aiding the green ones in the attack on the mage city. The Invader was assisted by an Orda. Since then, Hazz has been searching for sign of both the Invader and the Keepers. Finally, he has found them both."

Turning to face Shinal, he was not surprised to see the Brother's eyes wide in shock. The idea that the Keepers would turn against them was unthinkable; the fact that a Keeper would aid an Invader was beyond madness. The S'Hael allowed Shinal's inner struggle to continue a moment longer before saying, "I know you are in pain over this revelation, Shinal. So was I. But I need you now. Are you with me?" Hazz watched the other Brother with a look of near disgust. He had urged the S'Hael to make use of an elder Brother for this new scheme. Shinal was too unpredictable, too weak. Gradually, Shinal's eyes lost their wild look, and he nodded his ascent.

"Good. Now Hazz will report his findings and we will plan." As Hazz began speaking, Shinal leaned closer to the older Hazz, soaking in his words. The S'Hael was pleased with his eagerness.

CHAPTER FOURTEEN

Fenn sat next to the Mage's Lady. She had insisted he call her Denna, but in his thoughts she was Jonathan Champion's woman and it was hard to change that feeling of deference. All around them, the residents of Haven celebrated the New Year.

The winter in the Lost Isles was not a cold time. Instead, the humid heat of the warm waters seemed to cool and provided a pleasant time of gentle rains and fresh breezes. Luckily, the rains had held off for the day and the sky was painted in a vivid blue, with a few patchwork clouds. In short, a perfect day for a party, and what a party it was.

With so many different races and peoples making up the diverse community, it was difficult to find a holiday that they all could share. The New Year, which in Fenn's experience was usually met with little cheer, had been transformed into a full scale festival by the Corsair community.

Dozens of booths had been set up all along the streets of the town each with its own theme. Some had games of chance and skill, others had candies and other delicacies that were not usually available. Fenn was shocked to find a yellow apple plum from his own home in the deep of the Blue Forest, far north of Hyberan. The crunchy sweet flavor had brought back memories of home. The streets were filled with children cramming their faces with sweets, people drinking ale and hard cider, and all of it free. Free!

After a long morning of festive fun and eating, the call went out for people to come to a cleared out area. Wooden bleachers had been placed all alongside a field. On either end, a wooden frame with netting had been built. Denna told him that they were called goals, and the game, soccer, was something that the Mage had showed them how to play.

Out on the field two teams of young people were lining up. Blue and red sashes around their waists identified what team they were on. At a signal, a circular leather ball was thrown in the middle of the field. Two men with white sashes ran up and down the field as the two teams tried to kick the ball into their opponent's goal. The spectators cheered loudly and Fenn could see some betting going on between the Corsairs. The game went on for almost two hours and the people ate, drank and cheered the whole time.

Later, with his belly near bursting, Fenn found himself seated next to Denna and Captain Spuros for a feast. Wooden tables and chairs had been set up in the town square surrounding the new huge clock. The large structure would sound out with a loud bell ring for each hour, keeping the town running timely. Fenn was still amazed at the size of the thing that now towered over the celebrants. The idea that such a thing could be made without the use of magic was still hard for him to get his head around.

All around him people ate and drank. Corsairs, bakers, smugglers, and craftsmen all passed large platters of cooked fish and bread, sharing food and drink giving no preference to race or magic-users. Even though he had been living in

Haven for some months, he had not witnessed such a large scale celebration in the town. Knowing he probably looked like a wide eyed fool, still he could not help turning his head this way and that to take it all in.

"Amazing, isn't it?" Denna asked him. Fenn swiveled his head back to his hostess. Dressed in a simple red dress, the Lady, as those in town referred to her, was an amazingly striking woman. Her eyes crinkled as she looked Fenn over with an amused expression.

"Yes, well, it is amazing, Lady. Truly." This brought a musical laugh that was so infectious that Fenn soon joined with his own laughter.

After their laughter had subsided, she asked, "Amazing, Honored Mage? Even in comparison to the Bright City? I am sure that the Mages of Hyberan could outshine this simple gathering." Taking a bite of some warm bread, she watched Fenn think carefully on his next words as she chewed.

"It's not that it is spectacular in what the Mages do for fanfare in Hyberan. But, here in Haven there seems to be happiness, and a pure contentment that defies the lack of . . ." He trailed off, not wishing to bring offense.

Swallowing her food, the Lady finished his thought, "Lack of magic?" At his nod, she continued, "Yes, I understand. I have never been to the Bright City, but I did travel the Mok Empire. While the Empress did not have the number of mages as your Mage Council, still there was evidence of Magic everywhere lighting the cities, cleaning the waters, growing the food." She stopped abruptly as if her words were getting close to an unsavory topic.

This time Fenn finished her thought, "The rawstones?" At her nod, Fenn said, "Yes, the stones are a symbol of civilization. At least that is what I had always thought. Yet, here is proof of what the world could be like without the rawstones or magic. Or rather, with limited magic."

"Yes, we still need our bit of magic, don't we Fenn? Haven could not exist without the Corsairs plundering, though we are becoming more self-sufficient. The Corsairs could not survive without the power of the Mage. So, it seems as far as we can go without it, still we have need of magic of our own in a world dominated by it. Which turns to my next thought, that it is getting dark."

Sure enough, the day was turning into twilight. Soon, the dark would make it impossible to see. Denna stood up on her seat, raising her hands for attention which gained her little attention. However, when Spuros yelled out for quiet, his Corsairs took up the call and in a few minutes the crowd was silent. From her perch, Denna spoke loudly, "As some of you know, the Mage had to leave us on an important mission." Many muttered excitedly at this revelation. While it was not a secret, the fact that the Mage might be gone was not something that Denna had wanted to be spoken openly about.

She waited until the mutters had quieted before going on, "But, he did not leave us defenseless. The Mages of Hyberan, in a great showing of support for our fight for freedom against the Mok's, have sent one of their own to help us." This was stretching the truth to its near breaking, but Spuros had advised that something needed to be done to show the people that magic could still aid them even in the Mage's absence. Denna waved to a pair of tall men who each carried an unlit torch. At her signal, each torch was lit and the men took their places opposite each other in the town square. Behind each man a group of children lined up each carrying an unlit lantern.

Fenn then stood and raised his arms. The silence of the hushed crowd seemed to deepen, as if everyone was holding their breath at the same time. Closing his eyes, Fenn called air. Gently, he coaxed the wind into two thin streams, one for each torch. At his signal, the children with the lanterns spread out from the torch bearers until they were evenly spaced along the edges of the square, twenty on each side.

Once the children were in place Fenn released the air streams, gently, slowly. Suddenly, the children gasped as the lanterns were all lifted out of their hands. Rising up over the celebrants heads, the lanterns drifted in lazy arcs to the torch bearers. One at a time, they were lit by the torches and Fenn then guided the lanterns until they positioned them twenty feet in the air above the feasting, bathing the town square in a warm orange light.

At his signal, Denna again addressed the crowd, "Eat and be well, everyone. Even in the dark of night we are kept safe through our own brave hearts and the magic of our friends." Waving to the cheering towns people, Denna allowed Spuros to help off the chair and reclaim her seat.

Still waving and laughing, she leaned close to Fenn as she asked out of the side of her mouth, "How long can you keep the lanterns up there?"

"All night, Lady. I have put a slight compulsion on each lantern, a simple thing. As long as no sudden storm blows in, they will stay put even without my attention."

Leaning over Denna squeezed his before saying hand, "Excellent, Fenn. Thank you."

"Good show, Mage Fenn. Good show!" Spuros barked out before he took a long pull of ale and slapped the skinnier man on the back, nearly knocking Fenn off his chair. With a smile, the Corsair Captain handed Fenn a full cup of ale and the two toasted to the uncertain future. After a few moments Spuros excused himself to deal with an argument that was escalating between two of his crewmen. With Denna chatting to a baker's wife across the table before walking off with the other woman Fenn was left alone at the table as he sipped from his cup. He smiled as two children tried to reach one of his floating lanterns. The smaller boy had gotten on a tall girl's shoulders and reached up with little fingers trying to touch the magical light. People gathered around the young pair, calling out encouragement. Fenn gave a small mental push and allowed the just out of reach light to lower so the boy could just touch the glowing lantern. The boy gave a cry of triumph as his fingers brushed the bottom of the light. Fenn sent the light upwards again to the clapping of the watching spectators.

Draining his ale, Fenn put his empty cup on the table, when a female voice said, "Let me fill that for you, honored mage." Momentarily startled, Fenn turned to see that a mundane woman had taken Spuros' vacated seat. Brown eyes brazenly appraised the mage, making Fenn's neck warm to an uncomfortable degree. She allowed her arm to lightly brush his shoulder as she filled his cup from a small pitcher. Taking a sip from his cup, his hand slightly shaking Fen took a moment to look more openly at his benefactress.

With black hair that was tied in a long braid down her back, the woman wore a low neck orange sleeveless dress that emphasized her sun browned skin. Unlike Ferrekei women who tended to be rather slim, this woman was all curves. Fenn's gaze drifted from soft brown shoulders to the low neckline of her dress which barely covered two rounded breasts that seemed intent on escape. A blue belt cinched at the waist emphasized the curvy outline of her hips.

"Do you often play with children?" The woman's voice seemed to have an underlying purr.

Caught in his ogling, Fenn ripped his gaze from her chest and stammered, "Ummm . . . yes. Well, errr, I do when I get the chance. I am not around children often." His mouth suddenly dry, Fenn drained the rest his ale.

The woman reached over and refilled his cup before asking, "Do mages in the bright city not have children?" With a casual air, she slid to the front of her seat, and Fenn felt her leg rub firmly against his own.

It was a well-known fact that many mund women performed sexual favors for their masters; or were required too. In fact, it was this treatment of female mundanes that the Sublime Sisterhood most complained of to the Mages Council in their campaign to help this magic-less folk. While he had never had sex with a mundane woman, he was still a bit unsettled at how forward the woman was being.

His heart beating faster, Fenn cleared his throat before answering, "Some do. Most feel that a family interferes in their duties. They . . . ." His words stopped in his throat as the woman leaned closer and placed a soft, warm hand on the back of his shoulder and slowly moved upward. Fenn nearly melted as delicate fingers began to dance slowly on the nape of his neck.

"What about lovers? Or would a lover interfere with a mages' duties?" Her face was very close to his own now that he could feel her warm scented breathe on his lips. Her free hand was now on his knee, slowly working up his leg.

His breathing was now harder as he quietly gasped out, "No. Many mages take lovers. We are people after all. We have needs . . . ahhhhhhh." Her hand now had reached his lap and expertly burrowed through his pants to grip him firmly. Fenn gave a quick look around and was grateful that no one was paying attention to the odd couple. He barely suppressed a groan as female fingers began to rub up and down, using the fabric of his pants for friction.

"My name is Laith, honored mage. I have been watching you for a long time. I am glad to know that mages take lovers. Very glad." Laith suddenly stopped her ministrations, causing Fenn to give out a low cry of dismay. Chuckling, Laith stood up and took his hand. Rising a bit awkwardly due to his aroused condition, Fenn allowed her to lead him away from the town square.

From around a corner, Denna watched the pair disappear down the street towards Laith's apartment. She smiled to herself. Laith had been cautiously stalking the mage since his arrival. The dark haired beauty had approached Denna about arranging a rendezvous. From all appearances, Laith had been most convincing.

Denna was happy for both of them. It would be good for Fenn to experience some tenderness here in Haven. Humming to herself, Denna turned and walked back to the celebration which had now moved back into the streets.

CHAPTER FIFTEEN

Denna stood on the wall watching the tiny dots in the distance get slowly bigger and bigger. It was months since the Mage had left, weeks since the New Year celebration in Haven, and yet those times felt like they were much further in the past. The only thing that mattered now were those tiny dots.

Kay waited in respectful silence behind her. The young Gurashi had been the Mage's personal aid the last two years and beside himself with disappointment when he had been told him that he could not accompany the Mage on his mission. Perceptive as usual, the Mage knew that Kay would need a new duty to occupy him. Thus, Denna was now the beneficiary of Kay's attentions.

In fact, the Gurashi had been amazingly resourceful and useful in the days that followed the Mage's departure. His ability to keep Denna on a schedule which allowed her to deal with the preparations for the defense of the town and also the everyday running of the community was impressive. Although he was her personal aid, she soon learned that Kay was not a push over when it came to her personal health. Just this morning he let her sleep in after a late night of preparations even though she had instructed him to wake her early for a meeting with Master Orkus. Knowing he had done it on purpose, she had proceeded to explain to Kay that if he could not follow simple instructions she would find a replacement. The young Gurashi had simply bowed, given an insincere apology, and began giving her the day's appointments as she glared at him over a simple fruit breakfast. In truth, she had needed the extra sleep and felt much more invigorated the rest of the day, but would not admit that to Kay.

The past few weeks had been a hectic whirl of plans going into action. Once the Mok fleet had been sighted Spuros and his Corsairs embarked on a campaign of delay and deceit. Attacking from fog banks, boarding ships at night to set fire to sails and fowl the rigging, slitting the throats of Mok captains and navigators, anything to delay the attackers and give Haven time to prepare.

The walls already were as strong as they could be. Looking down the wall she saw that men and women manned the battlements armed with arrows, spears, and blades all ready to defend their homes. The children and elders had already been taken to the Mage's windswept mountain cave. With the aid of an ingenious rope and pulley system devised by Master Orkus, Sister Ella was able to get all of those unable to defend themselves to the safety of the cave and make use of the hide holes that honeycombs the place. Thinking of Master Orkus, she looked down the wall where the good Master was now making some adjustments to his new toys.

They were in fact not toys, but the concept had started that way. Mage Fenn's dose of life without magic, or at least minimal magic, had resulted in the current machines when the mage had seen a group of children hurling small rocks at each other with toys Master Orkus had made. The result was a wide wooden box with a large spring lever, and a bowl-shaped bucket at the end of a wooden arm. The first attempts at using the contraptions things on a larger level had met with disappointing results, but Fenn's idea had lit a spark in Master Orkus' head that could not be quenched. The final results were four machines that could hurl projectiles up to one thousand feet from the walls. Wheels had been added to allow movement, but it still took three strong men to roll the machines any distance down the wall.

Master Orkus finished his adjustments and approached her with an odd limping gait. His walk was not the only thing odd about the good Master. In fact, he looked as though two very different sets of body parts had been welded together for some unfathomable purpose. The right arm was large with sculpture like muscles, with strong thick fingers. In contrast, the left arm was shorter and slim, the fingers thin and delicate. Likewise, his legs followed the same pattern, one large and thickly muscled, the other shorter and slim. In testament to his ingenuity, Master Orkus had constructed a flexible leg brace for his weaker leg, with small tightly fitted gears at the knee and ankle that allowed some stiff flexibility. Over his large shoulder he lugged one of the wooden arms from his machines.

Denna called out a greeting, and Orkus opened his mouth in what for him was a smile. Drool dribbled out the side of his mouth, a normal occurrence given that the man's tongue was a bit too large for his mouth. A wide, plain face that would have been pleasant but for the thick dark eyebrows that gave him a constant thunderous look turned toward Denna. He shambled over to her and gave a clumsy bow, "Thu nees som fix."

Listening to Orkus was like hearing someone try to talk with a thick sock in their mouth. After dealing with the odd man for the past two years Denna had learned to translate his speech. "Excellent, Master Orkus. I hope it will be up to speed before our guests arrive?"

"Oh, yef fady. Oh yef." Orkus bowed again and walked down the wall toward his shop, cackling to himself as he went. Denna watched his retreating back for a moment before turning her gaze back out to sea.

THE ARMADA arrived in the night. The ships slid quietly toward the harbor, or where the harbor had been. The wooden docks had long since been taken down to make any landing difficult. This was the only location on the island that a ship of any size could hope to make landfall. Still, small groups of armed defenders patrolled the rest of the island in the event the Mok's attempted to gain a different foothold.

The stone walls had been built to an impressive height over the last year. Arrow loops ringed the top of the wall giving archers prime views of their targets. Thousands of arrows in numerous bushels were the result of months of work by the residents and lined the wall every few feet.

The only entrance through the defenses was the large oak double doors that connected the harbor to the town. Behind these doors another set, this one of metal, provided an additional protection should fire be used. Now shut and reinforced with iron bars the two sets of doors would have to be rammed down to have any chance of being used as a way to breach the defenses. Evil looking murder holes in the archway over the doors would prove the death of any invader who could expect a warm welcome of flesh burning oil and boiling water.

In the event of a breach of the wall, the wood from the harbor docks had been used to make bridges connecting the roof top of each building in the town allowing defenders to fall back from the walls. Clay pots filled with oil would ensure that the temporary bridges could be burned to avoid the attackers using the bridges themselves. The oil would also be used to burn down the building as the defenders abandoned it. This would prevent the attackers from using a rooftop as a base and ensure that the defenders maintained a higher vantage point to fire arrows down on Mok heads.

Wooden palisades had been built at certain places on the streets. The blocked intersections would provide vicious obstructions. The invaders progress would be stopped for a time at the palisades, making them sitting targets for defenders to pour down arrows from the rooftops.

Finally, the last line of defense was the Manse itself. Little had to be done to the building due to its location on the heights above the town. The narrow winding path leading up to the Manse would make it difficult for any attackers to reach the top in force. Additional arrows and weapons awaited any fortunate defenders that survived to this last defense. In the event that the Manse was overrun, the defenders would make for the Mage's cave to help protect the elders and children. This was a final outcome that the defenders, watching the approaching ships, did not wish to contemplate.

Denna, Liss, Kay and Master Orkus waited on the walls together. Fenn was stationed back behind the walls, giving him some added protection. Since he was their only mage, it was decided that he should stay back from the walls and apply his skills on an as needed basis. They had gone over the possible scenarios of how the battle would play out so many times that it had invaded their dreams. Now, under a full moon night they watched as six Mok ships coasted towards them. There was only space enough for two ships at a time to enter the harbor area, and nowhere to tie up due to the recent absence of the docks.

Denna watched as the first two ships glided silently into the harbor and lowered their anchors. She could almost feel the tension from the Mok sailors and marines at the inactivity from the walls. As part of the plan, no torches were lit and all of the defenders were to stay low and out of sight until the signal. As she watched the sailors' ready skiffs to begin offloading the marines, Denna mentally calculated with a fearful twinge in her stomach the numbers they faced.

Spuros had explained that a crew of fifty sailors was required to sail a Mok ship. Most of these were not really sailors but engineers and mechanics that operated and maintained the rawstone engines and equipment of the vessel. A fighting force of up to two hundred Mok marines would be on each ship. Six ships would mean that there would be over one thousand of the Empires elite warriors to be dealt with. That did not include any rawstone artillery and armaments, and the additional three hundred crew members that could participate in the attack as well.

It was quickly decided that any hand to hand fighting would have to be limited if the defenders were to have any chance of survival. Going blade to blade against Mok marines was a challenge for veteran soldiers let alone residents of a coastal town like Haven. Arrows and other projectile weapons were the only way that Haven stood a chance. Kill the enemy from a distance to avoid any face to face confrontation if at all possible. Kill and bleed the enemy from a distance. Use the Empire's arrogant faith in its military juggernaut against itself by presenting an elusive target that continued to fall back on defenses while raining down death from above.

Denna's stomach continued to sour as she watched the first skiffs reach the sandy shore. Even in the moonlight, the Mok's appeared as dark shapes jumping from the small crafts to the beach. Soon, a large group of marines milled quietly on the shore, waiting for their fellows to join them. At her nod, Master Orkus lit a torch and waived it over his head.

Along the walls, braziers were lit, flooding the night with firelight. Fire arrows were shot onto the beach, sticking out of the sand like flaming snakes bathing the shore in orange and red light. The soft thrum of bow strings filled the night as archers used the firelight to find targets. Soon, the cry of wounded marines filled the night.

At another signal from Master Orkus, his grown up toys were pushed up to the walls on squeaking wheels. A few minutes later, large clay balls filled with oil soared through the air toward the motionless two ships. On impact the clay shattered, spewing oil over deck boards, rigging, and Mok sailors. Oil doused sailors could be heard cursing as they scurried and slipped on the now treacherous ship decks. A moment later large balls of fire made slow arcs toward the ships. In the fiery light, Denna could see the terror of the sailors as they realized the horrible death that traveled through the air toward them. Moks began jumping in the black waters, trading a fire death for a watery one.

Once the fire balls reached the closest ship, its wooden deck was encased in the flames. The second ship first caught fire in its mast and rigging. The two blazing vessels seemed to be having a race of sorts to see which one could burn down to the water line first.

The sounds of burning and dying Moks caused unwanted tears to leave streaks down Denna's cheeks. Not wishing to wipe at her face to bring attention to her predicament, Denna kept her gaze forward, watching the deadly scene before her when she felt someone touch her hand. Startled, she turned to see the strange grey clad Liss step closer and offer a handkerchief. Smiling with silent thanks, Denna quickly wiped her tears away and offered Liss her hand. After a moment's hesitation, Liss took her hand and the two stood quietly and watched from the walls.

THE BLUE waters sparkled in the sunny day. White puffy clouds floated in lazy patterns in the sky. At any other time, the view would have been beautiful. Now it just made Admiral Jesh's anger smolder even more as he looked on the un-breached walls.

The battle plan had initially worked out to perfection. Twenty six ships sailed from the Capital. Twenty ships set out to seek out and destroy the Corsairs to prevent any interference with the attack on the island. The remaining six ships transported the fighting force that would be used to raze the island town to the ground.

Given that his small fleet had not seen a Corsair ship on their journey indicated the success of one phase of the plan. Now Admiral Jesh was feeling that odd mixture of fury and fear. He was furious that the first attempt at creating a beachhead on the island had suffered disastrous failure. Twice again he had attempted to gain the walls with nothing to show for it but more dead marines. He had no rawstone artillery or weapons of any kind to throw at these island wretches. Such weapons were too valuable to use on such an easy task, he had been told. His superiors had thought an elite fighting force of Mok marines more than enough to raze the town. They had not counted on any type of formidable defenses in place.

Jesh ground his teeth together as he contemplated the current situation. He had lost five hundred of his marines. Even if he managed to take the walls now he had six hundred marines left to deal with the defenders. He had no idea of what other nasty surprises awaited past the walls. Of their own accord, his eyes found his two strange 'guests.'

The two creatures filled him with an uneasy feeling. They had joined the force at the very last minute, at the insistence of the Empress. Black cloth covered everything except dark alien eyes, and long fingered black hands. His two guests had kept themselves to the ships hold until they had reached the island two days before. Since then, the pair had emerged and simply watched the battle, never taking their gazes off the tall stone walls. No eating, no drinking, no sleeping for the last two days; just watching. As if sensing his scrutiny, one of them turned toward the admiral and slowly walked toward him.

Stopping a few feet from him, the thing tilted its head at a sinuous angle and asked, "Are you finished, Admiral?" The voice made Jesh's flesh crawl. He was the survivor of numerous battles, had ordered thousands of soldiers to their deaths for the glory of the Empress, yet this thing had unnerved him; with its voice.

Calling up his courage, Jesh spoke harshly, "What do you mean, you? Finished with what?"

Again the head tilt, "Why, killing your soldiers, of course."

Jesh now bared his teeth in a snarl. Voice or no voice, he did not so cheaply sell his men on the battle field, "You are guests of the Empress, so I owe you that courtesy. But have a care how you speak to me of my men, you cursed . . . thing!"

At his words, the 'thing' made a strange sibilant noise, like hissing laughter before speaking, "Of course brave admiral, but perhaps we could assist you in not killing *all* of your troops before taking the walls? Would that please you? Would it please your green empress?"

Hours later, Admiral Jesh watched the skiff approach the beach where so many of his men had died. The two black clad creatures stood at the prow of the small craft, their eyes locked on the walls in front of them. Four Mok marines manned the vessel's oars, their strokes swift and sure. Jesh hoped he would see the men again.

WORD HAD spread quickly that the Mok's were sending in another ship. Denna was a bit surprised at the sight of the small skiff as it made its way toward the beach. Before now, all the attacks had come at night. This incursion in the bright light of day was bizarre. The fact that only a single skiff with six figures in its hold seemed like suicide.

As the skiff came into range, defenders arrows flew from the walls towards the easy target. Just as the missiles reached the boat, they suddenly disintegrated. Denna hissed in frustration as a second flight of arrows met the same end.

"Master Orkus!" at her shout, the good Master loped over. Guessing her question, he said, "No, goof, fady. The boat ifs too shmall for my beaufies."

Denna nodded and replied, "Too small? Well, we shall just have to wait and see." Giving his awkward bow, Orkus strode back down the wall to his machines. Kay and Liss joined her and the trio silently watched as the skiff came to rest on the sandy beach bellow the walls. Two tall black figures disembarked. Hurriedly, the four Mok rowers pushed off from the beach and made their escape.

Wrapped in black cloth of some kind, their bodies and features were completely covered. One of the black clad figures began tracing something in the sand, the other stood, arms wide waiting. More arrows from the walls fell on the duo, only to be burned to ash. Liss stepped forward and put her hands on the ledge of the wall, peering down at the two below.

As the defenders watched, the figure below completed its scratching in the sand. A square with a circle in the middle of it stared up at the defenders, like some odd shaped eye. The black pair then stepped back, each standing on either end of strange pattern. In unison, the pair on the beach drew daggers from their belts. Putting the blades to their arms, the figures made three precise cuts to each arm. Slowly, they walked around the pattern, dripping blood into the recently made shape. Their bloody business done, they stopped and simply looked up at the defenders, waiting.

Suddenly, where the blood had dripped, the square was engulfed in black fire. Even from the height of the walls, Denna could feel the heat from the dark flames. The fires roared higher, higher, until they towered ten feet into the air. Then just as suddenly, they went out. In the middle of the square where the circle had been, another dark shape now stood.

This new arrival was not dressed to conceal. A bright white garment of some kind covered its pelvis and torso. A reptilian like face looked up at the walls. Black scales covered long arms that ended in jagged claws; claws that clutched a staff with a white stone attached to it. Instead of a nose, two thin slits came together at a point. Plump lips formed an almost sensuous mouth that a pair of long fangs protruded over. Dark alien eyes regarded the defenders.

Liss hissed, "S'Hael."

Denna and Kay each gave Liss a questioning look. A grey hand held up forestalled any questions, "No time for questions now. You have to clear the walls, fall back to the wooden bridges. I can delay him for a time, a short time. Now. Move!" At the last word, Liss leapt over the wall down to the beach below. Denna cried out and rushed to the wall only to see Liss floating slowly down, until the grey creature landed lightly on the sand in front of the dark ones.

Her mind awhirl, Denn did not hear Kay's question until he asked it a second time, "What do we do?" The young voice had a touch of desperation in it. Looking down the length of the wall, hundreds of faces watched her intently, waiting for her orders.

Below on the sand, Liss faced the three dark creatures, blocking the wooden double doors. The one with the staff began speaking in a commanding voice. To Denna's ears, only a garble of unintelligible sibilant hissing noises.

Liss responded in the common tongue, "The Mothers have rejected you, S'Hael. Leave this place." It was obvious that Liss' answer did not please the scaly skinned S'Hael. Pointing a black clawed finger at Liss, it shouted something and pointed to the defenders at the wall. Liss spread arms wide, and a grey twilight glow spread out like a shimmering plate, covering the space in between the two. Black fire hit the plate, making it waiver. Liss took two steps back, as if being pushed by a great weight. Slowly, like a slow tide, the black fire crept closer to the walls.

Kay grabbed Denna by the shoulder and pulled her away from the wall yelling, "We need to listen to Liss. We need to run. Now!" Struggling against his grip, Denna broke free from his grasp in time to see black flames leap up to the left side of the wall. Men and women screamed in torment as their clothing and hair caught fire. In moments, all that remained of a hundred defenders were burnt husks. Denna's mind went numb as she looked at what had, just moments before been her friends and neighbors. Arms hung loosely at her sides as she stood rooted to the spot, unable to move. She barely noticed that Kay had picked her up and ran with her over his shoulder. Sitting her down gently, Kay pushed the wooden bridge to the cobbles stones below.

A large explosion rocked the wall, making great cracks in the mortar. A second later, the large double doors first buckled and then broke open, sending bits of wood and metal flying through the air. Denna feared that more black fire would boil out of the now broken doors but nothing followed. Through the doorway the Mok ships could be seen making steady progress towards the shore.

A grey shape appeared on the top of the wall and gracefully leaped to the safety of the rooftop. Liss sat down with a tired grunt next to Denna. Grey cloth smoked as if Liss had been cooked in a coal filled oven.

Denna leaned over and demanded, "What was that thing?"

Liss was silent, eyes staring off into space, then answered, "A S'Hael. A very powerful one in fact. He and I have met before, though I don't think he remembered." Liss shuddered then as if recalling a bad dream. Seeing that Liss was not going to be forth coming with any additional information, Denna rose from her seat and surveyed the situation.

All of the wooden bridges had been removed. Men and women now scurried on their designated roof tops, testing bow strings, heating oil and boiling water on small cooking stoves, and of course dressing wounds. Denna watched as Fenn flew down to pick up a middle aged woman whose arms were black and red with burns. The mage would be shuttling the wounded back to the last row of roofs where they could receive some medical attention from the herbalist, Master Thurga, and his assistants. She wondered how long the mage could keep this up before he exhausted himself.

For the first time she realized that besides Liss and Kay, Denna was alone on the roof top. Peering around, she saw that a number of roof tops were empty or had few defenders. When her eyes fell on the blackened part of the wall where the black fires had claimed so many, she realized that they no longer had the numbers to maintain the first row of defenses. Calling out to the nearest roof, she got the attention of Master Orkus. It was time to change the plan.

CHAPTER SIXTEEN

He both loved and hated the Mok Capital, Hett thought to himself as he squeezed through the mass of bodies that logged the Grand Market. He loved the excitement of so many peoples coming together in one place, hearing multiple languages arguing and laughing back and forth through the air, the wonderful tinkling sound of silver and gold coins exchanging hands. It was all very intoxicating.

But, what overshadowed this wonderful commercial camaraderie was the oppressive presence of the Moks and their damned Empress. Many of the people who made up this wonderful mix of commerce and diversity were members of conquered races from all corners of the Empire. The Empresses hunger for more and more lands, slaves, and wealth for her people was an appetite that in the long history of the Empire had never been satisfied. Hett's own Riskh people, though they shared the swampy origin of their Mok cousins, were treated like lesser class citizens, a servant race.

Hett had visited numerous cities in his travels, even the Bright City of Hyberan. Yet, no other metropolis compared to the Empress' Capital. The Mok city held the normal bureaucratic buildings, the military barracks, markets and other structures of a large city. But what set it apart were the Brood Houses.

Dotted throughout the metropolis, the Brood Houses looked like nothing more than large mud colored ant hills sticking out of the ground. Most were over three stories tall and as wide as a whole city block. Here, the Brood Mothers, daughters of the Empress, plotted and schemed to gain advantage for their brood kin. It was here that the Mok young were trained in the methods of empire. In the Brood Houses rested the true power of the Empire.

But now, things might change. The Empire's resources were stretched to their limits in this costly war with the mages. In fact, Hett's sources within the Imperial bureaucracy informed him that the war was expending more resources than what had first been predicted, far more. Whispers filled the streets that a fleet of Imperial ships had been defeated by the Corsairs of the Lost Isles and that now the Empire could not afford any additional conflicts until the mages were defeated. This is what Hett was counting on.

His plan with the Mage, Jonathan Champion, did not rest on the creation of a new conflict, but a disaster; A disaster for the Empress that would lead to the downfall of the oppressive Mok Empire. Such a monumental event would create opportunities for the Riskh and all the other enslaved nations under the yoke of the Empress. Hett's mind filled with the possibilities of a future without the Mok's, without the Empress. So focused on his own internal musings that Hett did not notice the large green hand that reached for him until it was too late.

Moments, hours?, later Hett woke with a bitter taste in his mouth. Almost involuntarily he tried to spit the vile taste from his mouth. Tagga Serum. He recognized the unsavory concoction immediately. Someone had doused him with the stuff, probably putting some of the liquid on a cloth rag and then placing it over his mouth and nose. Grimly, he shook his wrists together and felt the dead weight of chains. He did not need to move his feet to know that all four of his limbs were encased in iron shackles and that he was, for the moment, at someone else's complete disposal. As he began to quietly work his way loose of the constraints, Hett took in his current surroundings.

He was sitting on the floor of a dimly lit room. A large desk against the far wall was covered with papers of various sizes. Crisp newly made white paper sheets vied with yellowed parchments for supremacy on the wooden tables' surface. An abacus sat to one side of the paperwork alongside several small leather bags. The glint of gold from one of the bags with its top open indicated the contents of the other bags.

Dim light seeped through a small dirty window over the table. At least, the glass seemed to be dirty. Hett knew that if he examined the window carefully it would show that the dirt was in fact a syrupy sticky substance designed to give the place the appearance of neglect and abandonment to a casual observer from outside. A thick wooden door with an iron bolt guarded the rooms only entrance and exit. The smell of sea water indicated that Hett was probably in or around the Imperial dockyards.

There were thousands of such rooms in the Empire. Hett had been in his fair share and operated three of his own. It was a fencing operation, probably operated by one of the local dockyard gangs. New owners of stolen or misappropriated goods from ships and local vendors would bring their newly acquired items here to obtain official looking documentation of ownership. The newly legal owners could then go on their merry way to sell their now legitimate goods to honest buyers who were unaware of the nature of the property they were about to purchase. Then, the fence would take his cut from the sale of the goods and document it here, where the off the book records of the gang could gage the gangs profitability.

Hett thought through all of this as he released his wrist from the first manacle. With a slight smile of triumph, he began to work on the second when the door opened and a Mok entered. A familiar face made Hett stop working on the manacle and just stare. He felt his mouth go dry as he watched the grey clothed Mok shut the door and reapply the bolt. Hett could not help the look of utter confusion laced with fear that covered his face.

The Mok pulled up a wobbly chair next to the Riskh and smiled, "Hello, my dear Hett. Have you missed me?"

"You're dead." Hett's voice sounded flat, as if the shock of this meeting had driven all emotions from his mind. The Mok laughed as if Hett had said the funniest of jokes.

"Now, my dear, sweet Hett. How could I go off and die and leave you all alone in this dangerous world of ours? Who would look after you?"

Calphan leaned back on the wobbly chair and watched as Hett grappled with his emotions. He knew that his appearance would shake the sneaky Riskh. But there was something else in Hett's mannerism that was unexpected. The normally dapper and quick thinking Riskh was terrified. He was doing well to hide it, but Calphan's appearance had unbalanced Hett in a way that for a brief moment, he had let undiluted terror drip from his eyes. A moment later Hett clapped his hands together, which made a clinking chain sound due to the manacles and exclaimed in a very convincing jubilant voice.

"Spy Master! How good to see you! I am overwhelmed with joy to find you alive. How your enemies must be squirming in fear at your return."

"Oh yes my dear Hett, they would be squirming if they knew I still walked the streets of the living. But, alas I must keep a rather low profile for the now." Removing a small key from his pocket, Calphan leaned over and opened the manacle that Hett had managed to remove from his wrist. Holding it out to his guest, Calphan waited until Hett sighed and placed his wrist back into the manacle and watched as it was clipped shut.

Patting Hett's hand affectionately, Calphan beamed, "Now, isn't that better, my dear Hett? You are free from those awful thoughts of escape and can now concentrate on simply answering my questions."

Hett licked dry lips before saying, "Of course, Spy Master. But how can an insignificant Riskh like myself be of any use to your august person? I am but a small fish in this large fishbowl, as you know."

Nodding in agreement at his words, Calphan said, "True, true, my sweet Hett. There are other of my little fishes that I could send my simple inquiries too, but none that have the reputation for being so, ummmmm, . . . what's the word I am trying to think of . . . ?"

"Reliable? Discrete?" Hett offered.

"I was thinking, 'More concerned with his own physical welfare to even consider lying to me.' Would that be accurate, my dear Hett?"

That's more of a phrase than a word, Spy Master, Hett thought to himself. But he could not refute the Mok's observation. Clearing his throat, he asked, "What can I do for you, Spy Master? You of course have all of my humble attention."

Leaning forward so his lips were almost touching Hett's ear, his eyes wide with insincere innocence, Calphan whispered, "Where are they?"

Hett's heart began beating like a hammer against his chest. Looking up at the smiling face of his captor, Hett's thoughts ran wild. *What does he know? Does he know anything? Does he know everything?*

As his mind raced, Hett watched with almost detached interest as the Spy Master removed a slim, wickedly curved knife that reminded Hett of something that fishermen used to fillet fish. Slowly, the blade came closer, and closer, until it lightly rested on Hett's throat. The smile got wider and warmer as if the Mok talked with a treasured relative. The warm smile did nothing to soften the hard eyes of the Spy Master. Cold, hard, calculating.

The blade rested for a moment longer before Calphan asked, "Why the hesitation, Hett? Do you know where they are? Why are they leaving?" Hett's dark terror filled thoughts were pierced by a small light of confused hope, *Leaving? Who left?*

"Spy Master, please I want to be as useful to you as I possibly can. My respect for you has no bounds, but if you could perhaps provide a small bit of . . . ." Hett's voice ended in a squeak as the knife bit slightly into his neck. A warm trickle of green hued blood dripped down the blade, but Calphan never lost his smile as he studied Hett's face. After a few moments, the blade was lifted and Hett blew out a breath of relief.

"Why Hett, please let us get to the end of this game. The Riskh have been leaving, I would even use the phrase fleeing the Capital and I wish to know why. I doubt that this revelation has anything to do with my current project, but I need to make sure you see before I myself, leave on an errand for the Empress. So, tell, tell, my good Hett."

Hett felt both relief and fear at this question. Relief that his three companions were not the subject of the Spy Master's inquiry, and fearful that any information he gave to his captor would lead the Mok to uncovering the carefully laid plan. He had hoped that with most of the Imperial Intelligence community concentrated on the war effort that the activities of the Riskh as a whole would be ignored, or at least viewed as a low priority. Hett had not told his three companions that he had sent a very discrete message to his people in the Capital to make arrangements to be elsewhere in the next several days. How could he not? He was sure the Mage would understand that if they were successful in their plan, that several thousand Riskh would be killed? So, Hett had sent the word out to ensure as many of his people as possible could reach safety. What he had not counted on was anyone, let alone one of the Empresses' own Spy Masters taking the time to pay attention to the comings and goings, mostly goings, of the Riskh. As he looked into the smiling face of the Spy Master, Hett felt the careful planning of this venture coming undone like so many threads in a cheap scarf.

"DAMN." JONATHAN Champion paced inside their quarters, his irritation increasing with each step. Tyrell watched the tall man walk to the far corner of the room, reach the wall, then turn smartly around and continue his march. While a large room, much larger than their ship cabin, it still was not a space that was conducive to the type of angry pacing that his friend was attempting. Though, in all fairness, irritation was something that all three of them felt at the moment.

Hett was late. The resourceful Riskh had been obsessive about his punctuality. Every day he checked in on the three of them, bringing food, drink, and an update on the happenings in the Mok Capital. As the days went by, the time for their great endeavor came closer and closer. It was vital that things be timed perfectly.

At the moment, the city was filled to bursting with Mok troops getting ready to embark for the front. The Empress had stripped her southern garrisons in order to allow her generals the troops to punch a hole through Hyberan's forces. Such an aggressive maneuver might sweep away all opposition and lead to the very walls of the Bright City itself. Tyrell was unsure that Hyberan and its allies knew of the size of the force that would very shortly be heading north.

Tyrell's unease increased as he watched his friend continue his pacing. He knew that the Mage had some important errand that needed to be performed today, and that required Hett to lead him to the harbor. Tyrell knew little of this errand but the lack of information did not bother him. It was just something that had changed about his friend that he and Grach had to accept.

At finding their lost friend, he and Grach, who now dozed in a chair, had been ecstatic. But, in a very short amount of time he and Grach had seen the changes in their friend. Jonathan Champion had become very secretive in the last two years. His lost memories seemed to have included the trusting bond that had once existed between the three of them. While being kept in the dark concerning certain parts of the plan did anger Tyrell at times, the fact that their trio was back together over road any other petty feelings.

"Damn." Champion's voice broke through Tyrell's musings. The Mage turned and looked at the closed door for a moment. As Tyrell watched the Mage closed his eyes in concentration. A glow covered the tall man's body, and he suddenly disappeared from view. The sound of footsteps toward the door was the only indication of where the man had gone. The door opened letting in the sound of busy city life, and then closed leaving the two companions in relative quiet. Tyrell kept his eyes on the door as Grach continued to doze.

WITHOUT HETT'S guidance it had taken Champion most of the remaining daylight hours to find the city's harbor. Now, it was dark, the only light provided by the smoking rawstone street lamps. He walked as far from the lamp light as he could, finding a secluded place of dark and quiet that still allowed access to the water. The wooden dock creaked quietly under his invisible feet. Stopping at the end of the dock, he gazed into the dark waters as if trying to peer below its dark surface.

"Waven." He almost whispered the name. He waited to the count of ten heart beats, the said again, "Waven."

The waters began to boil and churn. He looked around the dock to make sure his clandestine meeting was a private one. Satisfied, he turned his eyes back to the water as a large body breached the surface.

Waven looked tired. At least that is what the kraken's appearance seemed to portray. The creatures many arms seemed to lack some of the animation that they exhibited while back in Haven. The red eyes seemed a bit pale as they glared up at the Mage.

"Hello, Waven."

"Foul cursed Mage! I hate this place. The Green Ones make the waters filthy with their stink. I should have eaten you when I had the chance."

Champion nodded at the harsh words as if the creature had simply inquired about his health, "So nice to see that you are doing well, my friend. How flow the waters?"

The waters churned again, the Kraken's arms began to swirl wildly. The large body rose slightly out of the water. Champion watched the spectacle for a few moments before asking again in an admonishing tone, "Waven. Do the waters flow?"

His words seemed to calm the creature. The waters quieted and Waven lowered its body back into the water. Champion watched as the creature calmed. He waited for the answer.

"Yes, mage. The waters flow."

CALPHAN WALKED the market square thinking of his talk with the unfortunate Hett. It only took the messy removal of one of the Riskh's ears and two of his fingers for Hett to begin to cooperate. Though Calphan did not believe the elaborate epic story that Hett eventually told concerning migrating Riskh due to fear of the Empire losing the war, still after the second finger he was fairly certain that Hett would go to his grave before he told the truth. But in reality, Hett was a valuable asset concerning happenings in the Capital and Calphan was never fond of letting assets go so easily. This was why unconscious Hett was now draped over the shoulder of one of the company of Mok guards that followed the Spy Master.

One of Calphan's other sources had informed him that Hett had been spending time in the Grand Market, a location in the Capital that was not one of the places the little scoundrel usually haunted. For some reason, Calphan's internal warning signs had gone off during his time with Hett. Call it a hunch, a sixth sense, or just a mental itch that needed to be scratched, he just needed to know. Calpahn knew before he began his mission to find Jonathan Champion that he needed to unravel this little mystery.

There were few merchants in the market place as darkness fell on the Capitol. After questioning a few of these late night venders in their stalls, Calphan learned that Hett had been seen going in and out of a building that was known to rent rooms out with few questions asked. Ordering that the guard holding Hett stay outside, Calphan and the rest of the troop entered the building as quietly as possible. Cowing the landlord into providing a key was a simple matter. Now standing outside the room Calphan waited until the guards had lined up three on each side of the door. At his nod, the largest guard kicked the door open and the other five rushed in. A moment later, Calphan entered.

The room was a mess of kicked over furniture, scattered clothing, and broken plates. Two figures struggled fruitlessly in the arms of the guardsmen. Calphan's face was first shocked, and then spread into a feral smile as he exclaimed.

"My friends, how I have missed you!"

CHAMPION ENJOYED the walk back from the harbor using a path through alleys that Hett had described to him. The night was pleasantly warm with a slight breeze. The moon was a slim sliver of white light giving the night a feeling of mystery. The enjoyable walk was short lived.

When he approached the Grand Market he noticed the number of lights. Rawstone lamps had been placed all around the large market square. Even stranger, the merchant stalls had all been removed to reveal a wide open space, filled to overflowing with Mok soldiers. The rawstone light glinted off of blades and rawstone weapons. In the air was a feeling of tense readiness. Champion stepped into the darkness of the alley to avoid the light. While his invisibility cloak was very handy, it still did not protect him from showing a shadow.

Peering around the alley corner, the sight made his guts turn into an unhealthy knot. In the middle of the square Hett, Tyrell, and Grach were there with heads bent and kneeling, all three bound in chains. Before each of his companions a large fire sharpened stake had been driven into the ground. Behind them three Mok soldiers stood, each with long curved blades resting on the back of the neck of the captives.

Next to the captives stood a group of Moks dressed in various colored robes. Champion could feel the faint tremors of magic from these Moks. Mages.

Taking on mages would be something new. At least, he had no memory of testing his powers against other mages. As he thought about his options a Mok dressed in a grey cloak stepped away from the captives and called out, "Jonathan Champion! I know you are out there! We have been talking with your friends here! Please come and join the party!"

For some reason the Mok's voice brought an inkling of a memory, something distasteful. But Champion did not have time to consider any clouded memories at the moment. He had to act. Removing the cloak, he stepped out into the middle of the alley.

"Aeris, Cinder, attend me."

The two apparitions appeared next to him, their countenances as grim as his own. In lock step unison, the trio stepped out into the light of the market square. Immediately the soldiers formed a protective barrier in front of the Mok mages. A shout from the grey clad Mok caused the soldiers to create a gap in their ranks. As the three approached through the soldiers, the Mok mages stood on either side of the three captives; four on either side.

Eight Mok mages. Eight. Champion thought to himself as they stopped just in front of the grey dressed Mok. The Mok smiled as he looked the three of them over.

"Jonathan Champion, you do show up in the most unexpected places! To think, if I had not decided to drop in on my good friend Hett, I would be on my way to the Lost Isles in search of you! But here you came to me. Truly, we were meant for each other, don't you think?" A part of Champion's mind thought that in another setting, he might think the Mok charming. "Do I know you?"

By the strained look on his face, the question seemed to knock the Mok off of his cocky pedestal, for a moment. But just a moment, he recovered his suave mannerism before saying, "Surely you jest my friend. I am Calphan as you know. We have such a unique history. We have so much to catch up on."

At an unspoken signal, Aeris and Cinder took two steps away from him, each seemingly squaring off against four Mok mages. Seeing this, Calphan moved behind the three captives spreading his hands in a placating gesture. "Come now my friend. At the first sign of magic my three companions here with the swords will remove three heads. Then what? A mage battle that you and your two friends have little chance of winning? Then I may be forced to use those nasty spikes that have been so recently sharpened. What a waste."

Champion ground his teeth at the truth of the words. Looking at his three companions Tyrell suddenly raised his head revealing a bruise blackened eye that showed that he had not been taken easily. Giving a sharp toothed smile and meeting Champions gaze the blue man growled. "Burn them all, friend Champion."

Fierce words. Courageous words. Which made it impossible for Champion to sacrifice their lives. With a thought, Aeris and Cinder disappeared. The tension in the air seemed to dissipate with the departure of the two manifestations.

Champion stood motionless for a moment meeting Calphan's gaze before motioning with his hand toward his three friends. At a word from Calphan the three soldiers sheathed their blades and stepped back. Giving Calphan a false smile, Champion asked, "What now, friend Calphan?"

CHAPTER SEVENTEEN

Champion tried to decide which part of his body hurt more, his arms or his legs. Thick chains stretched his arms over his head with just enough slack to slightly bend his elbows. His feet were manacled to the floor, allowing limited movement. He had no idea how long he hung there, hours, days? It felt like an eternity. He passed the time by trying to distract his attention with mind games, thus the question about his arms and legs. But this mental exercise was really an attempt to keep his thoughts from what hung from his neck.

The chain was his only clothing. The Mok's had stripped him naked almost immediately. Attached to the thin chain, resting against his bare chest was a strange triangular stone. Calphan had shown him the stone before it was draped over his head. The thing made his skin crawl, and his first instinct had been to call on his power. Immediately, his body began to spasm and he got violently sick, spewing his stomach's contents on the Spy Masters boots. Again he tried, and again he got sick, this time Calphan had wisely stepped out of the way. Champion had not seen the Spy Master since.

He had been confined in a strange room. Rawstone lamps on the walls provided dim amber light. Green root like appendages covered the walls. The floor was also covered in green roots, but these were so thin and packed together that they looked to the unobservant eye like grains in a green colored wood. The air was humid with warm thick moisture that felt almost oppressive. Moisture dripped and dribbled down the walls joining together to make a shallow pool on the floor. The temperature of the water was surprising cool and served to dull a bit of the room's oppressive heat. An immense throne had been placed in the middle room. The throne stood empty.

Though he could not see his secured feet, he could feel them getting wrinkled as they rested in the cool liquid. It was a strange sensation to be so thirsty and yet have wet feet. Lack of food and water had made him fade in and out of consciousness. Feeling his chin lower to his chest, his eye lids were heavy. He dreamed.

He was back in the cavern again, looking down from a great height. Below, the large serpentine body still lay where it had been since his last dream, half of its great body sticking out of a large glowing hole. Except now, they were not alone. Grey figures that reminded him of Liss now surrounded the serpent.

The dream shimmered and he was suddenly down on the stone steps next to the serpent. Being so close gave him a better perspective on how massive the serpent was. Green scales covered the skin, each one bigger than his hand. Closer to the shimmering hole, a crystalline type crust had formed over the scales. Where the crystals touched the skin, the scales were turned into various colored creations. The body heaved quietly as the large creature breathed, making the cavern light dance over the multicolored skin.

The grey ones were definitely kin with Liss. Same grey clothing, same long grey hands, and same eyes. Also the same quiet, gentle way that they moved reminded him of his grey companion.

Liss's friends would approach the serpent and carefully place hands on the skin where the crystals formed. They each placed a wide bladed tool against a scale, and giving a firm twist, the piece popped away from the skin. Large oozing sores dotted the green skin where the crystal scales had been removed.

As soon as the scale was removed, the grey figures would hand it to a mund standing respectfully off to the side. Each mund was marked with a spiral mark or tattoo on their faces that seemed to jog his memory. The munds then took the scales and placed them in a large wheeled cart. There were dozens of grey figures with their mundane assistants surrounding the serpent. The process seemed to be very efficient, and never ending. Hundreds, no, thousands of scales had to be removed each day.

A mund came close enough for Champion to get a better look at the scale he held. Even though it was a clear crystal color, he drew a sharp breathe as he recognized what it was. A rawstone.

Champion's dream mind reeled. The rawstones were not really stones. They were crystal scales. What?

The large serpent head swung towards him, one cloudy white eye regarded him with a blind stare. The eye was as wide as he was tall. The serpent seemed to be the only one who was aware of him. The munds and grey ones continued with their harvesting, unaware of his presence.

He stepped forward, coming so close that he could have reached out and touched its skin, before asking, "What am I supposed to understand? You make the rawstones? You are the stones?"

His question was rewarded with a slight shake of the great head and the whiter than white eye seemed to glow a bit. Champion felt caught watching the eye as it seemed to get larger and larger, until he felt his dream self to fall into it. He felt dizzy, then staggered and almost fell to his knees until a pair of arms caught him.

"Whoa there, stranger." Champion looked up into a round face that was set in a grouchy expression. Slowly he was put down on the floor with a grunt. Standing back up, this new stranger looked down on him as if he were a much unexpected, very unwelcome guest.

Champion felt sick, which is really unfair in a dream, or was this a dream within a dream? His surroundings were grey and cloudy. As if a morning mist had somehow been made into walls and a floor. Groaning, he lifted his head a bit to get a better look at this new aquaintance.

Hair. At least, all over except the man' bald head. Thick curly brown hair covered chubby arms, chest and legs. Large tufts of the stuff even poked out from his ears like thick whiskers. He was dressed only in an orange loin cloth which resembled a comfortable diaper. An impressive eyebrow spanned the man's forehead and he was regarding Champion with a curious scowl. Was this a man or a bear?

Champion must have said the last out loud, because the scowl deepened for a moment before the bear man let out a bark of laughter that did sound a bit like a bear's growl. Reaching down, he hauled Champion to his feet in a surprising show of strength.

Giving him a hearty slap on the back bear man said, "Been awhile since I have had someone speak such straight words to me. Been awhile since I have heard anyone speak to me, in words anyway. I am Kern."

Hair man stood there as if giving his name explained it all. At Champion's confused expression the scowl reappeared.

Stepping back, Kern spread his feet and put his hands on beefy hips and looked him up and down.

"Here now, son. We have been here a long time. Longer than we ever thought we would be. Are you here to tell us it's finally done? Are all the damned Drakes dead? Are we finally allowed to rest?"

Champion's confused look only deepened, "Drake? What is a Drake? Where are we? Are we inside a snake?"

Hair man waved hairy hands as if to swipe Champion's words out of the air. Stepping forward he gripped Champion's head between his hands. Before he could object, Champion found his thoughts reeling, and he blacked out. When he opened his eyes, he was again laying on the mist colored ground. Kern was sitting by a gently crackling fire close by, eyes glued to the flames as if in deep thought. Champion had no idea where the wood for a fire would come from in this world of grey mist, but it was comforting. He stood and cautiously approached the fire. Sitting down, he waited in silence for Kern to break the silence.

"Damn, boy. We had no idea things would happen this way. No idea." Champion stayed silent, listening. "But the answer to your question about whether we are inside a snake is no; and yes. She prefers to be called a serpent, by the way. Snake is kind of an objectionable term from her point of view. How does she look?" Champion's bleak expression told him enough.

Kern said in a hushed voice, "That bad, huh? Well, she made her choice. As we all did." Kern sat motionless, looking into to the fire, but not really seeing it. Keeping his eyes forward he explained, "The Great Mother, the serpent, has been inside the portal so long now she has become a part of it, and we, because we have become a part of her, have changed as well. But we knew the risks. Some will disagree, but I am going to tell you what I can. What I think you should know . . . ." Suddenly, Kern was interrupted by what sounded like hundreds of people *trying to whisper at the same time. The whispers made the misty walls and floor vibrate and shake. Clapping his hands together, Kern yelled out, "On my head be it then. He deserves to know something!"*

The Whispering stopped, Kern nodded once at the silence and continued, "We were called, boy, we mages. Called from our world, your world too, to this one. We had been given a message, a strange message that made us believe that by saving this world, we would save our own.

In this world we found snakes walking upright on two legs wielding black fire. They worshiped the Drakes as gods, their creators. I watched their bloody rituals, their sacrifices of thousands. Blood and pain for their Drake Masters. But the Drakes were gone when we arrived, though we could feel traces of their presence. Believe me boy, if those powerful beings had challenged us we would have lasted no more than a bloody moment." Kern paused then and rubbed his jaw as if by speaking so many words he was using muscles long unused.

Putting his hand in his lap, he looked back into the flames, his voice softer now, "Even without their masters, the snakes were powerful. We had fought them to a standstill. But we were tired. So tired, and so many of us had died. We just wanted to go home. It was then that the grey skins came to us. They told us that it was their Great Mothers who had called for us. Called us to help them rid their world of the snakes and the Drakes. They told us that the Drakes could use this world as a stepping stone, a gateway to other worlds, to spread their terror and blood. The Drakes had all left on some journey, and the Great Mothers were afraid they would come back some day. So, they told us of a plan, a way to keep the Drakes from ever returning here. From ever coming to Earth." Kern went silent again. This time both hands rubbed his face.

"What plan?" Champion's voice surprised even himself. Kern stopped rubbing his face and gave a grimace and a growling chuckle. The Whispers returned again louder, stronger, almost with wildness to them.

This time Kern had to accede to their wishes, "Fine! Damn your mutterings. I will tell him no more." Placing a hand on Champion's shoulder, Kern said quietly, "You need to go now, son. You have stayed longer than most and my watch is almost up and another will take my place as I rest. Tell Terra we still hold fast. For how long I don't know."

Champion felt the world shiver and vibrate. The misty walls disappeared and he was once again in front of the serpent, the Great Mother, her huge white eye like a full length mirror.

"Who was on watch?" The voice made more of a deep vibration than a sound. He winced at the question. The words seemed to push on his senses, as if they were a heavy mental weight that his mind could barely lift.

He cleared his throat, "I met Kern."

A warm rumbling laugh ran through him that made his senses feel like a recently wrung wash rag. "That one would still be on watch. His stubbornness is his greatest vice, and virtue." He had the distinct impression that the serpent was trying to tone things down so that her voice did not blow him to dust. Already his head began to hurt as she continued, "The stones that come from me are empty of power. They must be charged. I guard the gateway, and the gateway charges a toll on me. A horrible toll. The stones grow on my skin, and would soon kill me if my children did not constantly attend my body. The stones are much like a killing fungus that continues to grow and must be removed." Champion's mind whirled a bit. In this dream place, he could feel the emotions of the serpent. There was no element of deceit, anger, or evil, just a sort of vibration of emotions that emanated from the creature. Emotional layers that seemed to overlap each other in a complex weave of thought that it made him dizzy in trying to understand them. Underlying all of this was a terrible feeling of loss, a feeling that seemed to well up from the serpent like a suffocating blanket damp with uncontrollable sadness. Reaching up to his own white eye, he felt tears forming.

At this the serpent spoke again, "You cry for me, child? For me? You shame me. For what has been done to your people, hate should fill your heart. But what we did, we did to save what we could." The serpent gave a tired sigh and the huge body heaved. Champion got a feeling of monumental age from the creature, ancient. Also of pain. A great physical and emotional pain. The creature was dying.

Answering his unasked question, the voice spoke, "Yes, I am dying, child. I have been dying for some time, though the process has taken centuries. The poisons of the stones have entered my body ages ago." It continued on,

"I cannot ever make up for the harm my kind has done to yours, human. And we do not have the time for me to answer your questions. But, I can help you with the green Empress. The object that hangs around your neck is from another plane of existence, a tooth in fact. Its very nature creates an imbalance in the natural order of this world. Thus, it disrupts your ability to access your powers and free yourself. At the proper time, I will help you."

Champion turned and looked up at the wall with the huge glowing hole and the serpent sticking out of it. Over the hole an immense arch had been carved into the cavern rock. Dotting the surface of the arch, in the thousands, were raw stones. Not the clear stones coming from the serpent's skin, but fully charged rawstones, each one representing suffering and pain. He turned to the great white eye, a horrible question forming on his lips.

"I know child, there is much to be forgiven. But now you need to go back to yourself. Kern was right in that it is not healthy for you to stay so long with us . . ."

Champion jerked awake. His arms and legs were almost completely numb. Only slight tingles reminded him that he had any limbs at all. He looked up to see that the throne was no longer empty.

A huge figure made up green folds of fat sat and watched him with bright golden eyes. Muscled arms rested on the throne as the eyes watched him with unblinking intensity. Champion thought maybe this thing was a lifeless manikin of some kind until it spoke.

"You dream deeply." The voice was melodious and beautiful in strange contrast to the bulging green body. Two rawstone lamps had been placed on either side of him, giving off their greasy smoke with amber light.

He shook his head weakly, trying to clear his head and spoke around a parched throat, "Who the hell are you?"

The beautiful voice laughed. "I am the only one that matters here, mage. Some call me Empress, others Mother. You however, are my guest."

"Nice hospitality you have here, Miss Queen Bee. Been a while since you had any guests?"

Again the laugh, then the voice continued on in a musing tone, "Yes, a long time since I have spoken with a guest who was not one of my children. A long time." Seeing his glance at the rawstone lamps, she made a sympathetic noise, "I know, I know. The rawstones are not your favorite things, are they mage? Well, don't judge me too harshly. If there were some other way, I would not use the stones. But . . . ." Her shoulders shrugged, sending a vibration of flabby movement through mounds of fat.

Champion locked gazes with her and gave the Empress a dry smile, "Yeah, you're a real treat, aren't you sweetheart? Countless lives are snuffed out because of the stones. Using people like cattle? Don't sit there and shrug your fat shoulders at me like all this suffering is some unintended consequence."

The huge body sat back in the throne as if considering a response. "My first memories are of another world. A world of warm waters. We were taken, my sisters and brothers and I. I remember huge leathery wings that blotted out a blue sun and black clawed hands that picked us up out of the safety of the water. Only one of my brothers and I survived the journey.

We were placed here, on a swampy stretch of land under a harsh foreign sun. My brother held my hand as we burrowed below the surface, to find some wet comfort. After some time, we learned what to hunt, where to hide from those that hunted us, and I gave birth.

The first brood died. Four females and two males. All were too skinny and half formed. Each year I gave birth to a new brood, each one a bit stronger than the last. Finally, some began to survive. My brother and I taught our children how to survive, how to hunt, how to build shelters. For years we watched our children grow and thrive.

There were scores of us when the dark ones, the black snakes, first came. We were told that we had been brought here by their Great Fathers, to serve them. Our people were now numerous enough to warrant their attentions. My brother refused." The voice paused and the large head bent low, bright eyes closed in memory. Even so weak from lack of food and water, Champion felt a glimmer of sympathy for this strange creature as she raised her head and the story continued.

"He was burned to black ash. Some of my children tried to avenge their father. All killed. I then promised to serve the dark ones, to save those that remained.

You think your people are cattle? You know nothing of how a people can be used. They used my children like playthings in some bloody game. I would wake mornings to find some missing, taken in the night. We lived in fear of when the dark ones would take others.

Then the Invaders came,the mages, and there was war. The dark ones forgot about us in their struggle. I told my children to burrow into the earth, to make us safe in the deep underground. There we waited, living off of slugs and bottom feeding fish. We were in the dark for years upon years until the war ended. To this day my eyes cannot bear anything but dim light."

"Wait." Champion's voice was strained but easily heard. He swallowed, trying to give his throat some moisture, "I appreciate your story, Queen Bee, and I am sorry that you need to stay in the cellar because of your eyes. But, if these dark assholes were the cause of so much suffering for you and yours, why the hell would you work with these guys?"

The bright eyes locked gazes with him for a moment, then a sultry chuckle, "I am not used to being interrupted, Mage. But, I suppose I can make an exception in your case. Besides, you ask a good question. Of course I was hesitant to deal with the dark ones. In all honesty, I had hoped that their centuries of absence meant they had all died out. But I was intrigued that they had offered a potential new source for rawstones. So, I agreed to an uneasy alliance."

Now almost all the feeling was gone in his arms. Champion's feet were just a pair of wet skin socks with slight tingling sensations. Still, he was able to concentrate on the pain throbbing on his chest from Calphan's recent gift; it gave him focus to ask, "So, why do you need to take the Isles? Why this war with the Mage City?"

The 'Queen Bee' sat back in the throne, crossing her huge arms she glared at Champion, "Don't judge me, Mage. We will never go back to hiding in the mud. My children will inherit this world. I will not allow the Isles or the cursed Mages to endanger me and mine. The dark ones will never use us again. We will use them and any others if necessary. We will conquer and assure our preeminence. Nothing will stop that. Nothing!"

Nodding and with a tired sigh, Champion said, "I thought you would say something like that. I ask that you reconsider before things get messy."

A pause, then that beautiful voice let loose in a loud, wild laugh. The fat body shook with laughter, the muscular arms pounded on the throne. After she calmed down, the Empress wiped a tear from her eye, "Your gall is amazing, mage. Don't you know what it is that hangs from your neck? A tooth from one of the dark ones' ancient Great Fathers, no less. The Great Drakes! It is probably older than time itself. The thing nullifies any magical use on this world."

Champion watched and listened, his bravado aside, a feeling of powerlessness seemed to overwhelm him. Was the dream of the great serpent just that, a dream? Kern? Where the hell was the cavalry?

Fear not, human mage, the sibilant voice of the great serpent said in the quiet of his mind. *I simply waited until the green queen was done with her story. We can sympathize with her wish to protect her children, but she still should not be allowed to kill you.*

He felt the weight on his chest shift. Looking down, he saw that the tooth began to crack. In a matter of moments, the ancient artifact had broken into a hundred pieces and fell to the watery floor.

"Impossible" The beautiful voice of the Empress exclaimed. Even before the broken tooth hit the water, Champion was reaching for fire. He gasped as the warmth of the element sent needles of feeling to his legs and arms.

"No matter your powers, Mage. You cannot hope to escape. Guards! Archen! Aid your Empress!" Even in fear her voice was beautiful. But, his thoughts were not on escape at this moment but on Hett's plan.

The clever Riskh had explained that the entire Mok Capital was built on top of a massive fresh water swamp. Over the centuries, dirt and other debris had accumulated over the thick rooted plant life allowing large structures to be built. But, the entire city still rested on the strength of the freshwater plant life of the swamp.

Like most ecosystems, swamps survive on a delicate environmental balance between plant and animal life. So, adding an alien element, like salt filled sea water for example, could have a very destabilizing effect. This is where Waven came in. The volatile kraken had been using it's powers over water to channel huge amounts of sea water into the dense network of roots under the Mok capital. The result of introducing so much salt water to the fresh water plant life would be an acidic process which literally ate away at the roots. Once the roots were weakened, then the entire stability of the city would be compromised.

However, that was not enough to bring about the dramatic result that Hett's conniving plan required. The large accumulation of dirt and debris would not be effected by the disintegration of the underlying root system for years. What the dirt needed was a large push of some kind; or better yet, an explosion.

Hett had explained that this push could be accomplished from the city's sewer system. Layers of a huge network of sewer and water pipes underlay the city. In order to ensure the free flow of the large amounts of sewage, hundreds of blue rawstones had been placed at junctions where the pipes met. The effect of hundreds of rawstones being destroyed at the same time would be similar to the stone room of a Mok ship being ignited, but on a much larger scale. Hett's plan ran through Champion's thoughts in a moment. Turning his head, he focused on one of the rawstone lamps before saying, "Cinder, Aeris, attend me."

Chapter Eighteen

"Fire!" Scores of arrows flew into the mass of Mok warriors that milled in front of the palisade. Green bodies fell to the ground, writhing in pain. Denna watched with grim admiration as other Mok's rushed in with hastily built shields to cover their wounded comrades.

In planning the defenses, the defenders had operated on a premise that the Mok Marines would be out of their element in house to house street fighting. That premise turned out to be incredibly inaccurate. The Mok's in fact excelled at this particular type of fighting.

It was horribly amazing to watch the green soldiers' ability to take a running start and be able to make a few loping jumps to scale up the side of a wall and reach the defenders on the rooftop. In the initial hours of fighting, Denna and her forces had to abandon the first two lines of roof tops to regroup. In all, it had taken the Moks only two nights and one day to push all the way to the last palisade in the town's defenses.

Denna could not remember the last time she slept. Dark soot smudged her face and her clothing was ripped and torn in a dozen places. Her fingers were sore and blistered from firing endless arrows. She looked at the two rooftops of defenders that remained. Like her, they were grime covered and exhausted while the attackers seemed to be tireless in their assaults. Green Mok bodies lined the roads and alleyways of Haven, but still they kept coming, refusing to stop. Master Orkus stood next to her, watching the Mok's below retreat out of arrow range. In his large hand he gripped a club that looked like it had at one time been a small tree. His small hand idly scratched at a badly tended blade cut on his face.

Denna had wondered if Orkus would prove to be a liability once his machines had been destroyed by black fire on the wall. In fact, he had been the difference in being able to slow the Mok's down as opposed to being immediately over run. Orkus' immense strength was a match to any five Mok Marines. Half a dozen times Orkus had singlehandedly cleared a roof top of green skinned warriors with the aid of his club. Heroics and strength aside, it was simply not enough.

The Mok's simply out matched the defenders in the harsh, face to face fighting. The only positive thing had been the absence of any of the black fire wielders. For some reason, the dark trio had disappeared shortly after firing the walls. If they had stayed, the fight would have been lost in moments.

Still, it was all for nothing. Denna looked back up to the Manse, where the last stand would take place. Fenn had been flying wounded from the Manse to the Mage's cave all day. Thurga the herbalist had refused to retreat to the safety of the cave until all the wounded had been evacuated. Denna loved and admired the fussy man, but she would have to order him to the cave once she and what remained of her fighters fell back to the Manse. Healing skills would have no use in the thick of the fighting of a last stand.

Sensing someone at her shoulder, Denna turned. Kay offered her a jug of water. Greedily, she guzzled the liquid down. She wiped her mouth and watched as Kay continued around the roof offering water to thirsty mouths.

The sun was high is the sky, beating down on them like a hot coal over their heads. Being on a rooftop provided no cover from the heat and Denna felt the sweat begin to soak her arm pits and back. From her position, Denna had a perfect view of what was left of the town, which was next to nothing. The plan to deprive the attackers of a high vantage point by setting fire to abandoned rooftops had been very successful. Yet, the idea that burning down their homes could possibly be considered a positive thing was a morbid thought.

Down below, well out of arrow range now, she watched the Mok warriors taking a breather. While battered and tested, the Empire's force could almost taste victory. There were over three hundred marines left to carry out their mission. Denna had just over fifty men and women left. Fifty shop keepers and fishermen against three hundred trained killers.

What she was feeling was beyond sadness, beyond anger. She felt the heavy weight of hopelessness on her heart. It was different to discuss a worst case scenario over a cup of wine with friends than to actually experience it in real time. To see those same friends die screaming, their life blood spilling from broken bodies. She did not want Kay and the others to see her tears. She turned away to find Liss standing near.

The two watched the other for a moment, then Denna buried her face in her hands, trying to keep the sobs quiet.

Liss was there then, holding her up. She put her head into the grey clad shoulder as her body shuddered with weeping.

Liss spoke quietly in her ear, "I understand, Sister. Males think that weeping is a sign of weakness, of female emotional inferiority. But we know that it is better to let it all out to clear the mind and the soul."

Denna pulled back a little, with a confused tear filled frown. Looking up into kind dark eyes she sputtered, "'We' know? Wait. You're a female?"

Liss gave a soft hiss of a laugh, "Now you know my secret. Our secret. I am glad that I could share it with you, here at the end."

TYRELL had to admit that the view was impressive. He and Grach sat on a tower balcony overlooking the Mok Capital as the sunset blanketed the city in warm light. From their vantage point the grid of the large metropolis spread out before them like a sculptor's masterpiece. Green veined marble was evident everywhere. Narrow streets and broad avenues all seemed to flow from the tower where they sat. Here and there, the immense shapes of the brood houses seemed to thrust out of the ground attempting to disrupt the careful city planning.

The table where Tyrell sat was filled with finger foods of all types; crumbly cheeses, cold cut meats, fresh fruits and vegetables. Refreshing ale had also been provided that seemed to bring out the flavors of the food. Grach sat quietly, a half full cup in his hand looking only slightly less comfortable than Tyrell himself felt. The pair listened to the other two dinner guests carry on a conversation.

Hett and Calphan spoke of the weather, the price of eels in the marketplace, and how some of the smaller criminal gangs in the city were becoming too greedy during war time.

An unobservant passerby might see these two down in the city, sitting at some café, having the same conversation and think it was two long absent friends getting reacquainted. However, there were some peculiar things that would stand out. One was the fact that the Riskh was missing an ear. While now dressed with bandages, the missing body part gave Hett's head an odd unbalanced look. A second was that the Riskh was now lacking the middle and little finger on his right hand. The dapper Hett did not seem to be bothered by his maimed condition as he agilely swiped up fruits from the table and took large swigs from his cup. Nor did he seem to be put out by the fact that he now sat and made witty remarks with the source of his injuries.

Calphan leaned back and laughed at something Hett said. The Spymaster, not a merchant, as the Mok had been introduced to Tyrell and Grach, seemed to be enjoying himself immensely. He had delivered the freak mage Jonathan Champion to his Empress, had taken into custody two agents of the vile Mages Council, and was now content to simply converse with his old acquaintance Hett. While Tyrell had not really considered himself an 'agent' of the Mage Council, he supposed that by standards of warfare and espionage that is exactly what he was. His service to Mage Gazell and her plans was secondary to his wish to find his friend.

While Calphan felt he had won the game, his relaxed and nonchalant mannerisms were is stark contrast to the six armed Mok guards who watched the table with hard eyes. Evenly spaced around the circular space, they could reach any part of the tower top easily. If anyone of the Spymasters dinner companions made so much as a move towards him, the guards would intervene violently. Tyrell made the beginning of a wry smile at the choice of foods as well. Having finger foods ensured that any utensils, or anything that might prove handy to any attempts at escape, would be absent and yet not hinder the diners.

The smile quickly died as Tyrell thought of their current situation. To come so close to achieving their goal was galling enough. But to have lost Jonathan Champion so soon after finding him sent Tyrell's emotions to the brink of dark despair.

They had no idea what had become of their friend. Calphan had assured them of Champions safety, for the short term. Still, the spymasters' assurances did little to engender hope. They were in the dangerous Mok's power and control, so the fact that he cared to try to calm any of their fears seemed more like a vicious mental game than anything else. The three companions were in the spymaster's power and if they had any chance of survival, they would need to play along.

Just then four robe hooded servants arrived struggling with a huge tray up the tower stairs. Placing their burden on a side table, Tyrell saw that the tray held numerous types of deserts. Small cakes and candied fruits were next to more exotic foods like sweetened meats and some sort of insect that had been cooked and wrapped in a translucent leaf. The servants stepped a respectful distance from the table and waited in hooded silence.

Calphan exclaimed in delight as he reached forward and plucked up one of the insects. Deftly, he snapped off the head of the insect and sucked its innards out from the neck. Smacking his lips in gusto, the Mok then popped the rest of the unfortunate insect into his large mouth and crunched away contentedly.

Seeing Tyrell's lack of interest in the desert tray, he leaned forward, "Come now, friend Tyrell. You must try something sweet. Before you are delicious tidbits from all over the Empire, made for you by the Empress's own personal cooks. Such a delight should not be squandered, regardless of the situation." Tyrell heard the unvoiced "or else" underlying the Mok's words. For a moment he locked gazes with Hett. The Riskh nodded towards the tray, indicating that Tyrell should not choose this time to be difficult with their dangerous host. But Tyrell was tired. He was tired of the war, tired from their journey and recent capture, but mostly he was tired of playing this stupid game dictated by the Spymaster and his horrid Empress.

Leaning back in his chair, Tyrell put his feet on the table in an obvious show of disrespect, "I remember a time, Calphan, when you were a simple merchant making his way through a forest filled landscape with two mundane servants. We joined you, Grach, Champion and I as travelers often do. Numbers can add a feeling of security on less traveled roads. In a very short period of time we were chased by a rabid horde of mesk, almost burned to death by black fire then finally forced to travel darkened tunnels far below the ground desperately searching for the open sky and bright sunlight. Such experiences usually allow people to know each other better. So, knowing me as you do, through our shared experiences, you know that I have little patience for this game you are playing. Speak plain."

Swallowing another insect, Calphan leaned back in his chair and placed his hands in his lap before answering, "I can appreciate your direct talk, my blue skinned friend. I will oblige you. You and your mushroom companion are in dire straits. You both are considered agents of an enemy of the Empire. I find you here in my beloved capitol, with my dear friend Hett, plotting something that I am sure is not in the best interests of the Empire. You also brought a volatile, freakish mund with destructive powers within striking distance of the Empress, the Great Mother of the Mok race.

Even now, the Empress is questioning your friend in her private palace. If he proves valuable to the war effort then perhaps he may live. If not, well . . . ." Calphan shrugged leaving the sentence unfinished with a generous smile. While the smile exsuded false warmth his eyes remained calculating and cold.

"Well, finally!" Hett exclaimed, gaining him the attention of his fellow table mates. Turning to Calphan he put a friendly three fingered hand on the Mok's shoulder and continued in a happy voice, "You have no idea how hard it has been pretending to enjoy the company of a low life slimy piece of Mok shit like yourself, Spymaster." Before Calphan could react Hett slammed his good fist into the Mok's face, filling the air with the sound of cartilage snapping. Calphan fell backward in his chair, clutching at his now bleeding face.

As if the sound of the Spymaster's nose breaking was a signal, the four quiet robed servants burst into action. In a matter of moments all six Mok guards were lying motionless on the tower floor. Tyrell saw a small feathered dart sticking from the neck of one of the guards explaining their sudden unconsciousness.

Tyrell watched as the servants removed their robes to reveal four stocky Riskh. One approached, handed him a robe and instructed him to put it on. Donning his robe, Tyrell turned to see that Grach now stood next to him, similarly attired.

The two friends now watched a very interesting face off. Calphan had regained his feet. Green blood soaked the Mok's face and shirt. A trickle still leaked from his nose despite Calphan's attempt to pinch it closed with two fingers. In his other hand, he held a dagger in a defensive position. Eyes blazing, the Spymaster faced off against the smaller Hett and his four fellows. Two of the Riskhs held short blow dart pipes at the ready. Seeing that he was out maneuvered, Calphan lowered the blade. Nodding graciously Hett motioned with a hand and one of the Riskh stepped forward and relieved the Mok of the knife.

Hett held his hands out imploringly, "I am sorry to have to leave you in such a hurried fashion, Spymaster. But now that we know where Champion is, we have a mundane to go fetch." Two small shapes buzzed in the air toward the bleeding Mok, appearing as feathered darts in his neck. A look of surprise was short lived as the Spymaster fell sluggishly on his side, unmoving. Hett stepped forward and smashed a heel into the unconscious Mok's face, crushing what was left of his nose. Turning Hett pulled a robe over his head as he walked back.

"Was that necessary?" Tyrell asked as he and Grach followed the group of Riskh down the tower stairs.

His disapproving tone did not phase Hett one bit who replied, "Fuck him. He cut off my ear."

KREK had always been somewhat of a disappointment to Brood Grist. Bright, articulate, and extremely personable for a Mok, his personal characteristics led his brood clan to believe that he had an exciting future before him. However, Krek seemed to fail at nearly every endeavor placed before him.

Believing that she had simply not found the right fit for one of her children, Krek's Brood Mother moved him from position to position trying to unlock his potential. Soldier, bureaucrat, scholar, he inexplicably failed miserably at every turn. Finally, it was concluded that Krek suffered from a simple, yet terrible affliction; horrid laziness. After his diagnosis, he was put in the position as a grain merchant for the brood. A merchant was considered one of the lowest tiers of Mok society since they were required to travel and associate with non-Mok's and lesser beings. Yes, Krek was a great disappointment.

Then, to the surprise of many, the war started. By order of the Empress, the Brood Houses were to enlist many of their children into the war effort. This turn of events left Krek as the de-facto head grain merchant for the House. Since Brood Grist controlled a huge percentage of the imperial grain contracts, and since grain was such an essential staple for the thousands of soldiers the Empress was sending north against the mage city, it became a very valuable commodity. The ever increasing price of grain led to larger and larger profits for the House. And by no additional effort on his part, as the now head grain merchant, Krek was given all of the credit for the huge sums of imperial coins that now filled the Brood House coffers.

This was why Krek now stood in the public receiving chamber of the Brood House, waiting to be personally thanked by his Brood Mother for his efforts. He stood there basking in the envious looks of his brood kin. Who would have thought that Krek, known as a great lazy disappointment, would ever be personally thanked by the Brood Mother for anything? Krek stood there in triumph, thinking that he would reward himself with a rich meal and a nap later that afternoon. Those were the last thoughts he ever had before the entire Brood House came crashing down, crushing Krek and his brood kin, ending Brood Grist in one bloody moment.

CALPHAN staggered down the tower steps. He could not feel parts of his face, and those parts he could feel were in agonizing pain. Blood seeped out of his crushed nose and the only thing that kept him moving was the furious fire that filled his belly at the thought of what Hett had done. The little Riskh would pay with his life, one finger, and one bloody inch at a time.

Coming to the end of the steps, Calphan stumbled over a stack of bricks that a group of stone masons were using to repair the street. The streets were filled with people, mostly Mok's, going about their early evening business. Ignoring the mason's protests, he staggered to a pair of Mok soldiers who warily watched his approach.

Trying to ignore the pain, Calphan began, "Fetch your commander, I need . . . ." A screeching noise filled the air, sounding as if the earth itself were screaming in agony. A huge tremor dropped the spymaster and the soldiers to their knees. The tall tower that he had just exited began swaying from side to side as the world continued to shake. Bits of stone began breaking from the towers' turrets, spraying passersby with sharp rocky like rain drops. With a groan of agonized granite the tower came down, crushing screaming victims under its great weight.

Somehow Calphan found himself on his feet. Another tremor shook the ground, buckling his knees for a moment. Gaining his feet again, Calphan could not see through the debris filled air, his tongue was thick with gritty dust. All round him the screams of the injured and dying surrounded him in a nightmarish symphony of sound. Terror filled him and he could not tell if his own voice had joined the chorus of the damned, or if it was only in his mind that he screamed. Lurching down the street, with the city falling down around him, he put one dogged foot in front of the other, hoping his steps would lead him to safety.

He did not know how far he walked, or how long, but at some point the destruction of the city had paused. Suddenly, the dust parted and Calphan found himself near one of the city harbors. The damage seemed minimal here and a group of soldiers had cordoned off an area of order from the chaos. Tents with tables, bunks, and chairs had been hastily erected to house the dazed and wounded citizens that had made it this far.

As Calphan approached a soldier came forward and offered him a large jug of water. Mouthing his thanks, Calphan swished the liquid around his teeth, spitting the grime and dirt from his mouth. The second swallow went down his throat making him cough. A third swallow went well, and he felt the cooling effects of the water taking hold. It was the dark of night now, and rawstone lanterns had been placed around the harbor, as if the amber light could give a bit of hope to the shocked residents. Finding a seat on the ground, Calphan felt the exhaustion of his recent activities spread over him. He knew that he should find a healer to look at the damage Hett had done to his face, but those few that could be seen now seemed overwhelmed with survivors who had more serious injuries.

Just as he felt himself drifting off toward a weary slumber he was rocked back to his feet by a voice, a summoning that no Mok could ignore, *"MY CHILDREN! HELP ME!"*

Every Mok in the harbor area went still for a moment, and then there was a mad dash back into the city of death, back to buildings falling and the earth shaking. Their mother was in danger. The Empress had called and their very blood answered. Those too wounded to walk, crawled or wormed their way on the ground toward the summoning voice. *We are coming Mother!*

ADMIRAL Jesh gave a fierce, savage yell of triumph. The defenders last stand at the Mage's Manse had fallen. Defenders now fled in all directions, most running toward the higher hills. The locals most likely had a hideout somewhere in the craggy heights. Later he would send parties of marines to flush them out, but for now he joined his soldiers in celebration.

The fighting up the hill to the Manse had been a bitter progress. Arrows, rocks, and boiling oils had been hurled at the attacking Moks trying to halt their progress. Inch by bloody inch, wielding huge wooden shield walls, the Mok's had made their painful advance up the steep incline. Finally, when they had reached the summit of the hill, Jesh had ordered his warriors to attack, holding nothing back. Days of frustration at dealing with an enemy who preferred to fight from a distance had built up a huge well of killing rage that was now unleashed on those defenders who remained. The final confrontation had been short and brutal, but final nonetheless.

Many motionless forms lay all around the low wall facing the steep inclined hill. This was where the fighting had been the fiercest. A cursory look showed him that the archer bitch was not among the fallen. It did not matter, he would find her and run a spike through her screaming mouth. He would spike them all.

Seeing that some of his men tried to run down those that fled, Jesh bellowed out for them to halt. He would not have his soldiers cut down one by one in the hills. Places like that had prime locations for traps and ambushes. When he saw that the pursuers had turned back at his order, Jesh walked down the wall to an odd shape sprawled on the ground. A strange looking mund with mismatched arms lay between the bodies of two large dead Moks. Jesh had seen this man's work over the last few days, smashing Mok's with a huge club of some kind.

Removing a dagger from his belt, Jesh leaned over to make sure the strange mund was dead by way of a cut throat, when a voice rocked through his soul, "MY CHILDREN! HELP ME!"

DENNA watched in disbelief at the fleeing Moks. From her hiding place, she could see the green skinned warriors skidding down the Manse hillside in their haste. Some even dropped their weapons as they raced back down towards their ships. Further out to sea, other ships of the armada had already hoisted sail.

Moments before she had simply thanked the cursed gods that she had made it to the safety of the rocks. Now, she was just exhaustedly grateful that the Mok's were leaving. It could be a trap of course, a way to bring the rest of them back into the open to be slaughtered, but right now Denna was just glad to be alive. She waited till the last green shape had fled the Manse before turning and walking higher up into the hills towards the safety of the Mage's cave.

GRACH was not a great fan of salt water. In truth, it was a very little known fact that if a molden spent too much time in the ocean his body would start to erode. However, he had to admit that while he did not look forward to sea travel he preferred to be moving away from the Mok Capital. At least what was left of it.

After Hett had engineered their escape from Calphan's tower, the three companions, along with Hett's Riskh henchmen, went on a search for Jonathan Champion. Hett led them under the city to where the Empress resided. After only an hour of searching they found the unconscious

Champion being carried by his elemental attendants. Aeris informed them that Champion had followed the plan by destroying the underground sewer systems. Things happened very quickly after that.

Given that there was no way to determine when the destruction of the city may occur, it was better to err on the side of swift caution and Hett hurried the group to a very dingy part of the city near one of the smaller harbors. A short wait in a warehouse ended with the party being escorted onto a midsized ship crewed entirely by Riskh. Before the day ended, the ship had put out to sea and from a safe distance they had witnessed the destruction of the city.

On paper the journey had been a success. Grach and Tyrell had found their lost friend. They then had embarked on a mission to bring the Mok Empire to its knees and effectively end the war. Yes a huge success. Yet, instead of the feeling of satisfaction that should have accompanied success, Grach felt a deep sense of sadness.

The day was a bright sunny beauty. Light blue sky and dark blue waters seemed to meet at the horizon like lovers. Sun rays made the ocean waters glisten and sparkle like brightly melting jewels. It was almost offensive to have a day like this marked by such incredible destruction.

As they sailed away, Grach kept his eyes on the shattered remains of the Mok capital, its huge towers and buildings still managing to hold some of their majestic essence even in destruction. From this distance the Moks looked like so many frantic ants swarming over the fallen hill with their queen trapped under it. He quietly hoped that the green skinned people did find their Empress under all the rubble.

From the corner of his eye, Grach saw Jonathan Champion watching the destruction that his powers had brought about. On either side of him stood his creatures; manifestations of his power according to Fenn. Eerily, all three held the same stone like expressions. As if a stone mason had chiseled three similar faces into a piece of granite and then forgot to give them even a flicker of emotion.

Grach had come halfway across the world to find his friend. But he was not sure who this stone faced person was. This man looked like Champion, talked with his voice, even had his laugh, but there was a savage edge to this man's soul that Grach never associated with his friend. For the first time on this long journey, Grach wondered if finding Champion had been a wise decision.

Hett approached Champion and spoke for a few moments. At the mage's nod, Hett bowed gracefully and went to confer with the ship's captain. The clever green man had told Grach that several ships of his Riskh kin had escaped the destruction of the city and were now making for Haven. Grach felt a bit better at the thought that many of Hett's people had survived. Though, the idea of hundreds of opportunity savvy Riskh flooding their quiet streets might be more than what the residents of Haven had bargained for. The mental picture brought a slight smile to Grach's face.

Almost immediately upon boarding the ship Tyrell had gone down below and fallen fast asleep. Still feeling the adrenaline rush of the past day's events, Grach had decided to stay topside. He was now regretting that decision. Seeing such destruction, and Champion's apparent indifference too it, made his heart sink a bit.

Feeling tired enough now to attempt sleep, Grach turned and began walking toward the steps leading to the hold of the ship when an unfamiliar voice rang out, "What a chase you have led me, my Champion!" Spinning around,

Grach saw that a strange short woman now stood with her hands on hips, facing Jonathan Champion and his two manifestations.

A strange assortment of mismatched cloths and threads seemed to form a colorful mess of a dress of some kind. Black hair without a single grey strand was wound in a lopsided pile on her head. Bright blue eyes and a wide shiny white toothed smile sparkled up at the brooding trio.

Cinder stepped forward, red flames turning blood red, smoke laced his words, "Leave us alone, you dumpy dressed toad."

Not fazed a bit, the woman put a finger to pursed lips, "My dear Champion, you have been busy! I leave you alone for a couple of years and you manage to dredge up not one, but two manifestations?"

Aeris placed a wispy hand on Champions shoulder and whispered something quietly to its master. Shrugging the hand away, Champion stepped closer. With an angry word he ordered Cinder out of the way and now faced the 'dumpy dressed toad.' For several tense moments the two looked each other over. Champion broke the silence first, "Terra."

The woman's face nearly burst in a bright white smile. Reaching forward she clutched his scarred hand between her own wizened fingers and brought it to her lips. At the contact, Champion's eyes rolled up to the back of his head, then he staggered, and fell to his knees. Before he fell further, Terra gathered him up in both arms and gently laid his head in her lap. Cinder and Aeris watched the scene unfolding in tense silence. Hett and the Riskh crew made to move forward but a warning look from the strange woman stopped them in their tracks.

Looking down, Terra brushed the hair gently out of Champion's face and his eyes fluttered open. Gazing up at her, Champion's arms and legs began to shake, evidence of the beginning stages of a seizure. A low moan escaped from the tall man's throat as the shakes increased. Putting her hands on either side of his face, Terra bent closer until her nose almost touched Champions cheek. The shakes slowed, and Champion's body eased and lay still, his eyes still open. Closing her eyes, the strange woman grip tightened and she began humming a low wordless melody.

"No!" Aeris and Cinder screamed as one. The two made to move toward their master but were suddenly sent to their knees, gasping and holding their throats as if lacking air. Slowly, as they writhed on the wood deck of the ship, their bodies began to lose substance, like a faded tapestry. In moments, the powerful duo was gone.

Champion's eyes now closed as if Terra's gentle music lulled him to sleep. A loud wet popping sound broke the quiet moment. Red black blood spurted from the man's nose and ears but quickly stopped.

Producing a clean white cloth from somewhere, Terra wiped most of the blood from Champion's face. Gently placing his head on the wooden deck she stood, swaying a bit as if exhausted. Steadying herself, Terra crooked a finger at Grach, motioning him closer.

"I have done what I could, plant man. He had a head wound that had turned into a tumor. I drained it and cleaned out the infection. Now he needs sleep. The damage to his memory could be severe or not. It is now out of my hands." Leaning closer to him, Terra gave him an appraising look. "You have no idea how much I wish to discuss with you your very existence, plant man. Molden indeed!" Turning, she snapped a finger at Hett and the crew, "Well? Take him down and put him to bed." As if struck by lightning, the Riskh jumped into motion and Champion was carefully bundled up and carried down to the hold.

Once the Riskh and their precious cargo were down the steps and out of sight Terra walked over and leaned on the railing. She took a deep breath as if enjoying the ocean air. Grach cautiously joined her and they watched the Mok capitol dwindle into the distance. Grach could not suppress a sigh.

Terra matched his sigh, "I know my moldy friend. So much destruction is a horrible thing. Even if it does happen to a race as stubbornly arrogant as the Moks. In the end, their Empress had developed a very warped sense of paranoia. In her wish to keep them safe, she has turned her children into a war mongering society bent on conquest and destruction. At some point, even the biggest bully on the block run's into someone bigger."

"Like Champion."

Terra gave a rueful laugh, "Yes, like my Champion. He definitely never does anything half assed." She placed a warm hand on Grach's arm, "He will need you Grach. You and Tyrell, his friends. Even with all of his powers, he is fragile, like a piece of delicate glass. One wrong move, one strike placed just so, and he could break into a thousand pieces. Please, take care of him." She gave his arm a reassuring squeeze and them she was gone. Grach looked down at his arm where the fading impression of Terra's fingers still lingered. With another sigh, he turned, his steps taking him to check on his sleeping friends.

FROM all over the Mok Empire, the Empresses children came flooding to her aid. From the south desert reaches of the Red Sand, from the eastern swamps and bogs, and from the northern war front they came. Thousands upon thousands of the Empresses children armed with shovels, picks, and even their bare hands, digging to find their lost mother.

EPILOGUE

Grach sat with Tyrell and Jonathan Champion swapping stories and drinking sour beer. At times the stiff ocean breeze would muffle their words so that they had to be repeated as the ship sped swifly back to Haven. But Grach was just happy to have his friend back.

Ever since the magical Terra had healed Champion it was like their old friend had been restored. Gone was the powerful, ruthless mage who had so dominated the Lost Isles. Gone was the warry acceptance that Grach and Tyrell had received on their arrival. Champion's face was now filled with the open friendly expression that Grach was used too.

But not everyone was as excited to see this return. Off to the side the Corsair Captain Spuros and the Riskh Hett stood and spoke in quiet tones together. While Terra's cure had the positive effect of restoring Champion his old memories, it had also deprived him of the last two years. Champion had listened politely, if in a bit of shock, to Hett explain his role in the destruction of the Mok Capitol. During this tale, Spuros had watched the scarred man's face intently.

Grach felt sorry for Spuros. The old sea dog had been through fire and death when the Mok fleet had chased after his own Corsairs. Of the fifteen Corsair ships that had set out to harry the Mok Armada, only eight had returned. The battered Corsair fleet had intercepted their ship the night before with an odd story of the Mok ships suddenly breaking off pursuit and heading in a straight course back to the Mok homeland.

But Grach knew that there was concern about Champion's recovery, and rightly so. The powerful manifestations, Aeris and Cinder had not reappeared and Champion claimed to have no memory of them. While his friend remembered how to use his power, it was nothing compared to having the two manifestations in attendance.

Grach's thoughts had intentionally not dwelled on the lady that awaited Champion back in Haven, but it was impossible not too. There had been no word of how the island dwellers had fared. But, if the lady had survived, then Grach did not look forward to the hurt in her eyes when she realized that Champion may have forgotten her. In his mind, he was still having a romantic fling with the exotic Sublime Sister, Kitla. No one had yet to tell him that he had two sons. One was Sann, the son of the Red Lady whom he had taken in as his own and the other was his biological son by Kitla, though Grach had never heard of a Sublime Sister having a child. Count on Champion to make the impossible seem simple. Grach sighed again, took a drink, and tried to pay attention to Tyrell's retelling of their journey to find their lost friend.

GLOSSARY

Aeris—Elemental manifestation of air bound to Jonathan Champion. It looks like an unscarred version of Jonathan Champion.

Admiral Jesh—Commander of the Mok forces attacking Haven.

Archen-Mok Water Mage. He is an advisor to the Empress and the most powerful Mok mage in the Empire.

Bacha Collar-A collar worn by munds indicating ownership.

Breg-Former mundane servant to Calphan. He was horribly mutilated and tortured by the S'Ahas in "The Meth Conspiracy."

Brood House—Central home of a Mok Clan. It is where the brood clan Mother lives and young Mok's are born and raised.

Brood Clan Mother—Without the Brood Mother there is no clan. Each Brood Mother is a daughter of the Empress and is charged with producing young Mok's to serve the Empire.

Calphan-Mok Spymaster who was brought back to life by the Empress.

Captain Drach-Gurrachi Sea Captain of the Swift charged with transporting Fenn to the Lost Isles to investigate.

Captain Hyad—Duwvar Captain in the Mage army. Tyrell is in his company.

Captain, The—Gurrachi Commander of the Green Guard, charged with the protection and defense of the Sublime Sisters.

Cinder—Elemental manifestation of fire bound to Jonathan Champion. It looks like an overly scarred version of Jonathan Champion.

Citadel-Fortress of the Mage Council. Located in the center of Hyberan, and is the center of Mage's power.

Corsairs-Pirates of the Lost Isles under the command of Captain Spuros.

Denna-The Mage's Lady. A former high end prostitute who was owned by the Mok Shaff. Her services were sought all over the Mok Empire even though she was a mundane. She has striking fair skin.

Drakes—Also known as Sky Fathers-These powerful beings are the co-creators of the S'Ahas and the Orda. In times past they ruled with ultimate power before embarking a mysterious journey. The S'Ahas hold them in near godlike regard.

Dryan-Dusky skinned people who live to the west of Hyberan. A long lived people, they are known for their good health and beauty.

Duwvar-Yellow skinned people who live underground for the most part. Well known for their skills in mining and working with precious stones and metals. The Duwvar are the most military of the race's who are allied with the Mages of Hyberan.

Fastness-Name of the S'Ahas fortress.

Feast Brother-A Ferrekei title for a close friend. In many cases, a feast brother will be treated as a member of a Ferrekei's family. Tyrell named Jonathan Champion as a feast brother.

Fenn-Ferrekei Air Mage—Sent to the Lost Isles to investigate the unauthorized use of magic. He later sets out with Tyrell and Grach to find Jonathan Champion.

Ferrekei-Blue skinned people who live in the forested lands north of Hyberan. Allies of the Mages of Hyberan.

Gam-Gurrachii member of the Green Guard.

Gazell-Ferrekei Fire Mage. She is High Mage and a member of the ruling council of Mages.

Grach-Molden warrior and friend to Jonathan Champion and Tyrell.

Great Mother-Large serpent co-creator of the Orda and S'Ahas.

Great Root-Often a Molden will swear by the "Great Root." Non-Moldens are not exactly sure what the Great Root is but it may have something to do with the Molden people's origins.

Green Tails-Sect of the S'Ahas.

Great Temple-Home of the Sublime Sisters located in the center of the old city section of Hyberan.

Gurashii-Red skinned people living to the far south of Hyberan. A sea faring race, the Gurashii live in cities along the coast.

Haven-community in the Lost Isles and home to the Corsairs and the "Mage."

Hett-A very clever Riskh employed to keep Jonathan Champion and the Corsairs appraised of the activities in the Mok Empire.

High Commander Rish-Tuak Mage in command of the Mage forces fighting the Mok Empire.

Humans-Mythical people-Jonathan Champion insists that Mundanes are in fact Humans.

Hyberan-City of the Mages. Also called the Bright City.

Jonathan Champion—He is a mundane that has magical abilities in a world where humans, or mundanes, are a magic-less people and considered inferior to the other races.

Kay-Gurachii Corsair who is the personal aid to the Mage and his Lady.

Kraken-A large squid like sea monster usually found in the deep oceans.

Kern-Mage who meets Jonathan Champion in a dream.

Kitla-Sublime sister who has miraculously had a child with Jonathan Champion.

Krek-Unlucky Mok who was about to be given special recognition by his brood mother until the brood house roof fell on him.

Laith-Friend 'with benefits' of the Mage Fenn.

Liss-A grey skinned Orda. It was rescued by Jonathan Champion and the Corsairs.

Lore-A language made up of glyphs and runes. The Lore is an obsession of the librarian Mosha.

Lost Isles-A group of islands located south and west of the Mok Empire. Powerful ocean currents make the Isles a difficult place to navigate.

Mage-A magic user. The Mages rule from their city of Hyberan. They consider themselves the caretakers of civilization.

Mage Council-The ruling body of the Mages of Hyberan.

Manifestation-A magical creature like construct that serves as an extension of a mage's power. Only the most powerful mages are known to have been able to create them.

Manse-Large house of the Mage and his Lady, located in community of Haven in the Losat Isles.

Marda-Washer woman in Haven.

Master Pulk-Mok disguise used by Jonathan Champion to enter the Mok Empire.

Mok-A green skinned people who look similar to a large catfish with arms and legs, without the tail. Mok's are in general, extremely arrogant and disparaging when dealing with people of other races.

Mok Empire-Empire of the Moks and their Empress located to the far south of Hyberan.

Mok Empress-Eternal Mother of the Moks. She is thought to be thousands of years old and traces her origins to the beginnings of the Mok race.

Molden-Grey skinned people who live to the far north of Hyberan. Molden are often referred to as 'Mushrooms' or 'Plant People' by other races.

Mosha—Mundane Librarian who has a colossal memory and an ego to match it.

Mundane-Magic-less people who often serve as servants or slaves to the other races. It is commonly believed that the mundanes are inferior due to their inability to produce magic users, or mages.

Nook-Mundane boy who lives in the Old Quarter of Hyberan. He agrees to take the librarian Mosha to the underground below the city.

Nurn-Island located off the coast of the Mok mainland. The island is best known for its black market trade.

Orda-Grey skinned creatures who have a close relationship with the Great Mothers.

Oracle Braid-A white braid of string that a Ferrekei with a talent for perceiving the future, usually through dreams.

Orkus-A hunchback mundane living in Haven. Master Orkus is a master craftsman who is a genius inventor.

Rawstones-Stones which are the main power source for the civilized world. Most believe that the Mages of Hyberan control the production of the stones. Mundanes are used in the creation of the stones.

Red Sand-Substance that is used to keep a mundane complacent and immobile during the rawstone process.

Riskh-A green skinned people who a servant race to the Mok Empire. The Riskh are well known for their ties to illegal activity and gathering information.

Rish-Tuak mage and Princeps. He is the High Commander of the Mage forces fighting against the Mok Empire.

Sann-Denna's son. Sann suffers from the 'Mund Fever', a mysterious condition that afflicts some mundane children.

Shaff-Mok pimp who was the former owner of Denna.

S'Ahas-Black scaled creatures who have strong ties to the Sky Father's, or Drakes.

Seren-Dog like race that are often employed by the Mages of Hyberan. Like dogs, the Seren have keen senses of hearing and smell.

S'Hael-Title for a S'Ahas leader. A S'Hael is a strong magic user and has powerful ties to the Sky Fathers, or Drakes.

Shinal-A S'Ahas.

Sister Ella-Tuak Sublime Sister who serves as a healer for the residents of Haven.

Sky Father-or Drake. They are the co-creators of the S'Ahas and Orda.

experiences in his first book which speculates on a fictional conspiracy where the Meth epidemic is traced to another world filled with

He lives in the Chicago Suburbs with his wife and two children and prays daily for a Cubs World Series. When not writing or practicing law, he is a full-time gymnastics/golf/baseball/swim dad for his kids.

He loves comments and questions and can be contacted at j.e.horn@hotmail.com.

ABOUT THE AUTHOR

J.E Horn was born and raised in Alaska. In 7th grade his family began moving back and forth between Alaska and Iowa giving him strong ties to both states. Over the years he has been a dishwasher, cook, commercial fisherman, Assistant Srgt. of Arms for the House of Representatives for the State of Alaska (mouth-full), construction worker, penny poor law student, and attorney.

His third grade teacher introduced him to the Chronicles of Narnia by C.S. Lewis. In the 4th grade he was banished to home confinement after contracting chicken pox where he read The Prydain Chronicles by Lloyd Alexander and was officially hooked. What followed were years of reading every fantasy and science fiction book he could get his hands on. In 7th grade he was encouraged to write by his journalism teacher and that pretty much started the ball rolling.

He was exposed to the horrors of Meth addiction in his legal career as a family law advocate. He experienced firsthand the devastating role Meth can play in the destruction of families, the abuse of children and spouses, and the erosion of the human soul. He taps these

http://www.whitehouse.gov/ondcp/meth-intro
http://meth-kills.org/resources.html
http://www.drugabuse.gov/drugs-abuse/methamphetamine

If you are interested in a literary work that does an amazing job of providing the history and background of the Meth Epidemic in the United States please read Methland: "The Death and Life of an American Small Town by Nick Redding."

It is a well written work and the information it provides is as interesting as it is shocking.

About Meth Use

Meth addiction is a chronic disease affecting the brain, and just about everyone is different. The drug affects different people in different ways. One person can take and use meth, yet never become addicted, while another merely has one experience and is immediately hooked.

The health consequences of continued Meth abuse are abundant and severe. According to the National Institute on Drug Abuse, these damaging health effects include:

1. Changes in the user's brain structure and function
2. Memory loss
3. Mood disturbances
4. Psychosis, including paranoia, hallucinations, and repetitive motor activity

In short, the Meth addict, after continued use, slowly loses his or her mind. If you have a friend or loved one who is using this stuff, you must seek help. Here are a few resources if you need a place to start:

Spuros-Gurachii Captain of the Corsairs.

Stone Room-Room in a water vessel where rawstones are used to power the vessel. Mok ships rely solely on their Stone Room to sail.

Swift-Name of the ship that transported the Mage Fenn to the Lost Isles.

Tagga Serum-anti-pregnancy drug used by the Sublime Sisters.

Tesh-Tuak member of the Green Guard.

Thurga-Mundane herbalist living in Haven.

Tuak-Black skinned race living in principalities to the south of Hyberan. Allies of Hyberan.

Tyrell-Ferrekei friend of Jonathan Champion. He has labeled Champion a 'feast brother' which is similar to being a family member.

Underdark-The name for the underground sewer system located under the city of Hyberan.

White Lady-A famous figure among the mundane race who had challenged the power of the mages.

White Tar-Another name for Meth. This substance is used, alongside red sand, is administered to mundane victims in the rawstone process.